Allegra Hyde

THE LAST CATASTROPHE

Allegra Hyde is the author of the novel *Eleutheria* and the story collection *Of This New World*, which won the John Simmons Short Fiction Award. Her stories and essays have appeared in *The Pushcart Prize*, *Best of the Net*, *The Best Small Fictions*, *The Best American Travel Writing*, and elsewhere. She lives in Ohio and teaches at Oberlin College.

allegrahyde.com

ALSO BY ALLEGRA HYDE

Eleutheria

Of This New World

THE LAST CATASTROPHE

THE LAST CATASTROPHE

Allegra Hyde

Vintage Books
A Division of Penguin Random House LLC
New York

A VINTAGE BOOKS ORIGINAL 2023

Some stories originally appeared, in slightly different form, in the following publications: "Adjustments" in *TriQuarterly*; "Afterglow" in *Guernica*; "Chevalier" in *Moon City Review*; "Democracy in America" in *The Massachusetts Review*; "Disruptions" in *Blue Earth Review*; "Endangered" in *American Short Fiction* and *Best of the Net 2017*; "Frights" in *The Sun*; "The Future Is a Click Away" in *BOMB*; "Loving Homes for Lost & Broken Men" in *Kenyon Review*; "Mobilization" in *Story*; "The Tough Part" in *Indiana Review*; "Zoo Suicides" in *The Normal School*.

Library of Congress Cataloging-in-Publication Data
Names: Hyde, Allegra, author.
Title: The last catastrophe / Allegra Hyde.
Description: New York : Vintage Books, a division of
Penguin Random House LLC, 2023.
Identifiers: LCCN 2022033229 (print) | LCCN 2022033230 (ebook) |
ISBN 9780593315262 (trade paperback) | ISBN 9780593315279 (ebook)
Subjects: LCGFT: Short stories.
Classification: LCC PS3608.Y365 L37 2023 (print) |
LCC PS3608.Y365 (ebook) | DDC 813/.6—dc23/eng/20220721
LC record available at https://lccn.loc.gov/2022033229
LC ebook record available at https://lccn.loc.gov/2022033230

Vintage Books Trade Paperback ISBN: 978-0-593-31526-2
eBook ISBN: 978-0-593-31527-9

Book design by Steve Walker

vintagebooks.com

Printed in the United States of America
10 9 8 7 6 5 4 3 2 1

For who we'll be —

Contents

THE LAST CATASTROPHE

Mobilization

We were multitudes, we were millions. We lived within dimensions up to fifty feet long, fourteen feet high, but never more than nine feet wide. We were drivers, asphalt-lickers, road-runners, gearheads: the denizens of motorhomes who rolled across the country en masse, a fleet of rubber-soled seekers. We were a city on wheels. A city on the go. A growing city: more motorists joined us each day. Newbies drove shiny RVs off the lot—Class A motorhomes with leather interiors, granite countertops, TVs, bonus sleeper sofas—or they purchased tow-along teardrops. Fifth wheels. Cab-overs. Pop-ups for pickup truck beds. A wealthy actor built a double-decker apartment on a tractor trailer—hot tub on the roof. We let him join, too. We didn't discriminate. We welcomed families of five crammed into campers as well as heavy metal screamers straying with bandmates from their touring paths. Oddballs joined in custom trollies made from salvaged wood and glue. *Whatever works*, we said. What mattered was that everyone was always at home but always away. Gas pedal down, we cracked the code humanity had wrestled with for too many millennia: How to have an adventure yet keep your home close. How to wander the world yet never get lost. If only Odysseus could have taken Penelope and Telemachus with him, could have taken the old lady and the looms, the goats and farmers and the grapevines and Ithaca's gravelly shores, because we did. We brought our Siamese cats and Welsh corgis. One man had a sixty-year-old Greek tortoise that rode in his passenger seat. He let it roam during pit stops; it never got far. We brought our children, cousins, parents, partners, best friends, neighbors—packing together, as condensed as the sardines we ate—everyone headphone-wearing, video game–twitching, knitting, audiobook-listening, steering wheel–gripping. The cramped quarters were worth having the whole country to roam. We furnished our vehicles with macramé. Strings of dried chili peppers. Prayer beads. Great-Grandma's ashes sat in an urn on the dashboard. *May she rest in peace*, we said, *forever in motion*. We stowed gold bullion in our glove compartments, just in case. Also a couple revolvers. Hydroponic pot plants trembled over speed bumps. Cacti we kept duct-taped to windows. Bicycles we lashed to the roof. We towed Jeeps. Ski-Doos. Kayaks. By Lake Erie, we splashed into the water, kept an eye out for snakes. In Telluride, we made hundreds of snow sculptures—left them to liquefy. Down south, outside El Paso, we lay in the sun and let its rays fry us. *There's always room in the desert*, we told one another. We meant it. In Quartzsite, Arizona, we purchased gemstones by the armful, installed amethysts by our sinks. *Helps with digestion.* We pulled into grocery stores, bought out their tuna, pita, eggs, cinnamon, pickles, OJ, Coke, basil, bananas, hot dogs, buns, ribs, batteries, ground coffee, Band-Aids, beer, Pop-Tarts, gummy bears, Gatorade, iceberg lettuce, salsa, ham slices, sugar-free gum, hand soap, toilet paper.

We moved on.

Sometimes stationary people decried us, jeered at and protested us. Local kids watched wide-eyed from scooters. Local teens shot our flanks with paintball guns. We waved back, nonetheless. We tossed candy from our windows in one long parade. We set off fireworks to show our shared patriotism: our love of the country we roamed. We played our radios loud, tuning them to many thousand frequencies, and once in a while to the same station—everybody loved Talking Heads. *Take you there, take you there / We're on a road to nowhere.* We pitied these stationary citizens: stuck, trapped, misguided. We pitied their homes rooted into the earth, the burden of a basement. We pitied the necessities of lawn care. Mailboxes bursting with bills. We pitied their scorn. *They don't know what they're missing.*

Sometimes they did. A few jeerers always slipped in among our ranks. They rigged up their minivans, followed our trail in the night. Or they made hasty romances—often a glance was enough—and found a seat in a cockpit. Teens stowed away in our storage spaces, emerged tousled-haired and sheepish a hundred miles from home. We never turned them away. We made arrangements, kept going. We flooded Walmart parking lots, NASCAR racetracks, dried-out lake beds. We coated mountaintops like cubed snow. We saturated cities. When we parked, we stretched for miles in every direction—and we parked where we wanted. *Who's gonna stop us?* We were too numerous to ticket; we always skipped town. Once, we took up the length of every bridge spanning San Francisco Bay.

We liked the view, the squawk of gulls. We tried not to litter, but we couldn't help it. Leaflets, leftovers, stray bits of plastic wrap—they fluttered from our windows. Sometimes our hubcaps detached and rolled away. *We'll get new ones later*, we told ourselves. *Can't stop now.*

We scattered seeds, too: the fuzzy inflorescence of Midwestern maiden grass; pine cones from giant sequoias; every kind of acorn. Flush with the miracle of our country's fecundity, we had sex, wildly, on the roofs of our motorhomes, the open plains of Kansas stretching big and balmy in every direction—the moon a voyeur. Afterward, in the night air, we kept driving. We stuck our heads out windows like dogs. We tasted snowflakes. Black flies. Smog. The sulfuric fumes of a chemical fire, burning to the west.

Motion spared us from disaster. In Oklahoma, we outpaced a tornado. We circumvented riots and "civil unrest." Infectious diseases. Mourning of all kinds. True: some phone calls found us. *Your great-aunt passed* . . . Even the occasional letter. *You owe the U.S. government $29,780 in back taxes* . . . We didn't mind—we could out-drive it all. We piped in Internet, but not because the news would affect us. A *grave tragedy in Rochester, New York, as rescue teams rush to* . . . News was a show we tuned in to—tuned out of, just as quick. And anyway, we tried not to read much, lest we get carsick.

True, there were times we broke down; leaks happened; we crashed; but we also got ourselves patched up, inflated, recalibrated, jump-started. We were good at using duct tape. We pooled knowledge, our tools. At rest stops, we intubated fuel lines, wastewater lines; we drank diesel, gasoline, suckled it from gas station pumps, guzzling with greedy abandon because we knew the fuel gave us more miles. We released gray water, black water—chemically sweetened—in an aqueous trade that lubricated our plumbing. We tightened lug nuts. We checked windshield wipers, batteries. We sizzled: liquid and limber.

And then—street signs, construction signs, political signs, lost children signs, personal injury lawyer signs, memorial signs— we whisked past it all. We honked. We whisked past dates, too, dangling lights on our vehicles for holidays—Christmas, Hanukkah, Chinese New Year, Eid al-Fitr, Diwali, Liberalia— though often we got these dates wrong. Time warped, minutes meaningful only in their relation to one place and the next. Women gave birth at sixty miles per hour, on highways stretching straight into the sun, the birth locale changing as we crossed state lines.

I'll call her Texarkana.

We added bumper stickers—line-drawn figures accounting for passengers, phrases for what we wanted to say: *Brake for Moose; This Car Climbed Mt. Washington; I'd Rather Be Phishing; USA; NASH; LV; LOL; Not Old, Just a Classic; God Bless America; COEXIST; Smoke Tires Not Drugs; My Collie Is Smarter Than Your Honor Student*—until we filled the back sides of our motorhomes, the text piling on top of itself.

The moon squinted down, a skeptic.

Like we cared—we were fiberglass and steel, plywood and polystyrene. We were a polymer-infused spray when the mood struck, and we waxed the sides of our vehicles. Rainwater beaded. Every droplet demonstrated our invincible ease. During storms, we hydroplaned, skidded—threw our heads back and laughed.

We pissed in restaurants and behind trees.

We forgot stuffed animals at rest stops.

We shoplifted Jolly Ranchers, Crocs, designer sunglasses; we held up the occasional mid-tier jeweler.

Keep the engines running . . .

We hurried onward, counting roadkill to keep our minds busy, death as distant as a possum in a mirror.

Children started school with new landscapes out their windows each day.

You're lucky to see the country like this, we told them. *You get to meet people from all over, hear every accent, every perspective. You see every side of a sunset. You know the meaning of a mile, of fresh asphalt and old potholes . . .*

We had our favorite places, sure, but we never let ourselves stay long. Not-staying kept those places special. Kept them loved.

. . . Leave while you still want more. Promise to come back, even if you know you never will. Don't let a place hurt you. Don't ever think of slowing down.

We were ephemeral. A current on the tar trails—the interstate webbing connecting the country—our movements a synaptic pulse, the wink and blink of possibility. We were everywhere and nowhere. We went on for generations, assumed we'd go on for generations more.

Then one day we heard the gas was gone.

We didn't believe it.

We'd encountered such talk before: theories about peak oil, unstable supply chains. We didn't think the news applied to us. It was someone else's problem, someone else's life.

Probably a localized issue, we said. *These issues usually are.*

And anyway, we were in Texas—in the wide-open country

between San Antonio and Houston—where the black beaks of pump jacks perched over the earth.

If there's fuel anywhere, it's here.

We pulled off the highway into a small town with roads that crumbled into dusty paths. Houses wore tin roofs. A quiet, closed-door church displayed a sign condemning sinners. Inside the town's gas station, there were bags of salted corn chips. Jerky. Lighters with American flags flying on their sides. No fuel. The clerk shrugged. Told us to try down the road.

We tried down the road.

That town was out of fuel, too.

So was the next one, and the one after that.

A newspaper outlined a disastrous trade embargo. Governments in chaos. A domestic strike. Delayed shipments. *Blah blah blah.* We took a deep breath.

Fuel could be found—we just had to be strategic.

We pointed ourselves southeast.

The highway stretched long and flat. We tried to coast—to let the wind push us, holding our speedometers steady. We lost a few motorhomes right away—folks with fuel tanks knocking empty. *We'll come back for your camper*, we said. *Climb in.* We gripped our steering wheels, willed ourselves onward.

We'd decided on Galveston. Maybe we'd already gone a bit mad. Among us, a hypothesis had circulated, swelled into inevitable reality: they'd have fuel in that island city. We remembered RV hookups flush with gasoline. Potable water. Propane. We recalled driving right onto the beach: the sand firm beneath our tires, the Gulf of Mexico sweeping open like a stage set. Dolphin fins dicing the surf. The island: an easy drive from Houston's energy headquarters—from corporate offices, refineries, chemical plants. The island, a vacation spot for oil executives and rig workers alike.

Yes, we assured ourselves, *it'll have what we need.*

The sky darkened. We lost more vehicles. *Climb in. Climb in. Climb in.* Those of us with spare gas canisters sloshed around our last cups, spreading the remaining fuel like a sacrament.

Nearly nightfall—I-45 ushered us through marshy fields, past the prickly watch of utility towers. We held our breath as we crossed the long, low bridge that stretched from the mainland to the island, our vehicles running on fumes.

Stoic palm trees. Boat dealerships. Chain hotels. Vacation homes whose windows winked with the fretfulness of lighthouses.

There was no fuel in Galveston, either.

One by one, we ground to a halt. We were stranded.

A few among us—the oddballs, really—had custom electric rigs, and they went for help, spiriting back over the bridge, their taillights as bright as brimstone in the night.

Come back for us, we called.

We'd parked along the shore. A frozen flock, we stared at the ocean stretching away into darkness. Sea grasses whispered. The night sky stood tall.

A *pause*, we told one another. *Temporary.*

Flashlights beamed. Beach chairs were dragged out of vehicles, unfolded. Cigars smoked skyward. Children Hula-Hooped. Grills sizzled. AC units were methodically unclogged.

Around us: the wet murmur of the sea.

Above: the moon as bored and unbending as a god.

Rain the next day; the day after. The ocean sloshed, sediment-filled, turning the color of chocolate milk. Algae on the jetty rocks: slick as hair, bright green and swaying. Thundery skies.

Skies hysterical, pinched by lightning. Then: a fever-flush of heat. Our vehicles deadened by stillness. Leaning, exhaling through leaks. Tires going flaccid. Garbage swirling. Sewage smells. Beach chairs rusting, sinking into the ground. Bumper stickers peeling. Flags shredding, sun-fading. Grills gone cold. Our bodies prostrate. Slumped over steering wheels, twin yellow lines racing along the backs of our eyelids. The road right there, waiting.

The others never came back.

Sand, wind-driven, making dunes of our vehicles. Making tombs of our vehicles. Heat as heavy as a fist pummeling the island. More rain. The sea kicked up, frantic—a storm surge rising over the beach, the ocean like a salt blanket: a bedcover pulled above our heads. A demand for dreaming.

Darkness comes quick—sucked down, down into the sea, our vehicles clasp us. Here: algae blooms to toxic proportions, maddened by phosphorus runoff, overwarm waters. The rotting carcasses of fish free-fall in slow motion. Expired zooplankton, phytoplankton: creatures too tiny to see. Bacteria get busy cleaning our skulls, achieve anaerobic ecstasy. The Gulf: a gullet. It swallows us, grinds us. Our caravan crushed, axles crunching, fiberglass fraying, cabinet doors already fallen to pieces. Those bones of our motorhomes buried with us. Mud and murk press down on top. Sediment piling, solidifying. The ocean boils, bulges with glacial melt that claws landmasses into muddy plains, stirs atmospheric anomalies into continual tempests.

We are pressed and squeezed beneath all that weight. In our lightless, airless underwater coffins—down where the moon can't find us—we are fossilized, liquefied, transmogrified. We ooze. The continents creak, make their slow passages. Fault lines find reasons to agitate, tectonic kisses making the whole planet shudder, blush hot, lava throbbing red. Rock steams into the sky. Underneath it all, we are chemicals, superheated; we are millions of years in the making. Time skids along, careless as ever. We wait—to be called up, summoned—to burst to the surface, burn into motion. We are ready.

I

Disruptions

**Tropical Fish Cause Trouble as Climate Change
Drives Them Toward the Poles**

Biggest Walrus Gathering Recorded as Sea Ice Shrinks

**Tiny, Rabbit-Like Animals Eating "Paper"
to Survive Global Warming**

What's a Ghost Moose?

—Headlines at NationalGeographic.com

The daughters stop painting their fingernails. Instead, they sharpen them on cheese graters, white flakes dusting their boudoirs. The daughters pee standing up, a single slender arm pressed against the wall, urine splashing jubilantly onto tiled restroom floors. The daughters walk around smelling musty and sour. Their skirts drag. When threatened, they flash their sharpened fingernails. Herd behavior is no longer advantageous. The daughters roam alone, nocturnally, pausing only to mark familiar territory—the frozen yogurt shops, the frilly boutiques—before moving on, moving farther, teeth bared.

The fathers have fewer and fewer places to hide. The basement man-cave. The TV den. The garage. These spaces no longer feel safe. They are no longer man-places. They have been refurbished, refurnished, and in some cases completely removed. The fathers move upward. On the second floor might be a guest room, or at least a large closet. A place where one can nap. But these places soon disappear, too: they get cozied with cushions, scented with cinnamon. Even the attic. The fathers move to the roof. This, finally, is a safe space. The fathers crack open the beers they've hoarded. They release farts. Football is mentioned several times. It begins to rain.

The mothers are busy getting naked. They jiggle and lumber through town, exposing their C-section scars and moles and hirsute terrain. The mothers are too overheated to care. They meander into supermarkets and begin pushing shopping carts, their bare feet slapping against the linoleum floor. Skin goose-bumps pleasantly in the supermarket chill. The mothers change their foraging habits. Flock to the freezers. Glass, cold to the touch, is soothing. The mothers fill their carts with puff pastry, coffee-flavored ice cream. The kinds of foods they never get. Still, the mothers use coupons. Still, they carry oversized purses and fret over the cost of things: Too much, too much, too much. Oh, fuck it.

———

There has been a drought of lemonade, a dearth of grilled cheese sandwiches. The sons adapt. The sons use their baseball caps to catch raindrops, to capture what trickles from chins. The sons are sprightly and keen-eyed. They nibble berries found in the bush. They vomit up berries, now recognized as poison. Their gaunt ribs show. They no longer make fun of the weak ones. They are all weak and the weakest die. The sons languish, lost and dizzy. The sons are easy targets for speeding cars and guard dogs and the lightning bolts that shimmer down from the sky. More sons die. Those who remain gaze at the moon with throats too parched to howl. Wearily, they climb rope ladders into tree houses and sit in huddling groups. After some deliberation, they take a vote: the rope ladders are cut. The sons feel themselves vanished. They wonder if this means they're free.

The Tough Part

There were only five moose left. In the whole world. Some-one had to save them. I was someone. So was Marissa. Also our daughter, Dottie, though in a less defined sense. We were going to save the remaining moose. We were going to make a few moose into many moose. What the fuck else did we have to do?

The important thing, according to Dottie, was to keep the moose wild. People needed to stop feeding them Cokes, even though it was adorable to see a moose suction its big rubbery lips around a glass bottle and then tilt its big goofy head back and take a swig. Pretty hilarious, actually. But people needed to stop that. They also needed to stop letting moose cool off in their swimming pools, even though it was really hot most of the time. Wicked hot, actually. The trouble was that these kinds of behaviors made moose unwild. Unwild moose got soft. Soft moose got dead.

Kind of like you, says Marissa. How you got soft.

She is talking to me. She is talking in her vengefully righteous yet surprisingly sensual voice about how I gave up my unsuccessful, albeit soulful, DJing career to become a cruel, self-obsessed real estate investor feeding from the poisonous hand of capitalism.

I'm the one who paid for this house, I say.

Marissa pretends not to hear. Instead, she paces around our comfortable and well-equipped home, muttering about how I'm no longer the man she married—that I'm a sellout, a corporate stooge—and that the man she married would be more enthusiastic about saving the remaining moose.

I'm just clarifying the situation, I say.

The situation, Dottie tells us, is that moose are most threatened by people, because people drive cars and moose like people, or more specifically they like Cokes and swimming pools. Are you writing this down?

I am. To demonstrate my commitment to the cause, I am also admiring the moose costume she's made. It is brown and furry with a pair of highly realistic antlers. I'm supposed to share it with Marissa, each of us getting half (Kind of like a divorce, says Marissa). Marissa was originally going to be the front half, standing upright, while I was going to be the back half of the moose, bending forward, my hands on her hips. Then she decided it would be weird to have my face near her butt all the time, even though butt stuff was never a big deal for us when we first got married, and really she's just being difficult because she thinks I got soft, having given up my unsuccessful, though soulful, DJing career, even though my new job pays for her health insurance.

The health of the planet, Marissa announces on cue, is more important than our own.

She gestures toward the moose costume, indicating that I should put on my half.

I balk.

The plan is that Marissa and I will wear the moose costume so that we can trick the five remaining moose into thinking we are also moose. Then we will lure those five remaining moose to a peopleless wilderness in Canada.

Dottie says: I would do it, but I'm four years old.

That's a good point, I reply.

Marissa makes her vengefully righteous yet highly attractive face into a scowl. Have you quit your job yet? she says.

I tell her I'm planning to telecommute, though quite frankly I'm nervous about how exactly I will fulfill the requirements of my occupation given the constraints of our mission.

If you don't quit your job, says Marissa, I really will sign those divorce papers.

Dottie: Remember, once an animal is extinct, it never comes back.

People get divorced and then remarried all the time, I say.

Dottie: It's a long way to Canada and will probably take you many weeks. Maybe months.

Is that going to be a problem? Marissa asks me.

I don't say anything. Instead, I try to think about the importance of making sure there are moose for Dottie to see in the future—about how she deserves the opportunity to show these big, weird animals to her children, and to her children's children, and so forth—and, envisioning my descendants' future appreciation, I ease my body into the moose costume. My legs fill the furry brown legs, my head the furry brown head. Marissa gets in, too: her legs becoming the back legs and her torso the moose belly. At last, I take a few steps forward. My back half

(Better half!) trots along behind me, her hands grudgingly placed on either side of my waist.

These antlers are quite heavy, I say.

Try walking in a permanent bend, says Marissa. You're just—

I pay for electricity, I say.

Electricity is killing the planet, says Marissa.

You look really legit, says Dottie. She claps her hands.

◆

Our first few days as a faux moose go well, mostly because Marissa and I can't talk. Talking would clue in the real moose to our human identities. Instead, we grunt and gallop around, locating the five remaining moose in their current unsuitable habitats—highway medians, golf courses, wastewater marshes—then herding them in the general direction of north. There's a GPS in my fake snout. I'm not a superhero.

The tough part is crossing swamps.

The tough part is eating pondweed for breakfast.

The tough part is eating pondweed for lunch.

The tough part is secretly eating the candy bar I hid in my faux moose earlobe without the real moose noticing—or, more importantly, without Marissa noticing and becoming vengefully righteous about me carrying contraband that could expose our identity and thus jeopardize the mission.

The tough part is avoiding hunters.

The tough part is avoiding bodegas and swimming pools where the moose might succumb to human contact.

The tough part is crossing roads.

The tough part is Marissa's guilt-inducing yet surprisingly sensual breath filtering forward from the back half of our moose costume.

The tough part is when there is no more pondweed to eat.

The tough part is crossing roads that have turned into highways.

The tough part is Marissa pinching my waist, then tapping out the beat to a track I used to spin as a DJ. *Tap tap taaaap ta ta ta'taaaap*, she goes, mimicking Adonis and Charles B.'s "Lack of Love." *Tap tap taaaap ta ta ta'taaaap.*

The tough part is when the other moose try to get away from us and each other, because moose are solitary creatures and unaccustomed to traveling in herds. This is something Dottie made sure we knew.

The tough part is missing Dottie and worrying about her, but also knowing she is a highly competent four-year-old and that kids mature faster these days. And, really, we're doing this for her. So that she'll be able to someday show her children the moose—albeit from a safe distance, so that the moose remain wild creatures and don't get soft.

Tap tap taaaap ta ta ta'taaaap.

The tough part is when one of the moose sees a swimming pool and dashes away and we cannot catch up to it in time and we have to leave it behind for fear of losing all the moose and that now, realistically, there are only four wild moose left in the whole world.

Plus us.

Maybe they won't have swimming pools in Canada. I can feel Marissa trace these words into my back later that night. *Or bodegas.*

The tough part is when all the moose get ticks because ticks like warm weather and warm weather is all we get these days. The ticks latch on to the moose and suck their blood and make the moose itch. The moose start scratching them-selves. They dig their hooves against their flesh and rub them-selves on trees and chain-link fences and electricity pylons, and one moose, the youngest moose—still downy-nosed and knobby-kneed—he starts scratching so hard he razes whole patches of fur. But still the ticks suck. The ticks suck so much blood from the littlest moose that his body goes from brown to white. He starts to look like a ghost. A ghost moose. Staggering north.

Marissa and I scratch at the ticks, too, but our faux fur is firmly glued on.

Soon there are only three wild moose left.

Three wild itchy moose. Plus us.

Maybe the ticks will die when we get to Canada. Marissa presses her finger into my back, spelling out the words.

The tough part is that we are actually already in Canada, but Canada, it turns out, is a lot like everywhere else, and not what we thought it would be: which is green and wild and people-less. There are lots of people in Canada. And roads and bodegas and swimming pools. I even recognize my own real estate signs on a few parcels of land.

We'll probably get there soon. Marissa presses her fingers harder. *Won't we?*

I say nothing because I can't speak for fear of the other moose knowing we're human. And because I suspect that Marissa already knows what I know.

The tough part is knowing.

Won't we?

The tough part is getting very, very tired.

And seeing the other moose get very, very tired. So tired that one of them is too slow crossing a highway full of too-fast eighteen-wheelers.

The tough part is wanting to walk slowly into the highway myself, and starting to do so, but having Marissa plant our collective back feet and then feeling terribly sad that I can't tell the woman I love that I love her and that I'm sorry I was a coward and gave up DJing—because, really, what's the point in living in any way except the way that feels right and true?

We stumble onward. We are all very hungry.

After a while, I take out my second—and last—candy bar, which I kept stowed in my other oversized earlobe. I pass it back to Marissa. Then I hold my breath, waiting to feel the angry pinch of Marissa's disappointment, but also hoping—really hoping—that she forgives me for this and every moment in which I've put myself ahead of the greater good, or in which I've sacrificed the future for the present.

I feel no pinch. Marissa eats the candy bar.

The tough part is feeling happy and sad at the same time.

The tough part is wondering whether we've gone through all of Canada and passed the North Pole and are now circling the globe the other way, still searching for a wild verdant place. A safe place. A place that may not exist.

The tough part is looking at the other moose and wondering whether they are even moose at all, or just other pairs of humans in moose costumes. Maybe there were never any wild moose left. Maybe we are all just people trying to show our children that we care enough about them to keep a species continuing on.

The tough part is continuing on.

The tough part is continuing on.

The tough part is continuing on.

The tough part is continuing on.

The tough part is continuing on.

The tough part is continuing on.

The tough part is continuing on.

The tough part is continuing on.

The tough part is continuing on.

The tough part is continuing on.

Zoo Suicides

After Donald Barthelme, and also Dana Diehl

The first one hopped the fence into the lion pit. We almost thought it was an accident, what with . . . you'd be amazed at the stunts people pull for photographs. But then we found a note in the guy's shoe.

The next two incidents were more clear-cut: an unauthorized dip in the orca tank, the tickling of our resident silverback gorilla with a three-foot wooden pole. That really got the media cooking. Especially with last year's . . . as zoo director I did what I had to do.

People were upset. Rightfully so. It upset me, too, that the lions had to be euthanized. Our orca released into the wild. The silverback shipped to a research facility in Kaliningrad.

But I assured everyone that things would return to normal.

Obviously, I was wrong. How, though, could I have predicted a man would disguise himself as shrubbery, spend three days in the python exhibit until the snake swallowed him whole? That a woman would glue birdseed around her femoral artery and walk into the aviary? And those warthogs . . .

Was I concerned about these people—these lost souls driven to orchestrate their own tragic ends? Yes, I suppose on some level I was. But the acts also seemed so . . . a fad maybe. Twenty years as zoo director and I'd seen some tough times. We started as a humble petting park—only open on weekends!— yet with a little perseverance (plus a lot of kibble) we became a world-renowned menagerie of keen-eyed animal trainers, loudmouthed hot-dog vendors, fat-faced little boys, and enthusiastically masturbating chimpanzees.

I will say this: I could have installed more security measures sooner. Padlocks on the artificial savanna, for instance, might have forestalled the giraffe stampede . . . though it's worth noting that until a star-crossed couple broke through the twig enclosure, their boom box belting "If I Could Turn Back Time," the giraffes appeared entirely nonconfrontational. Now we know better . . . and that's good for science . . . and science is what the zoo is all about!

Okay, *okay*—there were times when I may have been a little sidetracked by ticket sales. March can be a slow month, but visitor numbers rose 65 percent. Sixty-five percent! We'd just renovated our Insect Annex—a real point of pride for me—so I assumed the crowds had come to observe the army ant colony's pheromonally driven hunting swarms, not to see someone . . .

So the Feds got involved and they really put on the squeeze. Carting off any creatures incriminated by their own natural impulses—namely, anything with horns, fangs, or stingers. Of course, I did everything I could to keep our remaining inventory intact. I increased fence height, lid tightness, mesh density—largely at my own personal expense—and still I underestimated the despairing human's capacity for ingenuity. I found rope swings into the porcupine enclosure. Tunnels into the meerkat den. And . . . penguins, it turns out, can be highly territorial.

A few members of my staff, I discovered, had accepted bribes. Did it hurt me to fire them all? Yes, tremendously. It caused me terrible pain. I had known many of these individuals upwards of two decades. Gary, the dung analyzer, was a close personal friend. And Janet, the toucan groomer, had recently invited me to her son's bar mitzvah. Still, the zoo was my life's work: a beacon of enlightenment amid the fog of modern torpor. I felt I had no choice.

Unfortunately, the new hires lacked the zoological expertise and surveillance experience to thwart a break-in to the Amphibian Arena—a tragedy of considerable loss, given that the rare poison-dart frogs . . . was it really so crazy of me to think I could run the entire facility all by myself? To be honest, my long hours likely did contribute to the downturn and eventual cessation of my relationship with Marguerite. They also did not help with my asthma. But with the zoo's inventory so depleted . . .

Such optimism, I admit now, was also a mistake. Though in my defense, the eight-person incident involving the Japanese-style koi pond had little to do with the fish and more to do with the asphyxiating effects of water.

It was my lawyer who insisted the zoo close.

"The good news," he said, "is that I've got a mini-golf company ready to make an offer on the property."

He looked rather squirrely as he said this: bucktoothed and twitching. His appearance filled me with tremendous nostalgia. Only hours before . . . those dear rodents.

"This deal should cover my fees," the lawyer added.

With a heavy heart I installed a closure notice on the zoo's front gates. What was left to do but take a farewell tour? After peering into empty cages, I wandered across the golden plains of the artificial savanna, through the cacti region, past the unmelting polar ice caps. The zoo air—once ripe with the smell of manure and cotton candy, melodious with squawks and bellows—hung stale and silent.

Perhaps I could start a new zoo, I told myself. A better zoo. A zoo unlike anything anyone had seen before, with Portuguese man-o'-wars, ribbon-tailed astrapias, jackalopes . . .

And yet, wasn't it true that any creature could kill under the right circumstances?

I walked faster, as if I might outpace my own answer. But even hurrying forward, more questions gave chase: Was it not the very nature of *nature* to rebalance unbalances within a network of interdependent organisms? To move toward a state of ecological equilibrium via the push-pull of life and death? Why should zoos be exempt from such natural realities, if zoos had always promised to put people in proximity to nature, and therefore, implicitly, in proximity to nature's equilibrial forces, which were bound to be particularly forceful given the unbalanced realities wrought by humanity's extractivist excesses and its rampant disregard for sustainable economic systems?

I hurried along faster—but this zoo, like all zoos, was encircled by borders. I soon reached its walled outskirts, the final exhibit: a geodesic dome housing the Butterfly Palace. Here were the only zoo animals remaining.

I went inside.

Inside, the air steamed ambrosially around red hibiscus and purple passionflowers, while butterflies—like miniature kites, or oversized confetti—flitted between blossoms. I stood motionless, listening to the whir of humidity fans, the rustle of leaves. *Any creature can kill*, I whispered to myself, the words a reminder, a consolation, a . . . suffice to say, I sat down beneath some ficus and closed my eyes. Minutes passed. Eventually, I felt the tickle of butterfly wings on my lashes, then against the warm planes of my cheeks. My breaths grew rapid. I braced myself. *Any creature*, I whispered again and . . . I wish I could say . . . it's hardly worth mentioning now, but in the end, I sat there, waiting . . . I waited a long time.

Afterglow

When her husband left her, the first thing she did was drink Gatorade®.

Red liquid—candy apple, fire engine, lollipop, stoplight, clown-nose red—she poured it down her throat, then other colors after: orange, purple, chlorine blue. A rainbow gurgled into her veins, carried on citric acid and sucrose acetate isobutyrate. On Red 40 and Yellow 6. All that artificiality made her less of the world, because she was no longer of the world—the world had left. She was a new species, radioactive, who bled coolant pink, neon green. Who peed blue. Who sneezed blue. Who sweated purple, just like the athletes in magazine advertisements she'd studied closely as a girl.

That she had stomach trouble was, according to her father, the fault of the liquid.

No wonder you can't eat, he said over the phone, his voice crackling from a thousand miles elsewhere. *You need real food.*

Saltines, maybe, he said.

Or pear slices.
Are you listening?
Mary, are you there?

To look at oneself in the mirror, though, blue-tongued as a lizard, eyeballs gone orange, was to see a woman who knew things she didn't. A woman who was not her. A woman whose husband had not left—or better yet, a woman who had never had a husband at all.

They had moved, that fall, to a sea-scraped island. Only seven trees marked the whole landscape—the island's old-growth forest axed centuries earlier for firewood—and those remaining trees were more like large shrubs, salt-black, bent by wind. There were many more houses. Shacks or Victorian-style mansions clustered over low hills and bogs and perilously eroding cliffs. Though on clear days the mainland was visible—a port city jostling with freighters—mostly, it was ocean everywhere. Chilled seabirds. Chimney smoke. Rockweed rot. A ferry had run between the mainland and the island, but the ferry had recently experienced propeller shaft issues, and anyway it was the off-season for tourism, so if you didn't have your own boat you had to convince a fisherperson to take you across the water, and the woman didn't have her own boat, she only had a house—unfortunately a large and beautiful house with a 360-degree view of the water—which meant a 360-day mortgage, for which she alone was now responsible. She had not yet unpacked most of her belongings, only a few appliances—specifically the refrigerator. When opened at night, the refrigerator glowed like a portal to another realm, its shelves stocked with liters of jewel-toned liquids, rainbow potions, her drinks.

I cried all the time, too, said her boss, *when I first got here.*

But you still need to do your job, said her boss.

Actually, said her boss, *we need you to show up at school, like, right now, because it's after eleven and all the students are waiting in the auditorium for their performing arts instructor.*

The school was a private middle school for mediocre preteens — fifth and sixth graders who were not sufficiently rich or intellectually gifted or even delinquent enough to attend the more prestigious mainland institutions. There were lots of middle siblings. Second-round casualties of child beauty pageants and spelling bees. The school itself was housed in a miniature castle that a minor Rockefeller had built on the island and then forgotten about. The building had a stone façade and several impressive turrets, though most of the turrets were inaccessible due to safety concerns. The auditorium was accessible, if underused: musty and dungeonlike, down in the school's basement. The woman appreciated its lush red stage curtains and red velvet seats, even if she couldn't be sure of the exact shade. The Gatorade® had by then migrated into her eyes—spilling across the white parts and into her corneas—so that her vision was filtered by a roseate haze. Nevertheless, the woman could appreciate this development, given that, culturally, the color signified a better outlook.

When she first walked into the auditorium, the students all went quiet, their faces rosy with unease.

———

We actually need you to do the job we hired you to do, said her boss, *which is not napping among the wigs in the theater supply closet.*

We're kind of on a tight schedule, said her boss.

We're kind of in a tight situation, said her boss, *with the donor visit coming up.*

There's no time for us to find someone else of your caliber, said her boss, *who would work for so little.*

When her husband left her, he'd announced he was doing so on the day they arrived on the island. It was mid-September, but they'd traveled on what felt like a leftover bit of summer: the sun high and bright, everyone on the ferry smelling like sunscreen and processed meats.

The woman and her husband had sat next to one another on the ferry's main deck, watched the other passengers feed French fries to seagulls. The birds would swoop down, pluck fries from outstretched fingers. Again and again, the gulls did this, and each time it was wonderfully funny: a miracle of human–animal interaction. A great sense of possibility had welled up in the woman, and she wondered how a scientist might characterize such an exchange—if it represented a coevolutionary development in which gull and person received symbiotic benefits. The woman had a great appreciation for science. At the parties for young professionals she'd attended in her former life—the life she was leaving behind, along with her family and friends and career, in a midsized, arts-centric, still-affordable city—she'd always made a point of seeking out scientists. She'd passed on conversations with up-and-coming pastry chefs and newscasters and exotic-animal trainers because she'd appreciated the scientists' restless, unsatisfied demeanors, their near spiritual commitment to failure in the pursuit of a granule of knowledge.

The woman had believed she shared an affinity for such pursuits. As a performance artist, a freelance director, she considered her work experimental in the scientific sense. Onstage, she hypothesized, tested audience reactions; she, too, sought stable earthly truths.

She was not yet famous, and might never be famous—especially having taken this teaching position—yet sitting beside her husband on the ferry deck, she'd felt a shimmering surge of optimism, a confidence in the inevitability of ground-breaking discovery, even as the ferry churned up to the island and she smelled the seaweed rot and diesel fumes, saw the low murky hills and stout cottages and the few trees.

I cannot overstate, said her boss, *the relationship between staging this performance and your paycheck.*

To the school's auditorium, the woman brought liters of Gatorade®, stowing them in her backpack the way a cosmonaut might carry extra air tanks. She sipped the liquid through a tube, paced the stage. To the preteens, huddled in the wings, she explained the situation: she needed to pay her mortgage, which meant she needed to keep her job, which meant she needed to organize a student performance, which under normal circumstances would be easy—she'd organized many productions, both avant-garde and traditional—but this one posed an added layer of difficulty. Their show needed to impress a visiting group of potential donors. It was hard to attract funding for a school such as theirs: distinctively undistinctive.

She asked the preteens if there was a play they wanted to perform, but the preteens couldn't think of any plays except *Romeo and Juliet* and that play was not an option.

The woman took a sip from the tube extending from a hole in her backpack, gulped a mouthful of orange. The preteens began to back away. The color from the drink had slithered down her throat, visible under her skin like an eel coursing through cloudy water. The color pooled by her collarbones, drifted down her arms to her wrists. The woman slid into a sitting position, her legs dangling over the edge of the stage. She rocked back and forth, side to side. It was true her stomach did not feel great; or else, no longer felt like a stomach. If anything, her insides were starting to feel indistinguishable from the outside air. At night, she talked to her father on the phone and he told her again that she really ought to start eating real food—it wasn't natural, what she was drinking—but he was a man who fed sugar to bees in the winter, who had married a woman who put syrup out for hummingbirds in the summer; he could not deny that those bees and those birds were robust, active, productive creatures.

A few of the braver preteens became curious—they tiptoed closer to the woman and peered at her.

She raised her head, grinned at them with orange teeth.

———

It's just not going to work, her husband had said, standing in the kitchen of their new home, the rooms empty, the walls blank—except for the uncurtained windows: lit up with the red flush of a sunset.

You need too much, her husband said, though only after the woman had signed the last of the paperwork, and after the real estate agent had left.

You need more than I can give, he said.

Your needs are exhausting.

Your anxiety, in particular, is exhausting.

And you won't take medication.

Also, you always make me drive when we go on road trips.

You are weirdly territorial about porches.

You tell long boring stories about your dreams.

You always expect me to make the plans.

You have no real pleasures.

You expect me to fill you up with joy.

You take your art too seriously.

You're still hung up on a high school debate tournament.

You can't take a compliment.

You expect my friends to be your friends.

You made fun of my favorite shirt.

You watch too much TV.

You get mad when I lie to you.

You expect me to tell you everything.

You chew loudly.

Do you think the ferry has left yet, or no? her husband said, though he wasn't looking at her when he asked. He was looking at one of the big bare windows, at what lay beyond. Before arriving on the island, the woman had been excited to have all those windows: vantages from which they could both watch sea mists and ocean swells and—oh god—the sunsets. She'd believed that was what he wanted; she'd believed that was enough.

The preteens told the woman their sad little stories about wildly talented older sisters and fabulously delinquent younger brothers. They told her about mediocre grades, mediocre looks, about pet hermit crabs that wouldn't do anything interesting but also wouldn't die. The preteens described JV soccer teams. Bullies who refused them the dignity of a black eye. Families who visited infrequently, but not so seldom it became tragic—had any cachet.

Some of the preteens started to cry and the woman teared up, too, purple liquid dripping down her cheeks. The crying made her dizzy; she had gotten so thin by then that losing any liquid felt hemorrhagic.

To make herself stop crying, the woman pressed her fingers to her temples. The skin beneath her fingertips turned silvery white—indicating the pooling presence of Gatorade Frost® Thirst Quencher in Glacier Cherry®—but the preteens had gotten used to such occurrences. None flinched.

The woman told the preteens that leading roles were overrated; it was the supporting cast who made a production come alive. A performer didn't need to be center stage, spotlighted, to mean something. In fact, you could remain largely unnoticed and be indispensable to a production. The industry term, the woman explained—feeling teacherly, revitalized—was *background actor*. Or if you wanted to be fancy: *atmospherian*.

Do you get paid? said one of the preteens. *In that kind of role?*

The woman sighed, long and deep, her breath so steeped in Glacier Cherry® it filled the auditorium with a white haze, smog-thick, densely sugar sweet and cloying.

Are you okay? said a preteen. *Hello?*

Once, at a party, a particle scientist had told the woman about the benefits of air pollution. Specifically, he'd explained how when the atmosphere fills with the right kind of particulate matter—aerosolized rocket fumes, volcano dust—sunsets can become more intense. The sky deepens into sorbet-sweet pinks, violently violet reds, heart-squeezing streaks of yellow gold. All that awful pollution could make the sky beautiful. There was something to be said, according to the particle scientist, for badness—in the right amounts, and in the right places—because what was better than a sunset, really? What wasn't there to like?

What the woman knew about sky color: red sky in the morning, sailors take warning; red sky at night, sailors' delight.

And yet, the sky had been red the evening her husband left—that was what continued to confuse her.

Is the show ready? said her boss.

You do know the donor visit is next week, said her boss.

You understand how important it is for us to prove to the donors how robust our arts program is, so we can build a new admissions office, a stadium, a bigger auditorium—so we can impress the donors more?

———

The particle scientist and the woman had been at a party in a cocktail bar on the top floor of a skyscraper when he told her about the benefits of pollution. The sunset had been extraordinary that evening—lush oranges melting into crimson-violets, clouds hovering near the horizon like glowing embers—which got the particle scientist talking.

That beauty, the particle scientist said, *the paradox of that beauty—that's what I'm obsessed with. How something can be bad and good at the same time.*

That's what I've devoted my life to, he said. *That's what I'll never get enough of.*

I could stare and stare and stare.

A sunset is always changing, you see.

Every second: something new.

At a certain stage of thinness, the body becomes all caverns and hollows, divots and disappearances. The body becomes an island: its surface a shoreline, eroded. For the woman, with her rose-vision—which became orange-vision, blue-vision, purple-vision—the hollows on her body were places in which a color might hover and commingle, drift away. Color moved through her: a vibrant shroud, a delicious mist, a billowing convergence of clouds, her own weather system.

The donor show, when it happened, was different from anything the woman had ever staged. Everyone was cast as an extra. The preteens drifted around the auditorium, dressed as restaurant patrons and townspeople and farm animals and anonymous soldiers and nonaggressive zombies, and no one entered any of the spotlights and no one spoke. When it was over, there was a long, long quiet, because it was hard for the audience to know the performance had ended, given that none of the participants had held a speaking role.

A gurgle from the woman's stomach broke the silence. Though she was ensconced backstage, the gurgle echoed throughout the auditorium. Despite the noise, the woman took another sip from the tube extending into her backpack— one of several tubes now, channeling yellow, purple, red. The gurgling grew into a roar: her stomach so full of color, so loud with it—the noise rushing up into her head—she couldn't tell if everyone in the auditorium was cheering, uproarious with the ecstasy of the performance, or if the ocean was making the noise: a gale brewing out beyond the school, wind battering the island. She tried to get a peek at the audience from backstage, but her vision had become too dense with color by then, swirling full of all she had consumed, which made it hard to see anything at all.

(A sunset, like a curtain falling.)

The particle scientist, if we're being honest, was her husband. Once, they had stood on the terrace of a cocktail bar on the top of a skyscraper in a midsized, arts-centric, still-affordable city. They had watched the sky—particle-filled—burn orange, then crimson-red, before bruising wine-dark purple. Together, they'd imagined owning a house with 360-degree views, like the skyscraper, where sunsets would be visible in full, every night. Those colors, beautiful and bad all at once, had reflected in her husband's eyes as he'd stared at the sky, a hunger on his face. And the woman had said, half-joking: *I wish I could drink those colors in. I wish I could consume them. Would you love me more then, if I had a sunset inside me? Would you love me, despite the bad parts? Would you look at me until the colors faded, all the way until the end, when the lights at last went out?*

Chevalier

Edith Eleanor Watts, who everyone called Eddy, hit her head when she fell off the radio tower, after climbing eight rungs high to impress Lyle Baxter II.

The swelling started immediately.

So did Eddy's inquests.

"Was Lyle watching?" she asked as we loaded her into the backseat of my Buick. "Did he look concerned?"

Trixie Everheart pressed an ice-cream sandwich against Eddy's forehead, proclaiming Lyle's paleness post-fall to be a sign of affection.

"He always looks pale," I said, but no one took any notice. Everything was already decided. Lyle's complexion offered irrefutable evidence: he would ask her out. Tomorrow maybe—or the day after. Once he'd had time to regain his composure.

A week passed, with no word from Lyle. Eddy's forehead, however, continued transforming—bulging—as if an egg were lodged in the center of her brow, and that egg was *hell-bent* on hatching. She kept her good looks, otherwise. Slim as stretched chewing gum, with brown hair blessed by a magazine sheen, and eyes like cracked geodes: full of crystals, depending on the light.

Her prettiness, though, made the swelling more conspicuous. An ugly person might have hid the disfigurement better.

Not that Eddy cared. She wore the swelling like a trophy. Told anyone who'd listen that she'd earned the lump by soaring through space for her One True Love.

I thought she'd earned it by being an idiot.

But as usual, I kept quiet.

"You should join a traveling circus," said Albert Hotchkins, who liked Eddy but pretended he didn't.

"Shut up, Albert," said Trixie, who pretended she did. "Eddy looks foxy-hot."

It was Friday night in Chevalier, and like most of the town's youth population, we'd wound up at the bowling alley. Albert sipped his cream soda and offered it to Eddy. Eddy had her own, but she accepted his beverage anyway. Drained it in a single swig.

"You consider seeing a physician?" I asked, unable to ignore her distended brow. "It looks like it really hurts."

You would have thought I'd brought up tax brackets, or fungal growth rates, or the dissolution of the former Yugoslavia, the way Eddy rolled her eyes. "Are we going to start bowling soon or what?" she said to the others. "Lyle might show up any minute."

Eddy, Trixie, and Albert trooped off to rent bowling shoes, but I stayed put. I'd always been the nice one in the group—a title I held with some pride—but I'd been growing increasingly fed up with Eddy, same as I'd been getting sick of cream soda and listening to the ABBA tracks my mother played every night during dinner. Of course I could suffer the soda, and even respect the way my mother had been deliberately driving my father insane the past five years, but I couldn't stand being treated like a doormat.

Especially by a friend. A close friend. A twelve-years-and-counting friend.

"Let's get this show rolling," said Eddy, who had installed herself in a lane with the others, on the far end of the bowling alley.

Albert selected a bowling ball and was cueing up his release when Trixie gave Eddy the signal for *boy-alert*: an alternating eyebrow lift.

Lyle had arrived.

It wasn't Eddy's turn yet, but she snatched the bowling ball from Albert and sent it careening into candlepins.

"Strike!" she exclaimed, doing a hip-centric victory dance.

Lyle squinted toward her, his hand on the lever of an arcade game.

Trixie's eyebrows began rapid-fire twitching.

I stayed watching, feeling like a lost planet—or a forgotten moon—orbiting the outskirts of a solar system that I maybe wanted to be part of. Maybe not.

It wasn't always like this. In fact, it wasn't so long ago that Eddy cried to me in the submarine darkness of a routine sleepover. "Cam?" she whispered, her voice trembling. "You awake? I really gotta tell you something."

I was awake. Bunked on the pullout couch in my family's den, I'd been listening to Trixie's chain saw snore and contemplating putting her bra in the freezer.

"It's a secret," Eddy added.

In those days, secrets came a dime a dozen—our incumbent crushes, the location of an older sister's nail polish—they were the currency of friendship, and Eddy liked to spend.

Still, a secret was a secret.

"I'm listening," I said.

Eddy's sleeping bag rustled in the pitch black. "I get this dream," she began. "I go totally invisible and everyone keeps walking by me, even when I yell and stuff."

She paused, as if struggling to describe something too horrible for words.

"I mean *everyone*," she repeated. "My mom, your mom, Trixie. Even Trixie's dog. Then I disappear."

The dream didn't seem like that big a deal. I'd had far worse involving my grandmother's collectible forks. But then Eddy's hand fumbled through quilts until her fingers found mine. She seemed genuinely spooked—squeezing my fingers like I was her only hope in the world—which made my heart beat harder than usual. I wanted to be brave on her behalf.

"You'll never be invisible," I assured her, in my most grown-up voice: solemn and unflustered. "That'll never happen."

"You promise?"

I squeezed her hand back and said I did. While it seemed highly unlikely Eddy would ever be ignored—by me or anyone—I firmly believed that what one asked of friends wasn't supposed to make sense. Because love wasn't supposed to.

"I promise," I told her, "you'll never be invisible to me."

———

Two weeks after the radio tower incident, Eddy's forehead had swollen to unprecedented proportions. So had her efforts to attract Lyle. We spent most nights staking out his place of employment: Pisa Pizza. That, or calling his house, then hanging up.

I decided to write Eddy a letter detailing her increasing disregard for other people's feelings and time. Specifically: mine. I brought the letter to school, and was about to hand it over during third-period English, but then—right as our teacher, Mr. Stiegler, started jawing on the *Epic of Gilgamesh*—the lump on Eddie's brow made a hissing pop and split open.

"Oh my god," I whispered, the letter forgotten. "You okay?"

Eddy patted her forehead. "Honestly," she said, "it just feels like a giant zit."

Trixie laughed so hard she almost choked on the pencil she'd been chewing. Mr. Stiegler's bald head swiveled toward our seats in the back of the room, and I'm sure he wanted to say something smooth, like: "What's so funny about an unsuccessful quest for immortality?" But high school girls had a way of making him blush. He tugged at the collar of his shirt, shushed, "Ladies, page twenty-three, please."

I noticed a bit of bone poking from Eddy's brow. A white nub, like an extra knuckle. "Maybe you should go to the nurse?" I said.

Eddy ignored me, doodled hearts on her copy of *Gilgamesh*.

Trixie glanced toward the classroom door, then sat up straight—gripped her desk as if she'd seen an antagonist-turned-friend return from the underworld.

"Lyle just walked by in the hallway!" she said. "He's wearing an argyle sweater—that's an enterprising pattern!"

Eddy nodded. "He's gonna ask me out today," she said. "I know it."

———

Lyle did not ask Eddy out. By sixth period, he had not even said hello, despite multiple opportunities orchestrated in front of his locker. Eddy's forehead, however, continued transforming: the bony nub lengthened, stretched skyward as a narrow pearly spire, six inches long and gleaming. A horn.

"It's like something you'd see on a mythical creature," said Trixie as we crouched under the bleachers during gym class. "Like a unicorn."

I could tell Trixie was impressed, borderline jealous. She wasn't very good at hiding that sort of thing.

"Unicorns aren't real," said Albert.

No one ever invited Albert, but he had a way of showing up in conversations.

"They're about done running laps," I said. Through the gaps between bleacher seats, I could see the other kids bent double over knees, tongues lolling, eyes blank as chicken broth. I'd been watching them to avoid staring at Eddy, about whom I wasn't sure what to feel. She looked both magnificent and ridiculous.

Eddy, clearly, saw herself on the *magnificent* end of the spectrum. Smiling faintly, she ran a finger along the length of the horn. Then she ducked out from under the bleachers and strolled in among her winded peers.

"Anyone wanna race?" she said. "I'm not even sweating."

I think she expected the growth on her forehead to cause a stir—and she did collect a few curious stares, probably grounded in her ability to skip laps once again—but then a red-faced kid projectile-vomited and passed out on a gymnastics mat.

"That's the coolest thing I've ever seen," exclaimed Lyle,

who'd faked chest pains to sit out of class. He was not looking at Eddy.

The bell rang. Eddy toe-kicked a dodgeball across the gym floor.

"Let's go, Camilla," said Trixie, tugging me out from under the bleachers. "Quit looking so smug."

So now Eddy had a genuine horn protruding from her forehead: hard as steel, beautiful as a narwhal nose. No one took much notice, naturally. Chevalier had its fair share of freaks and celebrities. Hell! We were the birthplace of running back great Bobby Chanel, and quilting champion Denise Dann. We had a guy with no arms who owned an antique store, and a couple of lesbians living on Abbott Street.

What was a girl with a horn to most people?

"You know, honey," said Eddy's mother, who was the only one to take any real interest, "horns aren't exactly the rage these days. Are you sure you want to keep it? I mean, do you even like it?"

"No," said Eddy. "Yes."

Trixie told Eddy that she'd heard Lyle thought it was fake. Eddy said she didn't really care what Lyle thought anymore. He was a bit of a bore, wasn't he? She wanted someone or something with a little more tooth.

"I've been thinking," she said one night as we browsed the whoopie pies at Speedie's GasMart, "I might go somewhere."

Her words filled me with a fountain of hope. A trip might be just what our friendship needed. It would be an adventure— like the kind we'd had before Eddy became obsessed with Lyle.

"What about Beauford?" I said, remembering trips to see

firework shows. Or to egg the other high school's mascot. Or to visit the town's larger, newer Speedie's GasMart.

"Get real, Cam." Eddy admired her reflection in a beverage cooler: the wet glint of lip gloss and an opalescent horn superimposed over packs of Bud Light. "I mean *go somewhere* go somewhere. Like leave town for good."

I laughed. Then I realized she was serious. For all Eddy's caprice, hadn't she always at least been original? Everyone talked about leaving Chevalier; the idea was a cliché. People generally planned to go west, to California, where weed was speculated to be legal and workweeks four hours long. Or they talked about Europe—especially the guys who studied French and used *très magnifique* to describe their girlfriends. But hardly anyone actually left, or if they did it wasn't for long. What else was out there, really? Lonely days? Lonelier nights?

Chevalier could be boring, sure, but at least we had each other.

"I'm thinking maybe New York," continued Eddy, her thin fingers pinching a whoopie pie, as if testing the idea.

For such a seasoned performer, she wasn't much of a liar; she'd obviously been considering leaving for a while—which felt like another slap in the face.

"The store carries these," said Albert, pointing to a display of road maps by the register.

Eddy selected a map, used it to fan herself. "Make me a purple slushy," she told Albert.

The map was only good as far as Connecticut, but I decided she could figure that out herself if she was really so keen on the plan.

"Red slushies are better," said Albert.

"Shut up, Albert," said Trixie. "No one cares what you think."

◆

Trixie married Albert five years later. They had an outdoor "open concept" wedding—Trixie's idea since she ended up studying interior design—and pretty much the whole town showed up. Even Denise Dann and Bobby Chanel's younger brother.

If I had to guess, Eddy was only invited to stroke Trixie's matrimonial ego. No one actually expected her to come. She did, though, unfurling from a taxi ten minutes into the service, her high heels grinding into backyard gravel over the minister's drone. Everyone seated on Albert's parents' front lawn ignored her—even Albert's mother, Mrs. Hotchkins, kept her eyes trained on Trixie's bouquet—but the effort was the stuff of heroics. It was one thing to arrive late to important occasions but quite another to take a cab. If you needed a ride in Chevalier, you called Patty "Jesus Saved Me from Cigarettes" Labash. Or you called one of your friends.

But I suppose Eddy didn't have those anymore.

After the service, I hunkered down on the Hotchkinses' screened porch. While I'd gained a bit of a reputation as a storyteller—specializing in elaboration—that night I wasn't feeling too talkative. Instead, I watched Eddy drift across the lawn like a loose newspaper page. No one said much to her, or if they did, it wasn't about her unusual choice in transportation, much less her five-year absence. Chevalierians are far too polite to badmouth someone to their face. Most folks went on ignoring her the same way she'd ignored us. We're a proud bunch, I'll give us that. Even when someone noticed her horn was missing, she was only asked if she'd met anyone famous in New York.

"I work in retail," she said, as if that meant something.

From the way Trixie carried on, one might have assumed she was too preoccupied by her nuptials to notice Eddy. But Trixie had seen her immediately. She was, like the rest of us, only doing her best to avoid the obvious: Eddy had been gone for years; she was a giantess in her heels; and, from the way Albert stared, he was clearly still in love with her. Even when Trixie did eventually swish over—cheeks flushed from champagne and a bit of frosting smeared across her upper lip—she just said, "Lyle got pretty fat, didn't he?" and whisked away before Eddy could answer.

I felt bad, in spite of myself.

Even so, I remained in my screen porch hideout. History hung heavy in the air; brought on by dusk and the cinder smoke of a chargrill and the rueful whine of an adolescent band, it clotted conversation, made even the mosquitoes drowsy with memory. A droopy-eyed woman mused on her first kiss: tongues gone xylophonic across teeth. A bearded man recalled working as a bag boy at the Phyllis N' Sons Grocery Store. I thought about the day Eddy left: how she'd caught a ride with a knife saleswoman the morning we were supposed to move in together. "Don't be mad, Cam," Eddy had called, leaning out the truck window, her horn glinting in the sun. "There's nothing here for me."

"I'm here," I'd answered, but by then she was already gone.

I'm here, I said to myself once more, having made a point of staying in Chevalier, having made a life of it.

Had this been the right choice? Rather than answering my own question, I turned to the others on the screen porch, asked them what they made of Eddy's missing horn.

"Bet she sold it," said Albert, who couldn't find anyone else to hang out with, even at his own wedding. "Probably to a New Age crystal shop or something." He peeled off a layer of sweaty tuxedo. "Rent's real high in New York. I've seen a movie about it."

From across the lawn, Trixie's laugh rang out like jangling keys. Then someone suggested that maybe Eddy's horn had just fallen off. We don't consider ourselves intellectuals in Chevalier—in fact, we deny the title given the chance—but we're not entirely unread. Even we knew that sort of thing happened.

"I still say it was fake," said Lyle, who hadn't gotten any cake and was cranky.

I got the real story, though. You might even call it the play-by-play. It was after the wedding, which stretched into the dingy part of the evening, long enough for the citronella candles to burn down and for Denise Dann to vomit in the birdbath and for the town's teenagers to sneak off with the extra booze. There were loud goodbyes from the newlyweds, whistles from a few guests, and the rattle of soup cans dragged behind Albert's parents' car. As far as I could tell, Eddy was gone, too.

I felt foolish. I might have at least said hello.

Then Mrs. Hotchkins hollered for help cleaning up, and everyone suddenly remembered a commitment to bedtimes. Guests stumbled into hydrangeas and foldout tables, looking for their shoes or an extra crab cake to take home. That's when

I saw Eddy. She was on the move: striding across the lawn, her high heels puncturing the turf. She was heading toward Mr. Stiegler, our old English teacher. She was smiling a big lipsticked smile—the first hint of happiness she'd shown all evening—and when she threw open her arms for a hug, I thought their reunion was rather sweet.

Then she held on too long.

I scanned the departing crowd for a reaction: for furrowed brows and tongues clucking. For Mrs. Hotchkins's shrill voice asking: "Who does that girl think she is?"

But no one said anything. It was as if I was the only one who noticed her.

Eddy unlaced her arms from Mr. Stiegler's and began twirling a strand of hair with one finger, her other hand on her hip. She giggled.

What are you doing? I muttered to myself as I watched from my screen porch hideout. *Of all people? Mr. Stiegler?*

Still no one said anything to Eddy. Wedding guests drifted away, oblivious, their shadows soaked up by the night. A tipsy Mrs. Hotchkins directed Trixie's brothers in the art of table-carrying.

Eddy reached out and stroked the bald dome of Mr. Stiegler's head, as Mr. Stiegler smiled stupidly. Was he blushing? Was he enjoying this? Then a more horrific thought occurred to me: Was she? I watched as Eddy held a finger to her lips. She did not seem drunk, but rather steely and determined. She took his hands in hers.

"Eddy!"

I burst out the screen porch door and ran toward my old friend, unsure what I was going to do, but certain that something needed doing—I could not stand to see her making a scene with our old English teacher.

"Oh hello, Cam," said Eddy, as if my panting appearance were the most natural thing in the world. "I was just chatting with—"

Mr. Stiegler, though, had already fled.

We ended up driving to the radio tower. Nothing in town was open that late, and for some reason I thought Eddy might want to see it. A fence had been installed in the past year, which we could have climbed if we'd wanted. Neither of us did. Instead, we sat on the hood of my car and looked toward downtown Chevalier: a low valley and a scrubby hayfield away.

Eddy didn't have much to say, so I did most of the talking. I tried to be curt, if not nonchalant, as I described what had happened in the years she'd been gone, but pretty soon my words trickled into a torrent. I told her about my job at the primary school. About my parents' divorce. About the spring rainstorms and the flooding downtown and how Pisa Pizza had closed from water damage. I told her how Albert courted Trixie: once he left a bouquet of chocolate roses in her car, but it was a hot day, so they melted. I told her that while I hadn't met the right person, I tried not to worry. After all, there weren't too many options in Chevalier, were there? "Besides Lyle."

Eddy didn't laugh. "You're serious?" she said. "Pisa Pizza is gone?"

This response irritated me. Couldn't she at least pretend to care about us, our lives? I considered bringing up Mr. Stiegler; it had occurred to me that she'd flirted with him because she'd known doing so would get my attention—a ploy that seemed excessive, even for her. Embarrassing, too. In a wave of mean-ness, I considered saying: *What? You can't find any decent men in New York?*

The question wriggled in my grasp, slick and ugly as a bullfrog.

"What? You can't find any decent pizza in New York?" I said instead.

Eddy looked at me, bored. My insides churned. I tried to think of something else to add, but in the ensuing quiet, the radio tower creaked, as if stretching awake in the night breeze. I remembered how, years ago, Eddy and I had carved our initials into the railing: *CAL+EEW*. Trixie hadn't carved hers because she'd been scared the police would later track her down. Albert had cut open his thumb.

I tried to read Eddy's face in the dim light—not far from mine as we sat on the car hood—to see if she was thinking about those initials, too.

But Eddy, with a yawn, said: "I suppose you want to hear about the city."

I didn't like the way she offered—as if I were desperate—and yet there it was, that dark sparkling thing: the answer to the question that had followed me around these past five years. What *had* she left for?

And then: What had been so good that she hadn't come back?

"I guess," I said.

Eddy drew in a breath, as if drawing in energy, sucking expectations out of the air. She'd always done this: made her audiences wait. It made me happy, despite myself, to see the old Eddy emerge from this lipsticked woman in a glove-tight dress.

"First," she said, "was the Empire State Building." She propped herself up on her elbows, cleared her throat, her voice slipping into a familiar lilt: musical and mesmerizing. "I caught a bus there and took an elevator straight to the top, a whole hundred and two floors up in the sky."

Eddy kept going: getting louder, sitting taller. She said she'd gazed out from the observation deck, feeling all tingly and respectful—the way a person does at church—until she realized no one else was looking at the view. Everyone was looking at her. Not casually, either. They were staring: eyes wide, mouths open, coffee cups dropped on the floor. People looked at her, it turned out, wherever she went in the city. With her horn, she stood out in a way she never had in Chevalier. People eyed her on the subway, peeping over the tops of their newspapers; they paused their Frisbee games when she walked through the park. Tourists took photos. She could barely stand to eat in restaurants.

"Halloween," she said, with a laugh that wobbled between amusement and ache, "was the only break I got."

Eddy told me about art museums that displayed plates of rotting meat and couches with curse words carved into them. Even there, people stared. They held toothpicked cheese up to their faces and missed their mouths. In the streets, everyone moved in human rivers, gushed through skyscraper canyons so frantic with light that invisibility became impossible, aloneness out of the question. People got shot, people got hit by buses, people won prestigious awards, and yet everyone looked at her. They—

"Stop," I said. I couldn't listen anymore.

She stopped, unperturbed, as if she'd been waiting for me to ask. Then we both looked toward Chevalier, as if the town might comment as well. Even from under the radio tower, we could see the matchstick glow of downtown streetlamps, the neon wink of Speedie's GasMart, and the odd bedroom window lit up in the night.

A dog howled its mournful assumptions.

"Not anymore, though," Eddy added quietly. She patted the place where her horn had been, almost sheepish.

It was a particular kind of summer night, the kind when young people skittered in and out of shadows, looking for something to do, trying to compensate for imagined cities: the unreachable wonders of other worlds. It was a night when people might fall in love—let their hands find one another's fingers in the dark—bravery made newly possible. It was a night, too, for mischief. On a night like this, teenagers might uproot the *Welcome to Chevalier* sign on Route 47. If everything went according to plan, they'd slide the sign into the town pool. I'd seen it happen before: the sign submerged underwater, the town's motto, *Cela est suffisant*, swimming like an alphabetic fish at the bottom of the pool. People were proud of that sign, even if they didn't always know what it meant, and even if they were the ones who splashed it into the deep end.

There remained so much more to talk about, but I noticed Eddy check her watch. It was a delicate silver number, the sort no one has a reason to wear in Chevalier: it would get busted doing dishes. I felt a hard knot of pride as I remembered my sturdy practicality, my foothold in a town to which she'd never really be able to return.

"Sounds like you've got everything worked out," I said with a spasm of cheerfulness. "And anyway"—I eyed the dark space around her forehead—"it didn't mean anything, did it?"

The question crawled around our shoulders, thick as sleepover blankets. From across the car's hood, Eddy looked at me. There was hurt in her eyes: an expression, I realized, I'd never seen before. She looked at me as if I'd failed to understand something important. Something crucial between us. It made me want to apologize: to tell her how much I'd missed her, that I'd only stayed in Chevalier to prove that I could.

Then I recognized the absurdity of such thoughts. Hadn't Eddy been the one to hurt me? What a reckless girl! What a careless friend! I wanted to push her right off the car's hood.

And I might have done it. Really and truly. But before I could, Eddy brushed the hair away from her forehead and leaned her face close to mine, so that for a moment I saw the place where her widow's peak pointed—a white circle, like a full moon or an inverse shadow—like a promise you can't remember, but can't forget.

II

The Future Is a Click Away

The Algorithm knew the timing of our periods. It knew when and if we'd marry. Whether we'd have kids. It knew how we'd die. It knew where we went, why we lingered, why we left. It knew what seemed unknowable: the hidden chambers of our hearts. When it sent us tampons in the mail, we took them. We paid.

We were a matrix of a billion-trillion data points. The Algorithm had them all. It saw patterns inside of patterns, heard the whispered implications of our every click, hover, scroll speed, misspelled search term. The Algorithm decoded our emails—our text messages, too. It could read a crab emoji like a rune, a dream symbol: our subconscious laid naked before its supercomputer mind. The Algorithm had studied enough crab emojis to know how people acted after using one. It synthesized this data with a thousand other patterns—stock market fluctuations, mortgage rates, the local weather—decoding our cyber DNA to peer through the looking glass of the space-time continuum and perceive our future needs. A crab emoji texted after *i luv you*; the Algorithm sent a pack of micro-filtering vacuum bags.

Deliveries occurred at least twice a day in most regions.

The Algorithm sent Sonya, in Fairbanks, AK, a box of sponges. Sonya already had sponges, but not the kind with a scouring pad on one side, which made the Algorithm's delivery fortunate—no, fated—because that night she burned a pan of lasagna.

Anastasia, in Harrisonburg, VA, received an ankle brace. The Algorithm had anticipated the sprain she'd suffer later that week on a hike up the High Knob Trail. Was the prediction predicated on a kink in Anastasia's posture—the reality of weakening cartilage embedded in a lifetime cross-section of bathroom mirror selfies? Or was there an air of recklessness in her email sign-offs that week (*ttyl, Ana*)? In the end, the Algorithm's methods didn't matter so long as she got what she needed.

Fatima, in Taos, NM, received a set of lemon-scented soy-wax candles.

Everly, in Great Falls, MN, received an all-weather wireless phone charger.

Jan, in Marfa, TX, received a twelve-ounce bottle of motor oil.

Deidre, in Detroit, MI, got a whole sofa: malachite green, velvet soft, curvaceous. Was it because she'd clicked on stain removers? Streamed too many David Lynch movies? Collected semiprecious stones as a child and uploaded images to multiple social media accounts? Didn't matter. Deidre loved the sofa: a distillation of her desires that materialized outside her door with the swift wonder of a miracle. Depending on where you lived, the Algorithm used drones to drop goods outside of homes in bubble-wrapped packages; or else, workers off-loaded cardboard boxes from unmarked trucks; or, in some instances, goods were whisked into apartment lobbies through pneumatic tubes—though that feature remained unavailable to people in most parts of the country.

You are always welcome, the Algorithm noted on every packing slip, *to send these items back.*

We never sent the items back. We knew we might regret the returns if we did—because the Algorithm was always right.

"Sure, but what if the Algorithm is in cahoots with certain for-profit companies?" speculated a few journalists. "What if a woman receives an ankle brace because Big Ankle Bruce is pushing their latest model—not because the woman really needs podiatric support for joint inflammation?"

These questions were rhetorical; the journalists took the Algorithm's goods, too.

"Perhaps we find uses for the items we receive because we have received them," suggested several behavioral psychologists. "Maybe it's a form of confirmation bias?"

But the behavioral psychologists confirmed that they also took the goods.

"Could be witchcraft," said the anti-witch agitators, who were suspicious of the Algorithm's uncanny accuracy. Yet this faction later disowned their prejudice, after receiving thought-provoking pamphlets on the topic—pamphlets that were constructed by us, using the paper and sparkly pens the Algorithm delivered to our homes for such purposes.

The Algorithm worked in mysterious ways.

Which isn't to say there weren't a few true nonbelievers.

There was a small contingent of people who sent the Algorithm's goods back.

People like Inez, in Denver, CO.

Inez wouldn't accept her deliveries from the Algorithm, even when she needed a particular item, such as socks—because hers were full of holes—and new beautiful socks arrived outside her door.

"But you have money from your pension," we said. "And these socks are reasonably priced."

"Also," we said, "it's a hassle to return stuff."

"And these socks would fit you perfectly," we added. "There's space for your one long toe."

Inez wouldn't accept the goods. A curmudgeon. Seventy-something years old, we estimated, though we could not be sure. Inez had also refused the sunscreen and wide-brimmed hats the Algorithm sent to protect her skin from the damaging effects of UV radiation—which was especially bad in Denver due to the city's high elevation. Inez sent the sunscreen and the hats back, along with a note to be left alone. She returned the socks, too, opting to darn her old pairs with yarn she'd acquired from the shantytown market: a motley bazaar at the far edge of Denver's sprawl, where a rough crowd bartered for used and broken bric-a-brac, wilted homegrown lettuce, amateur ceramics. Inez acquired most of her goods at the market. Or she went without.

"No wonder she's grumpy," we said to one another.

We did not understand her resistance to the Algorithm. All we knew for sure was that the Algorithm understood us. After all, we'd been inside its system since before we knew how to type—back when our parents first posted photos documenting our infant-bodies, swaddled and squishy in hospital beds. Although we had no proof, we suspected that the Algorithm might have known, even then, the fates that lay before us: not only what items we'd need, but who we would become. The Algorithm had already predicted that Umi would be a helicopter pilot; and Kendall a veterinarian specializing in equine treatments; and Arley a nicotine-addicted fashion model, who would sometimes take horse tranquilizers and require medical evacuation via helicopter. From our first uploaded image, the Algorithm had been invested in our futures. It had analyzed the texture of our baby blankets, the micro-musculature on our crying faces, the awkward cradle of our parents' arms. Then again, perhaps the Algorithm had known us before we even officially existed—extrapolating likely outcomes from our parents' data points, and our parents' parents' data points—a long legacy of information digested and decoded, transformed into the deliveries that appeared outside our doors.

It brought us comfort to be known so fully. Through the long march of adulthood—in which we lost our friends to distance, our parents to age—we never felt truly alone. We had something looking out for us, didn't we? We had the Algorithm at our side.

To be fair, there were a few deliveries that gave us pause. For instance, there was the time the Algorithm sent one among us packages of ground coffee—decaf—and we were mildly annoyed. Decaf? Really? What good would decaf do when we had emails to answer, charts to consider, customers to serve? How would we stay awake? We almost called the Algorithm's customer service, but our doctor's office called us first. Our test results had come in. The cardiologist recommended we reduce our caffeine intake.

We were grateful; we gave thanks. We praised the Algorithm for its insight and the gift of individualized commodity distribution.

We took our goods. We paid.

"See how much better our lives are?" we said to Inez when we passed her on the street. "With all these products selected for us by the Algorithm?"

She was carting a wheelbarrow full of wild mushrooms, bits of wire, tattered out-of-date almanacs. Her white hair was damp from the exertion. Beside her walked a drifter—dressed in a fake-fur coat and rain boots—who Inez had likely met at the shantytown market. The drifter carried a large ceramic jug filled with a sloshy liquid; he grinned at us toothlessly.

We ignored the drifter, focused on Inez. It upset us to see this elderly woman performing such taxing labor, her body sweating and un-sunscreened as she pushed her wheelbarrow forward.

"Why," we said, "won't you accept the packages of pre-prepared meals and the easy-yet-entertaining craft items the Algorithm has delivered to your home?"

Inez grunted, continued pushing the wheelbarrow. The drifter made a birdcall noise.

"If you did," we went on—our voices growing shrieky with agitation—"you wouldn't have to haul these odds and ends all the way across the city!"

Inez sighed. She stopped pushing the wheelbarrow and turned to face us—and for a moment we thought we'd achieved victory: we'd helped this old woman relinquish her unneces-sary stoicism—but then Inez said: "What could the Algorithm know about me that I don't? How can it possibly perceive the true depths of my soul? The Algorithm is a corporate robot, not a god. It was programmed by people and I've met people. I will not worship at the altar of capitalistic codependence. I will live freely and of my own accord."

The drifter hooted.

We shook our heads, retreated into our houses. We knew Inez was misguided, but it would be a lie to say her words did not linger in our minds. It would be a lie, too, to suggest that those of us in Inez's neighborhood did not peer through our windows at night, watching as Inez and the drifter—or maybe multiple drifters?—drank moonshine and sang sea shanties on her porch. Because we did. We also watched as she staggered outside the next morning to water her tomato plants, her white hair wild, her belches loud as she ignored the box of electrolyte-filled coconut water the Algorithm had delivered to her doorstep to help with her hangover.

We did not understand Inez's thinking. We were glad, though, that the Algorithm understood ours—it sent foam stress balls to everyone living in Inez's neighborhood, having anticipated our anxiety. It sent batches of sleeping pills as well, so that everyone's rest would be unpunctuated by sea shanties or doubt. The Algorithm knew we were simply trying to live our lives: to attend our dentist appointments and our children's soccer matches and our parents' funerals, and to do our jobs well enough to pay for it all. The Algorithm saved us time and preserved our energy. It sent us baby clothes before we had babies. Bigger clothes before we gained weight. The Algorithm always remembered our birthdays. It sympathized with our struggles; for instance, when we missed our friends—who were too busy or far away to grab a casual coffee—the Algorithm sent us photo albums containing images of past coffees that it had culled from our social media accounts. We wept over those curated pages. We happily paid the four installments of $39.99. The Algorithm was always looking out for us; we were grateful when it delivered new home security features, anticipating a rise in local crime. It sent us bottles of milk before riots broke out in some cities, predicting that tear gas would be carried on the wind and irritate our eyes. In Denver, where the air was thin and dry, our noses sometimes bled—dripping like faucets—even on the days no riots occurred, and so the Algorithm sent us tissues. It sent home humidifiers. Gas masks. Air-moisturizing houseplants. It sent earplugs for helicopter noise. Air purifiers for wildfire smoke. It sent us charcoal water for general bodily purification. The Algorithm sent us more and more, ever striving to make our lives better. It intuited the larger television we needed as a distraction from the chaos outside our homes, as well as the blouses and indoor golf putters and candy bars and fountain pens and hand towels and salt rocks and macramé plant hangers and chess sets and watercolor paper and glass unicorn figurines and frying pans and tweezers and duct tape and decorative wall prints and toilet paper and antacid tablets and hair dye and cat beds and mandolins and exercise bikes and plastic orchids and rare Roman coins we coveted, delivering these items like a fairy godmother, making our lives easier, brighter, making us feel known.

Years passed. The world went on, tumultuous as ever—but thanks to the Algorithm, we could tune that tumult out.

We were damn lucky, we believed.

Then one day, Lacy—who lived a few houses down from where Inez had lived—came home and found three huge boxes in her driveway.

The boxes contained a scuba suit—too large for Lacy's small frame. A lifetime supply of mayonnaise. And a coffin.

Could the Algorithm have made a mistake? We wondered this as we peered from our windows, watching as Lacy walked in circles around the items, poked at them.

"What the hell?" she said.

The sentiment rang true, and yet, we'd questioned the decaf coffee, hadn't we? And how wrong we'd been. The Algorithm was always right. If Lacy was meant to have these items, then it was only a matter of time before she understood their purpose.

The Algorithm never sent us more than we could handle. It knew the scope of our desires, but also our limitations. For instance, a single mother with two children, who earned a modest living as a dental hygienist —someone like Ernestine, let's say—would not receive a genuine South Sea pearl choker, made with white gold and inlaid with diamonds, even if her search history revealed compulsive price-checking, page-saving, and an otherwise deep consumer interest in such a necklace. No, the Algorithm would not put Ernestine and her children on the street because of the woman's fixation. But it would send her a tasteful stainless steel and imitation-pearl replica. The Algorithm knew our hearts, and also where to draw the line.

And when the items we received were a little beyond our budgets, well, we made our budgets bigger. We took extra night shifts, weekend shifts. That's what Deidre had done, for instance, when the green sofa sent by the Algorithm turned out to be a *touch* pricier than she would have preferred. All of us did what we needed to do to accommodate the small extra costs. Who were we to question what the Algorithm knew we needed? We did our best to optimize, the way an algorithm might. We skipped our softball league to work more. We told our kids: no camp this summer, sorry. We turned down the AC in our homes, even when the weather got wickedly hot.

Inez had, back in the day, called us fools for working so much, back when we asked her if she thought we were fools. This had made us upset. "You asked," she replied. Which was true. Also, to be completely honest, even though the Algorithm never sent us anything prohibitively expensive—and even though we worked constantly—over time, the small extra costs had added up. We'd come to owe a lot of money to the Algorithm. We also owed money on the money we owed, on what our parents had owed, and their parents before them. So we worked. We worked all the time. We let the Algorithm take care of our shopping. Easier that way, we told ourselves. The Algorithm could be so thoughtful, we thought, opening a newly delivered box, filled with more foam stress balls to squeeze. New fluffy slippers. An acupressure mat—which was a bit over the top, yes, but that would surely help with the back pain we felt from sitting hunched over our desks for hours on end. *Thank you*, we said. *Thank you so much.* We doubled down on loving the Algorithm, because the Algorithm loved us. Because the Algorithm would take care of us—of that we were certain. And so we bought what it sent us. Praise be: we paid.

And yet, looking at the items on Lacy's lawn, we couldn't help wondering.

A day passed, and then another. Lacy left the boxes in her driveway—still unsure of what to do with them. The items were also hard to move. So she waited.

More days passed. Lacy did not grow three sizes and fit into the scuba suit.

She did not develop an intense craving for mayonnaise.

She did not die.

We remembered, then, how Inez had knocked on one of our doors, a few months back, to borrow sugar. She was making muffins, she'd told us, to share with visiting friends. The shantytown market had been shut down for health-code violations; she wasn't sure when the market would reopen.

"But, Inez," we said, "isn't there a box of sugar on your lawn?"

We pointed at the cardboard box on her lawn, marked *Sugar!*

Inez scowled. "I don't want that sugar," she said.

We ran our fingers through our hair. We wanted to help Inez, but we couldn't stop staring at the box of sugar the Algorithm had sent. "It's right there," we said, "what you need. And while, yes, I have sugar in my pantry, I'm hesitant to give it away. What if I have sugar in my pantry because I might need it to make muffins for a surprise bake sale, and if I fail to do so when the time comes—because I gave my sugar away—my daughter will not be well-liked by her teachers and classmates, and will fall behind in her education, and will end up homeless and destitute, and will have many unresolved emotional issues about how her mother did not properly take care of her, which she will not be able to address because quality mental health care is prohibitively expensive?"

Inez said: "Are you sleeping okay?"

"Haha," we said, and held up a bottle of sleep medication the Algorithm had sent us, along with decaf caffeine pills to balance us out, because getting up in the morning was hard sometimes, on account of the sleeping pills.

Inez cracked her neck, peered up at the sky: murky with smog and wildfire smoke and a stray puff of tear gas. She looked tired. She looked even older than we had originally guessed her to be. Maybe, we thought, she shouldn't stay up so late drinking moonshine with wandering vagrants. Maybe she should use sleeping pills, too. Also, a self-massager for her neck and dark-circle-reducing eye masks. It pained us to know that these items had been delivered to Inez's home and she had not accepted them; that she had the opportunity to live a more comfortable and dignified life—but chose not to.

"Maybe I'll skip the muffins today," said Inez, and smiled at us, which was odd, because we had not helped her. Also she did not smile very often.

She walked across the street and back into her house.

The box of sugar stayed on her lawn.

The next day it rained. The cardboard box melted into a misshapen lump, and then the sugar melted, too, disappearing into the grass.

Inez was arrested soon after that, because she did not pay for the sugar, which she also did not return. And because the Algorithm had flagged her as a risk to society, given her well-documented social delinquency and her predicted behavioral trajectory. There were many overlaps between the Algorithm's analytical insights on consumerist and judicial fronts.

We never found out what happened to her.

Though, to be honest, we also never looked into her fate; we worried what the Algorithm would think about such online searches—if the Algorithm would infer that we had lost our faith in its judgments.

And yet, we also found ourselves whispering *a shame*, because we kind of missed Inez's late-night sea shanties and the drifters tramping through the neighborhood—though we were having trouble remembering precise details from those memories. The sleeping pills made our minds foggy. We were working so many hours by then.

Plus, when Lacy's strange deliveries arrived, we were distracted by their mystery.

If there was one person we would have asked about the scuba suit, and the mayo, and the coffin, it would have been Inez.

Inez was gone, though.

And so Lacy bought the items. She paid.

A month passed. More items arrived—large items, odd items—that surrounded our doorsteps, blocked our driveways, covered our lawns. An inflatable bouncy castle. Sherlock-style hats. A crate of AK-47s. Hundreds of yards of rope. A live Philippine cobra. A twelve-burner barbecue grill. A moped. A cannon. Endless filing cabinets. Used hotel furniture. Brand-new hotel furniture. A very long knit scarf. Very small dentures. A life-size doll that looked like our least favorite child. A plastic palm tree. Arsenic-laced wallpaper. A twelve-gallon drum of antifreeze. Flags for countries we'd never visited.

We wrote to customer service. "A mistake?" we asked, because by that point we could not help asking.

Haha, said the AI representative. *Thank you for contacting customer service. The Algorithm has a special treat for you.*

An unmarked truck delivered a box containing more sleeping pills. A yoga ball bounced off the back of another truck. Then a light-block sleep pod arrived. Followed by blackout curtains. Turmeric powder for inflammation. Lavender-infused moisturizer.

"These items are wonderful," we said, trying to smile—then coughing politely. "They are also very expensive."

Stress balls dropped from the sky in a colorful foam rainstorm.

"Thank you," we said, "thank you, but actually, we—" We had long ago run out of storage space. We were running out of credit as well. Also, it had started actually raining. "Please," we said, "just let us get organized." But the deliveries kept coming, more every minute, and the items were getting soaked on our lawns. We thought of the sugar. There was something to remember, notice. Our minds spun.

We raced inside, logged on to the Internet. We looked up *sugar, dream symbols, neighbor relationships, prison*. Articles floated by. We squinted at screens, exhausted, grasping for meaning. Outside our houses, more items arrived, piled on top of one another. Hours passed. Our eyelids twitched from the strain. No meaning materialized. We fell asleep on our keyboards.

In the morning, the Algorithm sent us new reading glasses.

Endangered

The artists were kept in cages. This was for their own good. The world had gotten really ugly, really fast, and the artists, generally, did not have the skills to survive. Most did not know how to shoot guns, for instance. Or how to make bombs out of soda bottles. The artists were a dying breed, in all honesty, which is why the government, along with a few wealthy do-gooders, put them in cages—nice cages—that resembled the artists' natural habitats. One pen looked like a gallery opening, with wine, cheese, and water crackers restocked daily. Another featured dumpster couches paired with a threadbare oriental rug. Nude models were occasionally sent into the enclosures, which sometimes interested the artists, sometimes not. These habitats were all very thoughtful—top-of-the-line, really—and tailored to the artists' individual needs. In fact, one could argue the environments were identical replications of how the artists lived in the wild, other than the glass walls installed for spectating.

Criticism of the artist preservation program was scant. When criticism did come, it came from little girls, mostly— who visited the zoo as the daughters of government officials and high-level bureaucrats and pop stars—who said the artists looked unhappy.

"He looks unhappy," the little girls told their parents. "Why isn't he painting? And why isn't she sculpting? And why are those ones over there lying motionless and staring vacantly into space?"

It's true, not all the artists took to art-making in captivity. Some, in fact, became quite ill. Of course, every effort was made to care for them. The artists were offered a spectrum of drugs, both medicinal and psychedelic. They were even issued awards, their names inked in bold letters across certificates and inscribed onto gold-plated plaques. Still, there were admittedly some incidents involving paint fumes, belt buckles strapped to ceiling beams. But these incidents were considered normal artist behavior. In the wild, after all, artists had often exhibited the effects of melancholia.

"Hush," the parents told their little daughters. "The artist is fine. Watch quietly now. Do not knock on the glass. Do not disturb the artist. The artist is sleeping, see? Oh, look, the artist is awake—look, honey, look, look, look—oh, wait, never mind. Let's go, honey, come quickly now."

Did a few of the artists make strange faces at spectators? Did they masturbate in public view? Smear feces on the glass? Yes. But, again, this was considered normal artist behavior. The artists were naturally provocative, subject to unpredictable compulsions, chronic irrationality. This was why they required protection. This was why they needed further study. There was much about them we still didn't know. There was much from them we felt we might learn.

Once—though the precise details regarding *how* remain undisclosed—an artist escaped. She got out of her enclosure, out into the streets, loose. She didn't get far, of course, not with the security cameras and the helicopters and the live broadcasts. It was quite a show, actually. The video became a viral sensation. I remember gathering with other citizens to watch on a public screen. We all laughed about it, I think. Or at least we paid close attention. The video showed the artist running down a neighborhood street while mothers called their children inside, and children pressed their faces against windows. The video showed the artist swerving sporadically, running as if looking for something—maybe a place she used to know—knocking over trash cans, ducking under shrubbery, before collapsing at the base of a barbed wire fence. Beyond the artist's enclosure was, of course, another enclosure: the wall surrounding an upscale habitat for beautiful wives. And then beyond that wall, another wall. And beyond that another. Our world was a series of concentric pens. It was safer that way. It also meant there was nowhere for the artist to go.

And yet, how serene the artist looked, how ecstatic, flopped down onto her back and breathing heavily as she gazed up at the sky. A satellite feed caught the moment; we could see her staring up—up at us, it seemed, as if we were gods—before the helicopters converged, the drones and the SWAT teams. Perhaps, in another life, it might have been her greatest work.

Loving Homes for Lost & Broken Men

I took in my first foster husband when I was thirty-eight. I knew, by then, that I would never have a husband of my own, and I wanted to do some good in the world. Fostering these abandoned men was a way to give back. There are so many husbands lost in the system—you don't hear about them much, but they're there—so many husbands looking for a forever home. I would be the one to help.

They say your first foster husband changes you the most, but I was forty-three and many foster cases in when I met Mr. Lionel Holm. I had a full house at the time: four husbands—all ages, all kinds of troubles. It was a big job every morning, fixing four settings of bacon, eggs, toast, and orange juice. Bringing each husband a copy of the daily newspaper. Giving them all short but motivational pep talks: "You're looking extra handsome this morning," or "I'm sure a raise is right around the corner." And to maintain structure in their lives, I also said things like "Remember to take out the trash," or "Be sure to give Spot his walk."

My methods were straightforward but effective.

Mr. Holm's caseworker showed up on a Wednesday afternoon. I'd been working with the woman for several years, and an unannounced visit had never happened in all that time. She said she was sorry she hadn't called ahead, though she did not appear apologetic. Rather, agitation crackled through her perm as she paced my living room. Her white pumps were scuffed; her shoulder pads lumped too low, like errant biceps. It was unlike the woman—usually fastidious, a staunch adherent to agency policy—to grab my shoulders, much less to say, "I've got a promotion on the line, but this guy—" Her grip softened. "Please, Claudette, you're the best we've got."

Like I said, I wanted to make a difference in the world. Husbands without loving homes could end up on the streets, eating junk food, openly farting, harassing young women, impersonating dead celebrities, joining white-supremacist groups. I didn't have much space left in my house—my resources were already stretched thin—but with the caseworker pleading, I said *okay*. I'd had tough husbands before. Husbands who got aggressive, husbands who skipped work to hit the bars, husbands addicted to porn, and I'd worked hard to set boundaries for them all. I established a safe and supportive environment. There were La-Z-Boy recliners in the living room, the PGA Tour playing like a lullaby on TV. Once a week, I organized simple home-repair projects as self-confidence boosters. Birdhouse installation. Grill maintenance. Garage door greasing. To be honest, I was proud of what I had accomplished: how I'd helped so many men get back on their feet. Though I'd never been good at much of anything, I was good at fostering husbands—even great.

But Mr. Holm.

As was standard for new foster husbands, he arrived at my house in his own vehicle: a red Cadillac convertible. Such sports cars were not an uncommon sight in my line of work. He must have hit his midlife crisis hard, I thought. Must have become a real monster. Maybe he'd started a garage band, or begun metal-detecting on public beaches, or become a little too curious about nudist colonies. Why else would the case-worker have fled as soon as I signed the paperwork?

When Mr. Holm stepped out of his Cadillac, however, he seemed anything but monstrous. He was trim, about six feet tall, and dressed in a tailored pinstripe suit, his silvery hair per-fectly coiffed. He took my hand and bowed slightly. His palm was warm, well moisturized. "A pleasure to meet you," he said.

Foster husbands never behaved this way. Usually, they slumped or waddled into my home without looking at me, going directly into the bathroom for some private time, before emerging puffy-eyed for chocolate chip cookies and a mug of coffee. Usually, it took a week of gentle coaxing to even begin getting acquainted.

Mr. Holm pulled a single hyacinth blossom from his sleeve, handed it to me. "My lady," he said, bowing slightly.

I did something I hadn't in years: I blushed.

Mr. Holm led me inside, as if welcoming me into my own home. "Please have a seat," he said, pulling out a kitchen chair. Then he reached into a cabinet and produced a bottle of champagne I had long ago received as a gift. He popped the cork and poured us each a glass. "To new beginnings," he said, clinking his glass against mine. Champagne sloshed over the side. Mr. Holm winked. I was so enchanted I didn't bother with the spill.

Upon returning from their respective workplaces, the other foster husbands made their unhappiness known. Quarters had been tight already, and with a fifth foster husband, the line to the bathroom did become long that afternoon. Mr. Holm spent a not unlengthy amount of time meticulously shaving and grooming himself. But it was also nice to be around someone who put effort into his appearance. And he was so charming, so regal, so kind. Though I was initially dismayed to discover that Mr. Holm had brought along his pet ferret, Ruffles turned out to be equally well-mannered, nuzzling my hand and making soft mewing noises.

I had never picked favorites among foster husbands before — doing so was strongly discouraged in the *Loving Homes for Lost & Broken Men* guidebook — but how could I not favor my newest addition? Mr. Holm could discuss sports, stocks, politics, fashion, cooking, and literature with equal and effortless grace. "I agree that *Emma* is underrated," he said. "But what is your stance on *Northanger Abbey*?" He seemed too good to be true, especially when he told me to put on my best dress: he would be taking me out to dinner that very night. When I explained, blushing, that I couldn't leave the other foster husbands unattended, he didn't bat an eye. "I've made a reservation for six," he said, "at La Strayvard." The best restaurant in town.

How long had it been since someone took me out? Well over fifteen years? Twenty? Back in the days when I still believed I might have a husband of my own, there'd been one close call. Mark Fabermore. My high school sweetheart. I pushed the thought aside as we entered the restaurant, concentrating on the atmosphere of winking chandeliers and violin solos and plushly upholstered seats. Waiters brought us arugula salads with truffle dressing. Red wine. Roast goose. Potatoes and cream. Chocolate cake. Brandy. Even the other husbands, squished together in a semicircle around the table, napkins tucked into their shirt collars, could not help getting into the spirit of things. Mr. Holm beamed at everyone, though mostly at me. I beamed back. A feeling stirred inside me, so unfamiliar that at first I thought it might be indigestion. Hope, I finally realized. Curdled by unease.

One of the cardinal rules of caring for foster husbands is that you remain supportive yet detached. That you care without becoming too close. To do otherwise violates your role as transitional vehicle. You are there to support the husbands as the courts work things out, make arrangements. Sometimes forever homes are found. Or permanent residencies with family members—brothers most often—and sometimes husbands return to their lawful wives after counseling. It happens. It would be cruel, when fostering a husband, to confuse his feelings by getting too close.

Cruel for the caretaker as well.

I knew all of this. I knew, also, that I had none of Mr. Holm's case history—his file contained little more than physical stats—and so whether he had left his wife, or if his wife had left him, or, worse, if she had passed away, remained a mystery. And yet, rather than worrying about the uncertainties of his past, I found myself considering my own future: was I really too old to have a husband of my own?

———————

By the time we left the restaurant, the other foster husbands were all chatting contentedly, their bellies swollen from the meal, cigars speared in their mouths—gifted by Mr. Holm, who offhandedly mentioned a business partner in Cuba. When we arrived home, he held the door open for everyone. Made pleasant jokes with the other husbands, as if they had been pals for years. Then he exhaled a good-natured yawn. "Well," he said, "it's high time for my forty winks."

At these words, the other husbands froze, cigars drooping. I could see their minds ticking through possible sleeping arrangements. There weren't many options. One foster husband was already lodged in the guest room, two more on the La-Z-Boys in the living room, a fourth in a sleeping bag in the craft room. Where else was there to go?

There was the bathtub—husbands had bedded there before, in a pinch—but to make Mr. Holm sleep in the tub seemed uncouth. Especially after such a spectacular dinner.

"Well," I murmured, without meeting anyone's eye, "I do have a sizable bed."

The other husbands' faces reddened. An argument ensued. There was much pouting. At least one kitchen chair was pushed over. It didn't matter. In the mêlée, Mr. Holm tiptoed upstairs to my room. I found him waiting on my bed in a fluffy white bathrobe.

He winked at me. Patted a spot on the coverlet beside him. "You must be exhausted," he said. "Let me give you a neck rub."

To accept his offer was wrong, I knew. According to the *Loving Homes* guidebook, receiving a foster husband's physical affection went against the Code of Caring. It would cross a line that could not be uncrossed.

"I can't," I said, looking away.

"It's only a neck rub."

"It's not fair to the others," I tried. "They—"

"They don't need to know," said Mr. Holm, his voice a balm of suave absolution. "And regardless, you deserve it."

He wasn't wrong. How many loads of laundry had I done for the foster husbands without so much as a thank-you? How many meals had I cooked? How many plates had I cleared? I wanted to do good in the world, but a part of me also longed for a little acknowledgment.

I went to Mr. Holm. I couldn't help it. He smelled like the expensive stores at the mall—like silk shirts and fancy oint ments and fine mists of cologne—along with the animal under current of his well-trained ferret, which could probably do tricks. There was something else there, too, something deeper. Retirement packages. Anniversary dinners. Public speeches at charity events in which I was hailed as a loving and supportive partner.

Mr. Holm smelled like appreciation.

His hands eased along my neck, then up the base of my head, fingers twirling strands of my hair. My hair: dyed coffee-table brown, limp as seaweed. How I looked hadn't mattered in years. Sometimes I forgot my body existed. But now, I became newly aware of my hips, the rise and fall of my breasts. A shiver shot through me. Mr. Holm absorbed it; his fingers gained energy. He whispered into my ear, "Oh, sweet Claudette."

The words made me dizzy. Motion diffused with memory, and I went spinning back across the decades, back to when Mark Fabermore had whispered the same words to me, back when my body was slender and smooth and I was sixteen and Mark was seventeen and we pressed ourselves into one another, kissing until our lips became puffy and raw, leaving red welts on one another's necks as if we were mollusks, back when we felt like the king and queen of our small town and our love was an empire that knew no limits.

Mr. Holm eased a hand, delicately, under my nightgown.

I had loved Mark. I had loved his serious eyes, the way his ears went pink when he felt something deeply. I had loved how he knew the capital of every country in the world, including Nauru. I had loved that he was an outfielder for the baseball team and how when I stood near him during games—just over the fence—he couldn't resist glancing in my direction. I had loved that his favorite meal was grilled trout with buttered corn.

We were reclining now, Mr. Holm and I, our limbs entwined.

Mark had proposed the day I turned eighteen. He'd said it wouldn't be any trouble at all, me commuting from the university to see him. It wouldn't change my chance for an education. It wouldn't change anything.

Mr. Holm switched off the bedside lamp.

But I had known girls who got married young, girls who had given up the chance to be a little wild. To have a big life: expansive and unpredictable and free.

"Oh, Claudette, sweet Claudette."

So I'd told Mark no. I'd given him up. It hurt terribly, but at the time it had seemed like the kindest choice for both of us: cutting ties. I wanted us each to experience the best version of our lives. I never found out if he did. It seemed easier if I never asked. Yet all these years later, I still see Mark's face, disbelieving and hurt, his ears turning pink as I told him my choice. And my life hasn't turned out to be wild and expansive after all.

Do not form strong attachments, the agency tells you, over and over, when you're training to supervise foster husbands. *This only leads to disappointment.* Always I'd thought myself above such mistakes. It was my gift: caring dispassion.

In the quiet darkness of my bedroom, Mr. Holm's lips brushed my earlobes. "Let's run away together," he whispered.

My bedside clock read 3:12 a.m. I was tired, but I played along. "Where would we go?"

"Las Vegas," he said. "We should get married as soon as possible. We could leave tomorrow morning."

I turned on the bedside lamp, studied his face.

"You're serious, aren't you?"

He nodded, a few strands of silvery hair sliding onto his forehead as he smiled a hopeful smile. My heart leapt and cavorted.

Was it crazy he'd made such an offer so soon after meeting me? It was. But I had so distanced myself from love that I couldn't remember what love really entailed. I knew it only as something seen through a telescope: a distant planet I'd almost given up exploring. Perhaps it was love, what Mr. Holm and I had between us. It was crazy, sure, for him to propose so quickly. But wasn't love often deemed a form of insanity?

Mr. Holm began kissing me again. Maybe it was the wine. His cologne scent. The late hour. I felt far away from my body: a universe of particles spread out and expanding.

What had people said to me when I turned down Mark? That I was cruel. Unjust. Unforgivably selfish.

How long was I going to continue punishing myself?

"Yes," I told Mr. Holm. "Yes, let's get married."

Our departure was a blur. We left before dawn, before the other foster husbands woke. I tried not to consider what would happen when they did. How confused they would be. How disappointed. Instead, I tiptoed through the house as quickly as I could, one hand holding a suitcase, one hand entwined in Mr. Holm's, past the guest room, the La-Z-Boys, through the kitchen—the table set with each of the husbands' placemats, their labeled coffee mugs—shutting my mind as I pretended I was someone else: a scientist in the Amazon, a tourist in a foreign land, a spy fleeing her own life.

Mr. Holm drove fast. We took his Cadillac convertible and sped along the highway with the top down, the breeze whipping our hair. We said little as the sun rose and the road filled with other cars. We're like those two bank robbers, I couldn't help thinking. What were their names? Mark would have known. He had had a memory for names. I wondered if he still did. I wondered if he'd turned out like the man I'd believed he would become: soft-spoken, hardworking, good.

I might have been hit by a wave of sorrow, but Mr. Holm gripped my hand. "We need to get you a dress," he said. With the sun glancing off his sunglasses, he looked like every handsome man in every commercial, his face a fantasy born of composite dreams.

"A dress?" I said. Mr. Holm's ferret, Ruffles, was in my arms, and she nibbled lightly on my wrist, as if chiding me for my hesitation. I had assumed we would get married as we were— me in slacks and a blouse, him in his suit—but the idea of getting a dress, the frivolous intensity of his plan, delighted me.

"It would be hard for you to look any more lovely, my darling," he said. "But I want to try."

The truth is, most women, at least secretly, believe they are beautiful. They just want their suspicions confirmed. I was no exception. A surge of glee bubbled through me like the carbonation in soda pop. Yes, I thought. I deserve this. This is my reward.

The dress was a creamy ivory color, silky, with lace and frills and pearls and tulle. A young woman's dress. But Mr. Holm insisted—not in a controlling or domineering manner; he insisted in a way that was honest about our ages, and therefore romantic. "Let's pretend we're young again," he said. "Let's start from the beginning." So I let my shoulders peek out, let my cleavage billow from the bodice like loaves of rising bread. The salesladies admired me. They, too, were charmed by Mr. Holm. His polite, inquisitive chatter. The way he addressed them using their first names.

"Remember, no returns," one saleslady said to me, cheerfully.

Mr. Holm made sure I got gloves, too. And shoes to match. A small tiara.

"Gorgeous," he said. "Just stunning. Keep the dress on. We'll go directly to the chapel. I cannot wait a minute longer."

So I shuffled up to the register. The saleslady beamed at me. Mr. Holm hunted in his pocket for his wallet.

"Well, I'll be damned," he said. He ran a hand through his perfect, silvery hair. "I must have left my wallet at your house."

The salesladies clucked their tongues sweetly. Their eyes turned to me.

"No worries, love," I said, producing my purse. "I've got it."

He kissed me, deeply and with tongue, as I handed the money over. The salesladies oohed and clapped.

We had driven all day. Barely stopping. Me in the dress, him clad in a new tuxedo. Las Vegas was close: *15 miles*, read a sign. I was getting hungry. I decided to stay stoic. It was more romantic that way. To remain charmingly brave. Mr. Holm drove faster and faster. Like he was desperate to arrive. This made my eyes well up, since I knew Las Vegas wedding chapels were probably open 24/7.

In the distance, the desert sky turned hot orange, then lurid purple. Saguaro stood silhouetted against the horizon like thick forks.

To distract myself from my hunger, and in the spirit of full disclosure, I decided to tell Mr. Holm about Mark.

"I almost got married once."

"That so?"

"To my high school sweetheart."

Mr. Holm said nothing, and I worried I had hurt him by bringing this mention of another flame into our relationship, which was still embryonic, fragile in its newness. "It was a long time ago, though," I said, trying to save face. "And really, I suppose I never would have married him. We were too young—way too young. I was only eighteen! How could a person possibly commit at that age? How could a person begin to know who she'll become?"

Mr. Holm made a small sound in his throat. I checked the speedometer: ninety miles per hour.

I couldn't stop talking. I had gone out on a limb and could only go farther. "Of course," I said, "at eighteen, you think you're going to have this big exciting life when you say no to such a commitment, but that turns out to be a delusion. Your life is small and quiet and boring anyway. Or maybe because you feel bad about giving up on someone, you become piously philanthropic. You make your life small and boring on purpose. You start to understand why people get married young:

it's because they are afraid to lose people. They understand they might not get a second—"

The car made an abrupt turn, and I thought we were pulling over. Instead, we peeled off the highway into a residential section of Las Vegas. One-story homes with beige walls and curtained windows and scrubby little yards, cloned again and again. Cul-de-sacs looped through neighborhoods like tangled yarn. It was not the Las Vegas I'd expected—with lights and colors and feathers and hundred-dollar bills blowing in the air—but I trusted Mr. Holm. He seemed to know his way around.

He parked the Cadillac outside one of the beige houses.

"Just a minute," he said politely, like a newsboy tipping his cap. Like a stranger.

He got out and went to the door.

I've pushed him away, I thought. This is my doing. All that talk about the past when it's the present that matters.

Ruffles the ferret wriggled in my arms. She also seemed agitated.

Mr. Holm entered the house without knocking. Must be a close friend, I thought. Maybe he's getting us a witness. I petted Ruffles. Minutes trickled by. The sun darkened. My mind went blank. My stomach no longer felt empty so much as filled with Styrofoam. I thought sadly of the other foster husbands struggling to make dinner—then I pushed the image away. The foster husbands were all grown men, I told myself. They should be able to feed themselves.

Shouting erupted from the house. I heard Mr. Holm's voice, elegant even at high volume. Then a contemptuous shriek. A woman.

She emerged in the doorway, dressed in a slinky sequined gown, skintight as scales. She had curlers in her hair, a cigarette in her mouth, another in her hand, a third behind an ear. One eye was garishly made up—a vivid magenta sunset rising from the lid—so that it seemed part of a separate creature. She was barefoot. With her one magenta eye she squinted at me, waiting in the car. Mr. Holm came out behind her. His face was taut. The woman stepped closer, still squinting. Then she laughed.

Mr. Holm, looking flustered—an expression I hadn't yet seen on him—said something I could not hear. She laughed harder, slapping a firm, sequined thigh, her hair curlers bouncing. "Go ahead and marry her, for fuck's sake, what do I care?"

Hearing the woman's voice, Ruffles popped out of my lap and climbed onto the dashboard. The woman darkened.

"Is that my ferret? Bloody hell—"

Mr. Holm grabbed at the woman's arms. He whispered in her ear, trying to tell her something—perhaps declaring his undying affections, saying I was a ruse, a mark, a fool—and as he did, he looked older, smaller. Not so handsome. More like a salesman: all flattery and distraction. The woman wrestled free and started toward me, a hurricane swirling in her eyes. I watched her approach—this furious, spectacular woman— and for a moment, I wanted the storm of her to hit me, to feel the full force of a rage like hers.

Then fear kicked in.

I threw my legs over the car's stick shift and plopped into the driver's seat, the wedding dress tulle cushioning my landing. The keys were in the ignition. I peeled out of the driveway in a screech of diesel and rubber. Ruffles squeaked like a chew toy.

It was easy to get to the strip. All roads in Las Vegas led there, so I followed these tributaries until I joined the thick river of traffic slugging through a jungle of lights and high-rise hotels. I cruised slowly, letting the desert breeze skim my cheeks. I felt numb more than disappointed. Marquees glittered and blinked. Along the sidewalks, bands of bachelorette celebrants stumbled into packs of bachelors. Businessmen ogled women wearing impossible heels. A child crouched beside a trash can, hiding from his parents.

My numbness gave way to a tingling curiosity. I drove slower and began to study faces. I started seeing Elvises, everywhere. Cowlicked and sideburned. Some fat. Some thin. Most in white jumpsuits. A few in powder blue. All these resurrected kings—come back from the past. All these men inhabiting an alternative present. A sharp pain twisted inside me, but it was a pain I'd long needed to feel. I continued cruising until I found what I wanted—which is to say, an Elvis of my liking. He looked both familiar and forgettable. He looked ready to have fun.

I pulled the convertible up next to him. My hair was wild. My dress twisted and bunched above my knees. Ruffles scurried around my neck like a live scarf.

"Hey, baby," I said. "Wanna go for a ride?"

Cougar

You couldn't go into the forest alone. Or at least the signs advised against it. *Carry a large stick,* the signs said. *Bring noise-makers. Don't go at dawn or dusk.*

It was dawn. LeeAnn sat on the trunk of a newly fallen oak tree, base spiky with split blond wood, leaves still greening its branches. If she'd had a phone, she would have checked it. Instead, she flicked her Rubik's Cube.

Sunlight clawed through the forest, brightening the twitch of ferns, huckleberries, the sprawl of poison oak and redwoods rising rootily from mud-raw gullies. Somewhere, water trickled. Rain had washed across California and the streams perked up like nothing had ever gone wrong.

The woods always rattled, full of sounds—LeeAnn wasn't one to diagnose them.

Then, Viktor's hand was squeezing her shoulder. He muttered about being late, a holdup at the front desk. Their kiss was awkward—LeeAnn half sitting on the tree trunk, him bending his too-tall body toward her, his necklace swinging and slapping her chin. He wore a dog tag, though he had never been in the military. LeeAnn found this distasteful, but she liked the feeling of forgiving him: the sense of her own magnanimity. Viktor also smelled like the popcorn made endlessly at the Center. And his nails, in LeeAnn's opinion, were too long for a man's—but maybe that was generational? He was more than two decades younger than her. He had dark hair, along with a downy fuzz that covered his whole body, which had repulsed her at first, though now she reached a hand down the back of his pants and stroked the fuzz on his butt as if it were the softest pillow. Her touch made him fumble with her bra clasp. The sun glowed brighter through the trees. She situated him behind her, placed her hands squarely on the trunk of an upright tree. He began. The bark was sharp against her palms; she inhaled.

"Did you hear that?"

Viktor paused, the silver plate of his dog tag cool against her neck.

"No," said LeeAnn—annoyed by the interruption—though when he remained motionless, she amped up her Texan drawl, added: "No, baby, didn't hear nothing."

Around them, ferns quivered. Viktor whispered that he *had* heard something, he was sure of it. He was still inside her, his body pressed against her own. A glimmer of anger—nay, indignation—stirred in LeeAnn. She needed Viktor to focus. She needed him to be committed to the shared endeavor of getting off. She needed to get off—and have her mind go blank for at least one exquisite instant.

But Viktor was withdrawing, pulling up his pants quick as he could, stuffing his belt back through its loops, his ears cocked as he scanned the forest's sun-dappled canopy, the shadows between tree trunks.

"I should get back," he said. And then, after a few seconds: "*We* should get back."

LeeAnn re-clasped her bra with the frosty air of a scorned queen. Viktor did not notice. He was mentioning breakfast, the morning session; he was already gone.

The sun rose higher. LeeAnn let the minutes expand, float away, if only to prove a point: the safety of being there, in the woods. Soon she'd have to follow Viktor to the Center for her first session as well. In just a few minutes. One minute. But for now, she sat and flicked her Rubik's Cube. It was supposed to help with her cravings. "Keeps a person occupied," a counselor had told her. "Brains like puzzles."

Red, blue, green, white, yellow, orange—the colors shifted like a disco dance floor: a party that wouldn't end. Three weeks she'd been fiddling with the cube, no luck.

The woods quieted. Oak leaves unwavering, even the stream stifled silent. LeeAnn's neck hair prickled.

Maybe something was out there; maybe it was watching her now.

"Fuck," she said—and hurried after Viktor.

The Center was, officially, the Udall-Meyers Treatment Center for Digital Disorders. LeeAnn had been there nearly a month. She felt the same as when she'd arrived—only now she was bloated by cafeteria food and gripped by near constant agitation and dread.

Coping had been easier in the beginning. Her first week,

she wandered all over the Center's 150 acres of protected land: an old-growth forest that bled into the wild peaks of the Santa Cruz Mountains—or what was left of them. LeeAnn could not explain why she was drawn to the forest. She'd never been an outdoors person. Didn't even like houseplants. But the fresh air was better, she supposed, than the claustrophobic atmosphere of the Center, with its too-cheerful staff and the inane conversations of other residents and the teeth-gritting hours of group therapy. Outdoors she'd felt a little peace.

Then the signs went up.

And while no one at the Center had encountered a mountain lion—the reports of mauled pets and claw-marked garage doors had come from the nearby neighborhood—the staff grew worried. The go-outside-with-a-buddy rule took hold. This hadn't seemed like a problem for LeeAnn, initially. She'd been taking buddies out there with her anyway.

"It's because there's no habitat for them," said Noreen at breakfast.

She was one of several residents seated at an oblong table in the Center's cafeteria, everyone's breakfast plates displaying a composite of toast, scrambled eggs, and, for unknown reasons, a cube of Turkish delight. Throughout the cafeteria, most residents had already picked away at the desired aspect of their spread; LeeAnn wolfed down her breakfast items indiscriminately.

"Yeah," said Sarah S., "mountain lions used to, like, live in the mountains, but now there's like not as much space in the mountains anymore. And like, less food and stuff."

Noreen and Sarah S. had identical faces, though they were not twins or even related. Rather, they had both gotten surgery to look like the same cartoon avatar: their eyes widened, noses narrow as a finger, teeth filed flat.

"God, it's so scary," Noreen went on.

The other residents at the table nodded; LeeAnn stabbed her scrambled eggs. They'd had this exact conversation before—a script followed on autopilot—because it was considered gauche to discuss what everyone really wanted to talk about: the ferocity of their cravings. Their restless, vicious, desperate hunger for a screen.

Viktor sat two seats down from LeeAnn. He had changed his shirt. He was cutting up his toast with a knife and fork. LeeAnn would decide later if this affectation counted as a pro or a con in his overall personality. She maintained mental lists of the other residents' tics—Viktor's especially—to keep herself from going totally nuts. Or from just having a run-of-the-mill meltdown, like the puffy-faced new resident seated across the cafeteria, who was weeping into his toast, eggs, and Turkish delight.

"You know you can't outrun a mountain lion," said Trevor, who was also seated at their breakfast table.

LeeAnn did not like Trevor.

"Though, realistically, you wouldn't even get a chance to *try* to run, because mountain lions sneak up behind you, silently, then deliver a crushing bite to your neck."

Noreen and Sarah S. gasped.

Viktor paused knifing his toast, his face pale. If LeeAnn had been in the seat next to him, she would have reached under the table and rubbed his balls, distracted him from Trevor's commentary. She did not want this speculative garbage to further diminish Viktor's willingness to go into the forest with her.

"So that newbie," said LeeAnn, interrupting Trevor's recitation of mountain lion kill strategies, "he must be a Documenter, right?"

She nodded across the cafeteria, toward the weeping new resident. Usually, there was interest in fresh arrivals. Longhaulers liked to guess people's particular digital disorders based on observable characteristics. Besides Body Modifiers, like Noreen and Sarah S., Documenters tended to be among the most conspicuous. They became paralyzed by the possibility of doing anything—eating a meal, selecting an outfit, reading a magazine—without photographing or filming the act. This was all part of a larger complex about control and mortality, LeeAnn had learned—albeit reluctantly—during one of the Center's education sessions. She'd also learned that Documenters, though initially dramatic in their meltdowns, usually improved the fastest. Other categories of resident included Excessive Gamers, with their stooped posture, prearthritic hands, and muscleless physiques. InstaQueens came in with muscle tone—though as soon as they were away from the mirror of social media, they tended to have hygiene issues. Online Gamblers kept making bets—*Five bucks it rains on Saturday*—but all of them had the same longing in their eyes.

"Or maybe he's a run-of-the-mill Nomophobic?" said LeeAnn, though the newbie did not have the telltale trembling that marked a fear of *no-mobile-phone*. "What do y'all think?"

Noreen and Sarah S. glanced with bleary curiosity across the cafeteria, then back at her. LeeAnn knew that, more than anything, these two—and others—wondered about *her* disorder. The Center was all about individually led disclosures; she'd never disclosed. She often felt the others scanning her, taking in her mildly sun-damaged but otherwise well-moisturized forty-something skin. Her dyed blond hair. Her leather cowgirl boots. Her press-on nails. Her drawl. She didn't fit in at the Center, not really. Not among these twentysomethings with their parents' credit lines and their lives unformed as putty. She knew the other residents gossiped about her, that the forest sex alienated some. But what did she care so long as that mystery got her through her stay at the Center?

"Mountain lions have been known to kill for sport," said Trevor, ignoring LeeAnn's attempt to steer the conversation elsewhere—typical tunnel-vision behavior for an Excessive Gamer like him. Viktor was also a gamer, but LeeAnn considered his version of the affliction less egregious. She considered Viktor, generally, to be less egregious than the others—even if he did eat toast with a knife and fork. He was less caught up in his own bullshit; less caught up in the Center's bullshit, too.

"For sport?" said Sarah S., nervously.

"For sport," repeated Noreen, in a tone of mystical reverence. "Like a housecat, killing just because it can."

LeeAnn willed Viktor to look at her so she could smile at him, shrug the conversation off—so they could keep doing what they'd been doing out in the forest and she could endure a few more weeks in this expensive analog habitat.

Viktor, though, gulped the last of his OJ, Adam's apple bobbing, and hurried away.

Across the cafeteria, the newbie blew his nose loudly into a napkin: a mournful trumpet of phlegm and surrender.

The Center wasn't advertised anywhere. It did not appear on maps. This gave the facility an air of privacy and remoteness. So did the price tag. Also, the location: up a steep winding road—gated at multiple points—and cloaked by forest on all sides. With no personal electronics allowed for residents or staff, the Center felt out-of-time. Beyond place. And yet, if a person walked the rambling trails through the forest—along a ridge that jutted from a stand of vertiginous redwoods—there was a lookout point with a sweeping view of Silicon Valley. Everything was still so close. The blue arc of San Francisco Bay bordered a glittering spread of tech campuses where thousands of engineers worked to find the levers that would light up the secret, soft parts of a person's mind, thereby refining the most potent drugs in human history—the virtual realities, virtual selves—that could drain bank accounts, disappear the hours and days and years of a person's life, mangle the membrane between reality and fantasy with pleasure circuits of likes and clicks and beeps, splashes of color and the warm full-body rush of being noticed, of having agency, of approval, of that approval actualized so sweetly and neatly in the infinite potential of a digital universe.

"It's not your fault," the counselor was saying.

LeeAnn's morning group had gathered in a circle of beige chairs in a beige room, the windows covered by gauzy curtains that made the daylight beige, too. California and its obsession with neutrals. LeeAnn supposed the color palette was meant to help keep people calm at the Center, but it just made her bored, which made her antsy, which made her cravings worse.

She twisted her Rubik's Cube while the counselor talked.

"Sigmund, you have your hand up. What does progress mean to you?"

Sigmund hadn't had his hand up. He'd been scratching his stringy neck, disappearing his fingers into a greasy mop of hair. LeeAnn liked him even less than Trevor. He was too flashy about his money, wearing multiple expensive watches on each wrist, each clock face equipped with subdials for air pressure, time zones, altitude, as if his body were a plane. LeeAnn could attest that it was not. She'd had sex with him once, early on, but a Porn Addict generally made a poor choice for a partner. She and Sigmund hadn't spoken since.

After a long pause, as if pulling the phrase from a deep well within himself, Sigmund grunted: "Better self-image."

LeeAnn snorted—too loud.

"LeeAnn," said the counselor, with an expression of bemused generosity that irritated LeeAnn further, "do you have something to add?"

LeeAnn shook her head, looked down at her Rubik's Cube: the traffic jam of bright squares. What right did this counselor have to give her a hard time? Nearly all the counselors were in digital recovery as well. She suspected they worked at the Center because they couldn't manage to live elsewhere without being consumed by digital temptations. The Center was a sanctuary, but also a prison.

Click, click, click, went her cube.

"Oookay then," said the counselor, barreling on, extracting a few more phrases from Sigmund. The other group participants seemed impressed by him. It made LeeAnn want to scream: this rich bozo spent twelve hours a day typing *cream pie, gangbang, MILF* into search engines, even when sailing around Saint-Tropez on his parents' yacht, bikini models lounging on the deck. And suddenly he's a hero for showing a modicum of self-awareness? LeeAnn felt no affinity for this strain of morality; in it the wrong people were always getting absolved.

"LeeAnn," the counselor was saying, "what were you trying to add?"

She'd been muttering to herself.

"Maybe you should put that toy away, just for a minute."

"But you said—"

"We'd like you to be a little more Present."

Everyone seated in the therapy circle nodded. They were all about being Present here. LeeAnn tried to catch Viktor's eye—they'd joked together about the undue worship of lived reality before. *Virtual world, real world, whatever,* Viktor had said to her. *If I'm alert and paying attention, it's all real.* Back when he was actively gaming, Viktor had dutifully performed his job in IT, even amid multiday binges in a zombie apocalypse simulation. Viktor's boss had been the one to send him to the Center—over concerns for Viktor's "health and well-being." *Wasn't necessary, in my opinion,* Viktor had told Lee-Ann. *As long as I'm not hurting anyone else, I don't see what the problem is.*

LeeAnn appreciated Viktor's gamer-boy nihilism; he made her feel like a digital fixation wasn't inherently bad. Which, in turn, made her feel like *she* wasn't inherently bad. In fact, maybe she had never had a problem at all. Her "problem" was really someone else's issue with it.

But then again, she hadn't been a gamer like Viktor, had she?

"It's been four weeks," the counselor went on, "and we haven't really heard from you, LeeAnn. Of course, there's never any pressure to share, but my understanding is that you'll need to demonstrate improvements here, as per your court order."

LeeAnn nearly dropped the Rubik's Cube. She stared at the counselor. Wasn't it a violation of privacy to mention the court order in front of everyone? The counselor maintained the same expression of bemused generosity, but the others in the therapy circle had stiffened—were staring at her—even the most languid of InstaQueens.

"You do understand, LeeAnn," said the counselor, with over-the-top gentleness, "that we all just want you to help yourself."

The room's beige light got beiger. The others' faces bent toward a grotesque pity—even Sigmund's, even Noreen and Sarah S.'s surgery-disturbed features. They were all so young and dumb, thought LeeAnn. Even the counselor, it occurred to her, was the same age as her eldest daughter, Gwyneth.

"Maybe you could start by explaining how you developed an early habit?" the counselor went on. "We've talked a lot about how small habits become bigger ones—like how Noreen and Sarah S. got lip fillers before moving on to permanent cosmetic procedures."

LeeAnn discovered she was sweating. Her daughter's face loomed in her mind, followed by the bobbling heads of her whole family. They'd all been shocked when they'd learned what she did online. Horrified, really. They'd looked at her like she was some kind of monster.

Was she?

No, LeeAnn reminded herself—her family just hadn't understood her. Because if they had, they wouldn't have sent her to the Center. They wouldn't have trapped her in a facility where her only ephemeral peace came from sex in the woods with various damaged twentysomethings.

The damaged twentysomethings stared at LeeAnn. Her sweating intensified, as did the beige blurriness of the room. Distantly, she heard the counselor say: ". . . or maybe you could start by telling us when your habit grew out of control. Because everyone here, in some way, lost control."

That's when the world began to fully melt. Beige slid into beige. Sound distorted. Faces, too—the counselor's features colliding with Sigmund's and Noreen's and Sarah S.'s and

Sarah Q.'s and Jasmine's and Mo's and Bianca's and Sun-Hee's and Rosy's and Trevor's and, horribly, Viktor's. The Rubik's Cube got hot, slippery with LeeAnn's palm sweat. She could feel her makeup dripping down her cheeks, the stares of the others stabbing her like a dozen electric prods.

So it was a goddamn miracle and a half when the fire alarm started blaring.

No one wanted to gather in the Center's parking lot—which bordered the forest—but they had to until the fire department showed up and declared the buildings safe. Residents huddled together in small groups, peering over their shoulders at the forest, as if a mountain lion might spring from the foliage and drag one of them away.

LeeAnn stood on the outer edge of these clusters. She was still woozy from the group therapy session, agitated by how close the counselor had come to voicing the habits that had brought her to the Center. In the old days, LeeAnn might have pulled out her phone, typed a post to regain balance . . . *Was just publicly humiliated by a self-righteous halfwit* . . . But, of course, she didn't have a phone. And this agitated her further.

She needed to get back into the forest, if only to clear her head. LeeAnn looked around for Viktor. Despite the embarrassment of the group therapy session, maybe she could get him to go out into the woods with her twice in one day.

Meanwhile, the fire trucks were arriving, groaning up the steep road leading to the Center. All the Documenters grew restless with their impulse to film the vehicles' approach. A Cyberchondriac cheered. Even the usually catatonic Compulsive Shoppers perked up at the approaching lights. Staff ran around, trying to answer questions, sowing confusion instead.

There was no sign of Viktor—though there was someone standing beside her.

"Hi, I'm Izzy."

It was a girl—maybe nineteen—a head shorter than Lee-Ann, wearing a Manson-girl-blue smock. Her hair was fine, almost smokelike, which only partially obscured a series of bald patches. Her skin was freckled. Her eyes tiny and fixated. A set of metal braces grinned at LeeAnn, who had never seen the girl before, didn't like her energy—didn't like that she'd thought of "energy" at all, which was appallingly Californian. But some of the other residents from group therapy were gawking at LeeAnn—like she had made the fire alarm happen with her mind—so she decided it would be wise to playact sociability.

"Thank god for this alarm," LeeAnn muttered.

The girl grinned wider. "Thanks," she said. "But I'm not God."

"What?"

"I'm not God, but you can thank me."

LeeAnn raised her eyebrows at the girl, then scanned again for Viktor. How good it would feel to get back into the cool forest, to have Viktor's long body pressed against hers, to stroke his fuzzy butt and be enveloped in his ambiance of casual tolerance. Out in the forest, LeeAnn wouldn't have to think about what she'd done—what she still wanted to do—and whether this was a problem. She wouldn't have to think about anything at all.

The girl shifted back and forth on her feet. "You can thank me," she said, after a minute, "because I pulled the alarm."

The girl's smile stretched so wide, LeeAnn wondered if her braces might pop off.

"Thanks?"

"Yeah, it was like this," said the girl. "They had me shut up in a room by myself and I kept telling them: No no no no no no no. I need to see other faces, or else."

"Or else," echoed LeeAnn—watching as a firefighter gave the Center's staff a thumbs-up. The buildings were all clear. Residents rushed toward the main entrance, eager to return to the safety of indoors.

LeeAnn trailed after the crowd, still looking for Viktor; the girl walked along beside her, arms swinging.

"You look familiar," the girl said. "What are you in for?"

"That's rude to ask," replied LeeAnn, in a tone she hoped conveyed a haughty carelessness—and not the shiver of nervousness she felt. She reached for her Rubik's Cube, her mind careening to the articles that had come out after her arrest, along with the gleeful cable news coverage. It had all been so humiliating. It had all seemed so unfair. Wasn't she just a Dallas housewife? A mother of two tax-paying adults? A middle-aged, run-of-the-mill woman?

Wasn't that the problem to begin with? a voice in her mind answered.

The girl kept smiling, braces glinting. It gave LeeAnn the creeps. She needed to get away—from the girl, and from all these people with their nosy questions and absurd moral reasoning. She needed to find Viktor and get back into the woods.

Three staff members, their heads huddled together, pointed at her—at the girl—while they whispered in an urgent way.

"I'll tell you what I'm in for," said the girl, cheerfully.

At last, LeeAnn spotted Viktor's lanky figure among the other residents. His dog tag swung from his neck as he reached for a held-open door. LeeAnn waved—but he disappeared inside before she could get his attention. She looked back over her shoulder at the forest with a sigh.

"I'm in for an addiction to sending death threats," said the girl—Izzy—who then skipped away into the waiting custody of several burly security team members.

Viktor did not want to meet again that afternoon. Or the next morning. Or the day after that. No one would go with LeeAnn out into the forest, away from the Center's oppressive beige walls, the boring analog activities, the popcorn smell, even for a no-strings blow job. They were all too afraid of the mountain lions possibly prowling the forest. Or else, that's what they were telling her.

To be fair, the corpse of another dog—a purebred Pembroke Welsh corgi, according to the owner—had been found in the neighborhood near the Center. And a local woman *swore* a mountain lion had peered into her solarium—though she later conceded it might have been a deer; she hadn't been wearing her glasses.

Viktor never asked LeeAnn about the court order their counselor had mentioned, but she suspected this detail had been the final straw in a mounting straw pile of which she'd been unaware. Viktor, it seemed, had been keeping his own mental lists.

Maybe he wasn't so nonjudgmental after all. LeeAnn moved *cutting toast with a knife and fork* into the con side of Viktor's tally. She put *dog tag* there, too. She considered moving *fuzzy butt*, then decided to address that trait later.

In the meantime, she endured. Or tried to. Without access to the forest—the release and distraction of sex—LeeAnn oscillated between craving the Internet and craving an escape from what she'd done on it. Was she a monster? The question grew loud in her mind, made it hard for her to sleep, hard for her to eat the Center's cafeteria food, hard for her to keep from rocking back and forth in her seat during group therapy—which in turn made it all but impossible to pick up new lovers, get back to the woods.

Help, she imagined posting, *a Luddite cult is trying to brainwash me into submission . . .*

Four days after the alarm—which was also four days since Viktor, or anyone, had agreed to go with her into the woods— LeeAnn's cravings grew so intense that she considered breaking the rules and going into the forest alone, skipping sex altogether. But a part of her, she discovered, *was* afraid of the mountain lion. She did not want to end up like someone's pet dog: torn limb from limb.

All she could do was keep busy. And so she paced the Udall-Meyers Treatment Center: up and down the beige corridors, around the rec hall, the reading room, the gym, the ceramics studio, the all-faith prayer pavilion, her cowgirl boots clacking, her manicured fingers gripping her Rubik's Cube as perfume contrails streamed in her wake. The other residents glanced at her, glanced away; they trained their eyes on table tennis games, pool volleyball, the pages of gossip magazines—as if enthralled by these activities. It made LeeAnn jealous: how untormented they were. But then she reminded herself that this contentment was likely often an act. Because she couldn't be the only one stoically surviving until the moment came to again press power on a confiscated phone, computer, tablet, gaming system. She couldn't be the only resident waiting to hear the delicious whir of noise and color, their machinery waking up: a portal opening to elsewhere. *Ping. Ping. Ping.*

Because for all the damage LeeAnn's online actions might have caused—to her and others—hadn't the months of her "downward spiral" also been the first really good ones in a while? Delicious months they'd been. Invigorating months that broke her out of the long slow slide of middle age and her dwindling sense of purpose as a housewife in suburban America.

LeeAnn almost felt okay when she remembered this—good even. If she could endure a little longer, she'd get to leave the Center and return to her former life.

But then, just as quickly, the beige walls of the facility would press in, her doubts along with them. Her family's disturbed faces would loom in her mind, and she would remember how they'd all assembled in the living room of her town house in Lakeview Heights. Her dumb, devoted husband. Her gossipy sister. Aunt Beth the do-gooder. Second Cousin Jeremiah, as if he mattered. And her kids—Gwyneth, most prominently. Gwyneth with her eyes glistening, tearful as she said: *But why, Mom? Why did you do this?*

An intervention, her family had called that gathering. An ambush was what it was. LeeAnn had felt cornered: a wild animal with nowhere to run. Even now, the memory made her want to scream and kick and claw at anyone and anything in her way—which in this case was the Center's beige curtains and smiling counselors and the Jenga tower some residents were building in the rec hall.

But she couldn't; to do so would have confirmed to everyone that she was the monster they all said she was.

"To be frank," said the Center's director, who had requested a special meeting with LeeAnn, "we aren't seeing you make much progress."

LeeAnn closed her eyes and nodded, as if she, too, found this to be irksome and puzzling—and not the fact that she was still at the Center, being lectured by a shapeless woman with tea-stained teeth. The director was LeeAnn's same age, but not nearly as well-preserved. She had no taste, either, as evidenced by the excess of crystals, prayer beads, and meditation gongs displayed around her office.

"You know that progress is required, as per your court order."

LeeAnn exaggerated the verticality of her nod.

"We talk a lot about being *in the moment* here at Udall-Meyers, but, for you, it might be useful to focus on the future. Have you visualized your first day out?"

LeeAnn had many times visualized firing up her laptop, her fingers hovering like hawks above the keyboard—pouncing. Text appearing. The sweet rush of reexposure.

The director narrowed her eyes, as if she knew what LeeAnn was thinking—even the bad bird analogy.

"You know," she said, "some of our clients leave the Udall-Meyers Center, only to later return several times. It's all part of their journey."

"*What a racket,*" muttered LeeAnn, but the director kept talking.

"You, LeeAnn," she said, "only have this one chance. And while there are more affordable detox centers out there, even state-run facilities have long waiting lists these days. And keep in mind that the treatment modalities at those places are largely pharmaceutical."

The director wrinkled her nose—then she gave LeeAnn a hard look.

"Your other path, LeeAnn, leads to prison."

LeeAnn shifted her focus to the director's office window. Outside, the evening sky had purpled with impending rain. Wind swayed a series of massive sycamores on the edge of the forest, their trunks like gateposts guarding the trembling, wild territory beyond. She wished she was out there. She wished Viktor was speaking to her. Or better yet: that she was out there with Viktor, and he was kissing her neck while she clawed her fingers down his back, the pair of them pressed up against an oak tree, inhaling the wet-earth smells of the woods, the concerns of the world made meaningless by nature's sheer indifference.

"Your family sacrificed a lot for you to come to Udall Meyers," the director tried again. "One of your own children paused her graduate studies for you to be here."

"Massage school isn't—"

"You have two weeks left, LeeAnn. To turn this around."

LeeAnn felt itchy. Outside, a crack of lightning splintered the sky, the sound shuddering through the Center. Then the rain picked up, lashing the office window, blurring her view of the forest beyond. In weather like this, she wouldn't even be able to pace around the Center's pool.

"We need to see some serious effort. We need to see you think about strategy. Lifestyle. Accountability," the director continued. "Which is why we've conferred with your family and decided to take extra measures to ensure that progress is made."

"Excuse me?"

"We're giving you a roommate. It'll be good for you, a little vitamin C—for *community*."

"But I paid—"

"Actually, you've been getting a discount."

LeeAnn opened her mouth, closed it. "Who?" she said, dread blooming in her stomach.

"Her name is—well, I believe you already met. Or she seems to think so."

Izzy was waiting in their now-shared room, where an extra cot had been pushed against one wall. She looked the same as before: blue smock, floaty hair exposing bald spots on her skull. She grinned at LeeAnn, braces glinting. Her breath was meaty and shallow.

"Told you I'd see you again."

"What?"

"Want to play table tennis?"

"No, god. Leave me alone."

"I'm not—"

LeeAnn fled the room. She hurried down a beige corridor, past a gaggle of anxious *Truman Show* Conspirators, until she reached the rec hall—blessedly empty of other residents. At one end of the hall, a bay window offered a view of the thunderstorm rumbling over the Center. Through the glass, Lee-Ann could just see the massive sycamores at the edge of the forest, their branches tossed by wind and rain. She curled up on one of the rec hall's sofas, twisted her Rubik's Cube angrily. Red, yellow, blue, green, white, orange. The squares traded places, shifted, refused to cohere into homogenous planes. To think there was only one solution and a million wrong ways.

Her only solution now: escape. Maybe she could stow away in the food service delivery truck, hitchhike to Delaware, or wherever, and start a new life. She had a knack, after all, for creating new identities.

"I know who you are."

LeeAnn dropped the Rubik's Cube—a scream spiking her throat. Izzy's face hovered a foot from her own; the girl had crept silently into the rec hall.

"I thought you and I could be friends," Izzy said.

Her grin flashed metallically. Outside, wind howled through trees, branches creaking, more rain slapping the windows and walls of the Center.

"When I saw you at the fire alarm the other day, I was sure you looked familiar," Izzy went on. "I needed to know more, so I identified the least experienced staff member and got him to smuggle me a phone by threatening to choke myself unless he did. Once I had the Internet, I read all about you. Turns out I was right! I'd seen you on the news before coming here—there was a story about all those scams you pulled. Boy oh boy! A lot of people hate you! That's how I knew we would understand each other. Because I used to send death threats, and sometimes malware-laced ransom messages, to senators and celebrities and former classmates, which isn't exactly what you were doing, but—"

"Get away from me," said LeeAnn.

"It's okay to be scared," said Izzy—leaning in for a hug—"of who you really are."

LeeAnn rolled off the sofa, out of reach. The girl was genuinely unstable. How could LeeAnn be expected to sleep safely in the same room as her? LeeAnn would go straight to the Center's director, demand a change be made.

While Izzy babbled more nonsense, LeeAnn inched backward toward the rec hall door, taking one step at a time. And she might have reached the threshold—might have escaped—had something tall and semi-firm not blocked her path.

LeeAnn spun around. "Viktor!"

He seemed surprised to see her, too. Or maybe a little sheepish—which wasn't necessarily a negative reaction. Noreen and Sarah S. lurked in the hallway behind him; Noreen held a deck of cards, Sarah S. a bowl of popcorn. Viktor must have come with them to play Go Fish, or some equally inane game. And yet, LeeAnn wanted to fling her arms around him. She wanted, really, just to be near him. The confession rose in her chest—an impulse further pressurized when he put a hand on her shoulder and asked what was wrong. She looked awfully pale.

Then Izzy interrupted: "Oh hi, Viktor—that's your name, right? LeeAnn's fine. She's just coming to terms with our innate connection. Because I also used to manipulate people using illicit means. Both of us disrupted dozens of innocent lives by—"

"Shut up, Izzy," hissed LeeAnn.

"—by preying on their weaknesses to satisfy our own selfish need for power and control."

Viktor's face clouded. He stared at Izzy, then at LeeAnn. "You did what?" he said.

LeeAnn opened her mouth to reply, but the situation suddenly felt desperately complicated. Her words came out in stammers.

Viktor shook his head. "Never mind, LeeAnn. I don't even want to know." To Noreen and Sarah S., he said, "Let's play Uno somewhere else."

"Wait," said LeeAnn, "it's not what you think—I mean, no one was physically hurt or—"

But the three of them were already walking away, disappearing around a bend in the corridor, and it was just LeeAnn and

Izzy—Izzy, standing there grinning—waiting with the Rubik's Cube in her outstretched palm.

"Here," said Izzy, "I solved it."

Heat spiked through LeeAnn's limbs. She slapped the cube out of Izzy's hand, emitted a stream of obscenities she hadn't known she contained. Izzy's grin melted into slack-jawed confusion; her eyes went puppy-dog sad.

"Oh no no no no no no," Izzy said. "I thought—"

"Get away from me," screamed LeeAnn. "Just get the fuck away."

With eyes downcast, Izzy ran to the rec hall's emergency exit—a fire door covered in bright red alarm warnings—and pushed it open. The room filled with the wet whoosh of wind and rain. Izzy sent LeeAnn one last wide-eyed look. Then, in a blur of braces and blue smock, she dashed into the stormy twilight, the dark mouth of the forest beyond.

LeeAnn's first post had been an accident. While walking around her neighborhood in Lakeview Heights, the clasp of her tennis bracelet had come undone, and the bracelet had slipped into a storm drain. Just like that: gone. The feeling of having, then not having—the swiftness of disappearance—had startled her. She'd needed to tell someone. Her husband, though, would be working his job as an accounts manager until late that evening, and he wasn't particularly perceptive anyway; her kids no longer lived at home; her gal friends were more interested in acquisitions than loss; and she didn't want to have to listen to her sister babble about her own problems. So LeeAnn posted the anecdote on the neighborhood's online forum. She'd never posted before, had only used the forum to ascertain disruptions in the local trash collection service. But in that moment, posting felt right. The story of the lost brace-let poured out of her. *To think,* she'd typed, *that an heirloom passed through generations could vanish in the blink of an eye.*

The outpouring of support stunned her. Her neighbors—some of whom she knew, some of whom she didn't—seemed genuinely sorry about her loss. Maybe people were less tongue-tied online? Or less preoccupied by watering their begonias than they were in person? Whatever the reason, a long thread of comments spelled out condolences. Some individuals shared similar experiences: an engagement ring lost on a beach in Fort Myers, an antique brooch slipped from a cardigan at a casino in Vegas. One lady, whose brother owned a jewelry store, offered to set LeeAnn up with a deep discount on a replacement pur-chase. *I know it won't substitute the REAL treasure,* the woman wrote, *but it's a start.*

LeeAnn hadn't actually liked the bracelet that much—she'd posted to convey the shock of loss, more than anything—but she *did* like the sympathy she received: attention she hadn't known she needed. LeeAnn understood that, all things con-sidered, she had a very decent life. A privileged life, even. She and her husband had almost paid off their mortgage. They took a vacation twice a year—never intercontinental, but a trip, nonetheless. She had her health, except for mild sciatica. She'd stopped working after her kids were born—and while her kids weren't geniuses, they weren't huge fuckups, either. LeeAnn had no reason to complain, really. She spent her days doing the odd household chore, browsing department stores, visiting the salon, lunching with friends.

And yet, with each passing year, LeeAnn felt increasingly that something was *off.* People stopped holding doors open for her the way they once had. Baristas chatted with her less. She wasn't catcalled, even when she wore heels. The world, she finally realized, had grown tired of her presence. She was a middle-aged woman whose looks were fading and whose kids were raised; she had no career to fall back on. Her existence no longer had a purpose—a point.

Then came that sympathy.

The Internet-compassion slid into her veins: a syrup so sweet, it tickled her whole body toward pleasure. All those people mourning *her* loss. She read their comments over and over.

To justify her second post, LeeAnn told herself it was simply an experiment. A test to see what would happen. She made a fake account for someone "new to the neighborhood." Then she posted about a lost wallet—had anyone seen it? It contained cash, gift cards, as well as precious family photos.

Condolences poured in. LeeAnn's spirits soared, lifted by the secondhand love—but even more by her power to summon it. She had agency. Talent, too. Why not see how far her talent could extend? And so she began to post on other neighborhood forums, and other social media platforms, describing other losses, along with catastrophic house fires, floods, illnesses, discriminations, harassments, heartaches of all kinds.

. . . *I thought the worst was over after the car accident,* she wrote, *but it turns out I have a rare brain infection. I'm worried I won't live to see my own daughter graduate . . .*

Her own daughter, of course, was doing just fine: studying massage therapy, dating a PE teacher named Thom. But LeeAnn's fake daughters—and husbands, and wives, and sisters, and friends—experienced tragedy alongside her, everyone suffering in the imagined realities of her posts.

A part of LeeAnn knew that asking for money was a step too far. But people offered it before she ever asked. And when she did ask, her crowdfunding pages were there to fit her stories—because her stories demanded authentic trappings—and because when she was deep in a post, scrolling through messages of support, she forgot who she really was. She became a victim uplifted by the grace of others. She became a survivor willing to battle the worst. She became, more than anything, a newly empowered creature, more confident and in control than she'd ever been before. There were times when, standing in the kitchen of her recently remodeled town house, afternoon light streaming in—along with phone alerts tracking her latest purchases: designer wedges, luxury moisturizers, better tennis bracelets—she'd shed tears of joy, reveling in the Internet's ecstatic capacity to make her feel alive.

Then one day she got caught.

LeeAnn stepped from the rec hall into the gurgling, dripping twilight. As the emergency exit slammed behind her, the Center's fire alarms trilled for the second time that week. Residents and staff would soon pour into the parking lot on the other side of the facility. Everyone would be running around in a panic. By the time LeeAnn explained to someone what had happened, Izzy would be long gone up the forest trail.

"Goddamn it," said LeeAnn, staring into the storm-drenched woods. "Izzy!"

She considered wiping her hands of the situation: joining the others in the parking lot, pretending nothing was amiss. But she knew that it was possible—likely, even—that Izzy would get lost or injured. And it would be LeeAnn's fault, even if she hadn't told Izzy to go into the forest, specifically. It would confirm what Izzy had told Viktor and the others: that she, Lee-Ann, was a monster who preyed on those weaker than herself.

But what if LeeAnn retrieved—no, *rescued*—the girl? Wouldn't that prove to everyone that their ideas about her were backward? That she wasn't a monster at all?

"Izzy," called LeeAnn as she started running toward the forest, her cowgirl boots wobbling in the mud-slicks made by rain. "Izzy, come back. I don't care about the Rubik's Cube. It doesn't matter."

No answer.

LeeAnn kept running, holding her hands out in front of her to keep tree branches from smacking her face. The rain had slowed, but the evening sky careened toward blackness, the forest canopy blocking out what little illumination might have reached the trail below. LeeAnn slipped, fell onto her knees, her wrist smashing against a rock. She cursed under her breath. Then out loud. In the distance, the Center's alarms pulsed. Trees swayed, creaked in the wind. At last, LeeAnn glimpsed what looked like the swish of a blue smock up ahead. She ran toward it, blundering through shadows.

Nothing.

How much easier this would be, LeeAnn thought, if she had a fucking phone with a flashlight.

"Izzy," she yelled again. "Where the hell are you?"

No answer.

LeeAnn considered going back—letting Izzy fend for herself—but then she remembered Viktor's disappointed face. His face, and Noreen/Sarah's face, and the director's face, and her daughter's face, and the faces of everyone who believed she was an active danger to society.

Was she?

No, LeeAnn told herself, as she had many times before. She couldn't be. Not her. She was just someone who'd gotten carried away. A woman who needed a little extra attention as she faced her own impending obsolescence.

"Izzy—wait," LeeAnn called. "I only want to talk. Everything is fine—I'm glad you solved the cube. I'm glad we're roommates. I—"

The wind picked up. LeeAnn could no longer hear the Center's alarms. A huge tree crashed down on the path directly behind her—a near deathblow—and she bolted, trampling ferns, branches scratching her limbs, poison oak gutting her mouth, bark tearing her clothes. She had to be bleeding, if not covered in mud. Her breath wheezed.

"Izzy, where are you?"

Another massive gust of wind ripped through the woods.

"The issue now," said LeeAnn, "is that I don't know how to get back."

To the Center, she almost added. The center of what?

"I'm sorry," she said—testing the phrase. "I'm so so sorry," she went on, louder this time, willing herself to mean it. "I'm sorry I hurt you. I'm sorry for everything. It's me that's the problem. I'm fucked up and I need to change."

A twig snapped.

LeeAnn peered into the dark forest, the trees knitted impenetrable by shadows.

"Izzy?" she said.

Another snap. LeeAnn's body tensed. Was that predatory breathing she heard? Hot breath, stalking steps, the sizzle of a stare perceiving more than she ever could know?

She should back away. She should run as fast as her body could take her. And maybe she would, she told herself. Maybe she'd stumble onto a trail that led all the way to the Center. Once there, she'd find Izzy safe and sound; she'd find the others, too—Viktor and Noreen and Sarah S., and everyone—and she'd hug them all. Even Trevor. Even Sigmund. She'd finally share with them what had brought her to the Center: her diminished sense of purpose in the world. She would summon the courage to apologize to her family, her friends, the strangers who had unwittingly given to a woman who hadn't needed their help, so that when she walked out of the Udall-Meyers Treatment Center, she'd leave as a new woman.

She knew that she should.

She knew, even, that she could.

Another rustle in the undergrowth; the neck-prickle of being watched. LeeAnn lurched forward through the darkness, barreling down the nearest trail—ready to return home then stopped short.

The trail dropped away into a ridgeline lookout. A sweeping view of Silicon Valley spread out in front of her, glittering in the night. The lights of all those cars and houses and tech campuses—LeeAnn had the feeling she could reach out and scoop them up like jewels, let the wealth run through her fingers. And yet, there was an awfulness about the lights as well. Against the darkness, she could see how they crept up the surrounding hills and mountains in a glowing encroachment—a beautiful ambush. They would never stop coming, those lights. Eventually their brightness would eat up the remaining peaks, consume them whole. It was only a matter of time.

No wonder the mountain lions were acting out, thought LeeAnn. If you didn't make a point of your own existence, you'd be annihilated. Annihilated without anyone giving a second thought.

She turned to face the forest. Panting breaths, wind, the slash of more rain—this remaining patch of wilderness rioted, violent and mean. Her pulse quickened. Her blood ran hot. She wasn't going back—she knew that now—despite the terror of what approached. Rainwater, sweat, dripped down her spine, carrying an electric tingle. She was Present. She was here. Anticipation thrummed through her as her eyes adjusted, and the dark screen between trees materialized into form.

What she saw was magnificent and terrible—svelte, long-nailed, ferocious.

LeeAnn's eyes dilated. Her skin burned. At last: the rendez-vous she'd been waiting for this whole time.

III

Frights

Brek liked attics, especially ones with dust motes raised by every motion, the air-whisper of particulate matter wafting like the shadows we no longer had.

Cornelia preferred a graveyard. Traditional, she was. A home-maker tending to her plot. She circled the rosebush planted by her husband as it grew thorn-studded, blossom-beautified, maturing into sawtooth-tangles that consumed her entire headstone.

Lamb lurked side-stage at the opera house: a ripple in velvet curtains, a glimmer under low lights. He got high on the sopranos' shrieks, vibrations quivering his ectoplasmic bonds.

It's not good for you, we said, as if anything could hurt us now. Lamb, we knew, liked that people came to see him as much as *Don Giovanni.*

———

We lapped upon our own legends. A soup of stories: the makings of our deaths. How delicious it was to be remembered—or to receive, at least, a lick of acknowledgment.

Prinne hovered in the supply closet of a candy factory, where workers spoke of a former night-shifter, unlucky: had slipped into a caramel vat and drowned a week before retiring. Workers warned one another of an angry apparition—sugar-blistered, vindictive.

Prinne had never worked at the candy factory but was plenty angry. Most murder victims are.

Others of us floated like seedlings on the breeze, blowing across the continent, over cornfields, subdivisions, byways and beaches, out to the Pacific. There, we were buffeted by gales, our translucent bodies cyclone-spun, our ghost-howls swallowed by storm winds until we were tossed to remote ocean corners. We moved slow once the weather died—we pondered our own ends—but we had all the time in the world to get where we were going.

The world, though, was on limited time: even we could see that.

This cheered some among us.

Ellie was a bedroom ghost: a dream-visitant, a gentle levitator, a classic cold-sweat presence-in-the-corner, but she felt undersung. *It's not like the old days,* she told us. *They attribute everything I do to Ambien . . .*

————

Eldorado was a bedroom ghost, too, but a different kind.

No complaints here, he said.

I liked mirrors most. In one, my phantom-face hovered over a viewer's shoulder—as if we inhabited the same plane, as if I wouldn't vaporize when the viewer spun around.

Call me a hide-and-seek spook. A tease. Really, it was a show of shyness, even after all these years.

Such reticence was unwarranted; the living wrote off our hauntings with escalating frequency. They explained us as air-pressure changes, as electrical short-circuiting, as geothermal discrepancies, as sunspots, as rats in the attic, as raccoons in the basement, as drafts, as bad dreams, as bad drugs, as signs of Alzheimer's, as carbon monoxide poisoning, as the Caputo Effect, as tired tales of superstition.

Imagine being believed in, we moaned. *The way we once were. Respected.*

Admittedly, we tended to take a gloomy outlook.

But, we told ourselves, told each other: little mattered in the end. And the end was surely nigh. We watched humanity's Doomsday Clock tick closer to midnight—seconds siphoned day by day—bringing with it all the unknowable repercussions of an undone Cinderella-spell.

MISS ME? I scrawled into mirror condensation when my unseen-ness became unbearable. The ephemeral tablet was conjured by shower steam, my wraith-writing spelled out in the Modern English I'd struggled so long to learn.

ЯM SSIM read the living, perplexed.

————

It was Za—haint of swamp cabins, rot-ravaged and creaking—
who saw the ghost flock first. Pigeons, he told us, fluttering
and coasting on winds that weren't there. Elegant birds, odd
birds—he followed the great mass of them for miles. They flew
unexhausted through rainstorms; their feathers shimmered in
and out of lightning strikes.

Never seen anything like it, he said.

We were curious, yes, but we had other issues on our minds:
namely our own obscurity. Some of us coped by dozing for
decades; others slept through whole centuries. Most of us wandered, waited. We hoped for a paranormal renaissance: a renewed
reverence for our presences, an investment in our fates. In the
meantime, we avoided bright lights, the scent of burning sage,
salt flats. We watched our former cities razed, or raised; the planet's
minerals plundered, land tilled, teased into crops—every square
inch strip-searched. Squandered. The living were ever industri-
ous, increasingly frantic. On the move. So we moved with them.
We hid in the exhaust ports of combustion engines, tagged onto
airplane wings, whooshed along high-speed rail lines. We let
Wi-Fi signals prickle the places where our spines once were.
We felt the stab-stare of satellites, sonars pulsing through us. We
even roved the Internet: striking poses in Google Street View—
ever hoping to be noticed—but digital imagery didn't carry the
same drama as the daguerreotypes of yesteryear.

When the newly dead joined our numbers, we shared with
them our doomed outlook: a dull eternity.

That is, until more among us noticed the ghost flock flying
overhead—pigeons traveling in a shimmering cloud, shadow-
less and vast.

See, said Za, who'd left the swamp by then, his former haunting grounds swallowed by rising seas. *I told y'all.*

What makes a ghost a ghost? Not every soul leaves a paranormal footprint. Some simply disappear. Bodies compost. Worms revel and writhe. Earth eats flesh whole while a spirit splits for elsewhere, uncaught between realities the way we were—in the thin veil between this and that, here and there, as sticky to us as a spider's web.

We cannot tell you if there is an afterlife; we've never been.

What we can say: we've stayed behind because something has held us. Unfinished, we are. Undercooked. Unsatisfied. A mortal coil unshuffled: a love we couldn't leave, an injustice we couldn't let go, a location we didn't dare depart.

We'd assumed this situation was anthropomorphic, only.

More ghost creatures turned up. Trig reported a ghost toad: hopped across the basement of a McMansion she haunted in the suburbs. Scowled at her with red demon-eyes, the toad did, before disappearing into a drainpipe—pulling a poltergeist plumbing job.

Icarus spotted a ghost moose. It specter-stepped across a ten-lane freeway as traffic blasted through its body.

Kova counted a dozen ghost crabs scuttling sideways down a subway car, pinching the toes of passengers.

We were perplexed. True, we'd seen ghost horses before—their gallops swift and silent beneath bloated moons, their riders often headless. Canine spirits, too, had nosed the grounds of abandoned churches, their owners flitting in the buildings' belfries. But these animal phantoms we'd understood as extensions of ourselves—as props, really—not unlike the top hats we sometimes wore, or the canes we carried, or the axes held with blades eternally blood-dripped.

These new paranormal animals were different.

We watched the ghost pigeons, the ghost toad, the ghost moose, the ghost crabs make their own haunted rounds.

Weird, we all said—even the witches among us. *Those are no ghost familiars.*

Things got weirder—

A bobcat, wildfire-singed, bawling, crossed death's door only to spring up, tail twitching, and stalk around an electrical grid in its new phantom form.

Ghost prairie dogs popped through the linoleum floors of ranch homes, chittering.

Ghost humpbacks spewed ectoplasm from blowholes— unbeached from where they'd washed up with plastic-gutted bellies. With them came schools of ghost fish: swordfish, white sea bass, gliding manta rays. Salmon swam through crowded city sidewalks, scales pellucid as they piloted upstream.

More ghost birds materialized—owls, woodpeckers, war- blers, parakeets, wide-winged condors—clotting the sky, their numbers dizzying, feathers smoke-steeped in an atmosphere clouded by fumes, their collective movements as graceful as any human ghost's swoop.

We looked on in awe, wondered if the living perceived what we did.

———

Most didn't.

But a few, at least, watched wide-eyed as a herd of ghost bison burst split-screen through a supermarket wall, their steps silver-swift, a pack of ghost wolves at their heels—howls eerie, echoing, making the fluorescent lights flicker. The observing patrons had clutched their shopping carts, unable to blame earthquakes or rolling blackouts for what they all had seen.

Soon after that, a pair of ghost sharks raised their fins in soup bowls. A revenant: making eaters faint.

Ghost mosquitoes—recently pesticide-poisoned—buzzed like live insects in the skulls of their killers. Brain swarmers, unswat table and relentless. They made their victims go mad. They made us a touch concerned.

Look, we said to the ghost mosquitoes. *Go easy. We have unwritten rules . . .*

Rules, though—unwritten or otherwise—kept shifting.

The ghosts of elms, redwoods, Joshua trees grew from the lobby floors of office buildings—their branches swaying, phosphorescent—trunks stabbing like spears through the metal hearts of skyscrapers.

Ghost grasses pricked through bedsheets.

Ghost mosses glommed onto television screens.

On door handles and inside keyholes, ghost oysters clustered alongside coral formations: the ghost shoals marked by sea anemones—already wraithy—that wafted their tentacles to tingle passersby.

More of the living took note. They felt these presences—our presences, as we came to think of all the ghostly organisms— and hid their eyes in terror. They covered their mouths. They trembled. They told their friends, then fled to places that seemed safer.

We were touched, but even we could see where things were heading; we'd seen this direction for a while.

In our paranormal realm, we welcomed the chilling creep of ghost glaciers, along with the shudder-touch of ghost snow-flakes dusting the corridors of air-conditioned malls.

We welcomed a ghost Gulf Stream—that oceanic ligament—flexing in the byway between life and afterlife. A swath of ghost wetlands spread across parking lots, cattails swaying. Ghost aquifers fed a ghost swimming hole, newly opened on statehouse steps, ghost water lapping at the feet of elected officials.

Look, look—

The living became desperate. They lay awake at night, sweating—their bodies so fleshy and physical, tender—as they read articles about us, exhuming the circumstances surround-ing our deaths. They rushed to make amends. They offered sac-rifices, pledged money, wrote letters, recycled bottles, planted trees—as if new life could exorcise what had already been lost.

We should have been pleased. We should be pleased: Wasn't recognition what we'd always wanted? A reckoning that might release our trapped souls—the ballast between this life and the next?

(In my haunted mirror, a ghost meadow yearns into being. Wildflowers burst open—honeysuckle, buttercup, Queen Anne's lace—blossoms redolent even as apparitions. Ghost bees bask in pollen, the nectar sweet here: infinite.)

Answers no longer seem straightforward.

Some of us do wonder what will happen after the end—the last catastrophe—be it brought on by bomb or sickness or famine. But mostly we've decided that such specifics no longer matter. Because while we cannot know what will happen to us after the last of the living lies down and dies, for now we do know this: in our paranormal realm, in this in-between place, we are no longer unnoticed. We are no longer lonely. We are vine-tangled, creature-shrieked—vibrantly alive.

Democracy in America

Where in the memory of man can one find anything comparable to what is taking place before our
eyes in North America?

—Alexis de Tocqueville

She was beautiful, which made things difficult. The planes
of her face cut to carry the light, liquid umber hair, pensive
mouth, nimble body—she looked good even when shoplift-
ing, sweatshirt-clad, her movements hunched. When I first
saw her, stealing cashews from a convenience store in Massachusetts, my breath caught in my throat. I nearly missed my
chance to follow her outside.

Honey was her name—or the name she gave me.

Her looks drew me to her, but they pained me as well. Soon
she wouldn't be her. Anyone with eyes could have predicted
this. Honey was beautiful and also broke. She was an ideal
candidate for consignment.

Not that the future had ever stopped me from pursuing what I wanted in the present.

I had been in America less than a month—in Honey's weathered township mere days—but courtship isn't complicated. After a second casual crossing of paths, a clever remark, a half smile, I had her looking my way. And I knew how to hold a look. For my trip to America, I had packed light, but my two suits were impeccably tailored to my narrow chest, hips. A swagger lilted my walk. No one would call me beautiful, but they might use the word *striking*. Close-cropped hair, razor gaze; I possessed an androgynous cool that flipped hearts. And Americans went mad for accents.

Honey was no exception. After a round of drinks at the local tavern, then a twilit stroll, her hand found mine: fingers small and cold. I wanted to suck them warm, though I did not tell her that until later. And by then there were more complicated matters to discuss.

◆

Honey's announcement arrived on a November afternoon. We had been seeing each other for several weeks by then; I had rented a room in town, and we had been meeting there mostly. We were resting in my narrow bed when she said: "So I talked to one of those recruiters who hang around the basketball courts—"

I pressed my eyes closed, braced for what I had known was coming.

"—and we actually had a great conversation," Honey went on, "about my future and my current financial situation. And, you know what? I think I'm going to consign."

From her tone, it was as if she had decided to dye her hair pink or get a tattoo.

"It just seems like the best choice for me. Especially right now, with how young I am and everything. It's a big opportunity. Plus, all my sisters have done it."

I kept my face impassive as she rationalized further: her oldest sister, Danika, had used her consignment payout to cover daycare for her toddler, which let her work full-time at the packing plant; Roxanne had used hers to buy a car, which allowed them both to get to the plant. And while she, Honey, didn't have a baby—and couldn't get hired due to her criminal record—maybe she would use the funds in other ways. She could start her own business. Or she could at least pay down her family's debt—her mother's MS wasn't getting any better, and the medical bills kept coming. Also their house needed a new roof.

I had once visited the family's house. A tired brick structure in a row of former mill homes, it leaned precariously over an eroded riverbed. Garish children's toys and dead lawn mowers lay scattered around an unkempt yard. The interior stank of chemically fake American cheese. The dereliction of the place had appalled me.

"What do you think, Alexis?"

I turned onto my back, my hands behind my head, pretending to ponder Honey's question. The rented room was above a local grocer and below us the register clanged with the afternoon rush, shrill with its clattering belly of coins, the swish of paper money, credit card beeps, as locals purchased pumpkin pie filling, mint ice cream, meat, for one of their culture's holidays. This was the kind of American town I had come to see, but it had not yet shown me what I wanted to know.

"My other idea," said Honey, "was that you and I could travel together. After consignment, I'll be able to pay my own way. More than anything, I've always wanted to see the world. I could even help you with your research."

She propped herself up on one elbow to gauge my reaction. The bedsheets fell away, exposing the smooth length of her torso. With a different woman, I might have guessed she had done this on purpose—to cow me—but from everything I had observed of Honey, she was guileless. Also: stubborn, striving, utterly provincial—a true citizen of her country—which did not change the fact that her body had a majesty of its own. Dark hair dripped around her shoulders. Her skin glowed. I ran a thumb along the ridgeline of her torso: down into the valley of her waist, then up the crest of her hip.

"Or do you only like me for my looks?" said Honey— emitting a loud, false laugh.

There was nothing to do except pretend her question offended me.

"Really, Honey?" I said. "You think I'm that shallow?"

She apologized immediately—relieved to be cast as the one in the wrong. I let her coax me back into her arms, our limbs entangling, the mood restored. Yet the ease of deception unsettled me. For all her rural coarseness, her petty criminality, Honey expected the world to be fundamentally fair and good; she expected me to be. And this expectation of hers moved me. It cut some ballast of detachment that had, until then, held me at a researcher's steady remove from the American experiment.

I might have been worried—I should have been—but then, Honey's lips found my neck. Her fingers teased my thighs. And all worries faded against the landscape of her body, its infinite potential.

◆

America had loomed in my imagination my whole life. Across the sea, yet ever present. An opposite and an endpoint. A fever dream and a nightmare—the force of its customs, values, ambitions, emanating outward. Consignment was a lever on America's slot machine of possibility. What if, it proposed, you could sell your youthful beauty? What if you could buy it back? Because in America, everything had a price. That liquidity pushed the nation down the river of equality—kept the country buoyant on its democratic raft—or so the story went.

I myself had grown up in one of Europe's obdurate second cities. You know the kind: with a decent cathedral, ruins a few tourists visit—though not with the vigor they might bring to a country's crowning metropolis. A city saved from tackiness by virtue of its elderly architecture and a stubborn commitment to constancy. A city with boulevards and outdoor café tables, small brutal espresso drinks; clothes shops selling cheap shirts, their prices in the windows. Dance music at night. Drunks. An old man on a bench, who has always been there. Schoolchildren in uniforms. Pigeons, papers fluttering. Cigarettes and crusty bread. Brisk winters. You know—I know, you know.

My family was well-off by many standards. They had afforded me the finest schools, access to the right circles, though most of our wealth was tied up in several crumbling properties too expensive to repair—a metaphor for most of Europe, really. My homeland longed to sit unchanged: comfortable in the ease of decay, drunk on its own history. Yet here was America, tugging on the reins of the new century, dragging the whole world with it. I wanted to know where she was taking us.

Officially, I had traveled to America on a government-sponsored fellowship, tasked with studying the nation's system of detention centers for undocumented immigrants. Europe was beset by its own refugee crisis; state officials were happy to have me research American methods—specifically, how America turned a profit on an outwardly intractable problem. I had been sent with a research partner, Beaumont—a longtime friend—but quarrels divided us early on. We had gone our separate ways in Boston. I cared little at the time. Detention centers were not my main interest. I wanted to understand America in its entirety; I had the idea that I would write a book.

Then I met Honey.

◆

On the scheduled morning of Honey's consignment, she and I stood together in a strip mall parking lot, in a small city a half hour's driving distance from her hometown. Honey's father and a jumble of her sisters were there, too—a bleary smear of faces. We had arrived early. The sun was coming up, the parking lot nearly empty: endless asphalt except for a few enormous American cars. Spilled motor oil fumed around us and I inhaled willingly. There was a primal quality to what was happening, as if we were all standing before a volcano, a Delphic vent, a pit of lions, knowing something awesome—in the terrible, incredible sense—was about to happen.

Was it wrong that a part of me felt excited? Consignment was outlawed throughout most of Europe. One wasn't even supposed to talk about it: religious types got uncomfortable. Then, too, it was simply déclassé. Technically, consignment may have faced restrictions in a few U.S. states as well, though with the sitting president's deregulatory push, red tape had loosened across every sector.

Which is not to say that consignment was without stigma in America. For discretion, facilities were often embedded within other businesses. The site where Honey would receive the procedure was housed inside a travel agency—images of palm trees foresting the windows—the front innocuously positioned between a nail salon and a sporting goods store.

At ten minutes past the hour, the agent who would coordinate the financial aspect of the consignment had yet to arrive. Honey's father—a wan, poorly shaved man—scanned the parking lot. In his hands, he wrung a sweaty handkerchief. His face twisted, presumably as he calculated the family's potential loss of income.

I felt a dual pulse of disappointment and relief.

Honey seemed in a similar state: holding my hand tightly, her whole body vibrating. She had been impulsive, bawdy, the week prior. Appearing at my rented room at all hours, she demanded feverish sex, late-night visits to the local tavern; she binged on peppercorn cookies; she leaned out my second-floor window, catcalling men and laughing.

Her outbursts fascinated me—though they disturbed me as well. They were cries for help, no doubt: efforts to prompt me to admit that her beauty was what kept me close, that she ought not to go through with consignment. But while I was a flirt, a foreigner, I was no fool. To have made such a statement would have ended our liaison anyway, and I wanted to observe what would happen in the wake of the procedure. For all the discomfort that would come from seeing Honey transformed, the consignment process was uniquely American. My observations of Honey's experience could be included in my future book.

That our relationship would eventually end felt like a given—but that ending was far enough in the future so as to feel unburdensome. And when our ending did occur, I told myself, it would likely appear to be for reasons unlinked to her physical form. Honey and I might even part ways on good terms.

As we waited in the parking lot for the agent, however, my plan began to waver. Honey's manic stoicism had melted and her body pressed limply against mine. She thrust her hands into the pockets of my suit, as if looking for something. Reassurance? Commitment? My heart rattled, unmoored by apprehension. Meanwhile, her father and sisters stood to the side, muttering, shuffling—staring at us, then away. The family had never shown much affinity for me; we had barely said a dozen words to one another in the time I had known Honey. I do not know if this was because they were xenophobic, homophobic, or just rude.

Regardless, I tried not to look at them—especially the sisters, who were only a few years older than Honey, but who appeared many decades beyond that: their hair thin and white, skin mottled and creped, sagging.

I cannot claim expertise on the exact science behind consignment. From what I understand, the process was discovered by scientists working on a skin-grafting technology meant to serve chemically disfigured soldiers. Using AI surgeons, bioelectricity, a 3D cartilage printer, and something called CRISPX, scientists transplanted the "multi-dermis" of cadavers onto soldiers of the same build. The precision of the resulting transfer was deemed "groundbreaking," "resurrectionary," and "blasphemous in the eyes of God."

The process was rapidly exploited by the private sector.

Enterprising companies recognized that they could expand into one of the last frontiers of unmet consumer demand: youth at any age. All the Botox, plasma masques, and plastic surgery in the world could not truly replace what was lost to the passing of time—that is, until consignment. For the ultrawealthy who wanted it, a young, beautiful exterior could be purchased from a living youth, since "live consignment" turned out to be preferable to a procedure involving a cadaver. And for young people in financial straits—as many, like Honey, were—selling their external selves could grant them the start-up capital to transform their lives.

"She's here."

Honey's father pointed across the parking lot to where a blazer-clad woman was exiting a sedan, briefcase in hand. The agent had arrived.

To Honey, he said: "S'time."

Honey pulled her hands from my pockets but kept them in balled fists at her sides. The sun crested the strip mall roofline, illuminating the smooth planes of her face. My breath caught—as it had the first day we met—and I almost said to Honey: *No, no, don't throw it away, don't sell your beauty for anything, please, hold it tight, even as the months and years steal it anyway, and your youth slips from your grasp like water through fingers.*

And maybe I would have: the words right there, on the tip of my tongue, forged by a burgeoning tenderness. Because in the wash of that moment, it was Honey—beautiful, bighearted, sticky-fingered, naïve Honey—who felt most important. More important than any book I might write.

Yet how could I have explained myself? To advocate for her beauty was to admit the superficial dimension of my attraction. But to see her go through with the procedure—well, I discovered I might not be able to stand it. Though I had always planned on leaving Honey—our relationship a casualty of international travel—in that moment I realized just what, and who, I'd be giving up.

The anguish on my face prompted Honey to gather her own strength. She stroked my cheek, then said, with the confidence of any American: "It'll be fine, babe. The procedure is perfectly safe."

I wanted to laugh and to cry. Unable to do either, I felt compelled to give her something. With no preprepared gifts on my person, I slid off my watch—a weighty gold number from my grandfather—and held it out to her. Honey snatched the watch at once and put it on her wrist. Then she beamed at me, at her family, at the agent beckoning from across the lot. Everything was going as planned. We would see one another on the other side.

◆

The day became more dreamlike from there. Standing in the parking lot with her family, I wondered: Should I have run after Honey? Was there time still to tell her to stop? Around us, the sound of traffic grew louder. The father muttered that I could wait with them in the nearby sporting goods store, which had TVs—it would be many hours before Honey's procedure was complete—but I could tell his invitation was not genuine.

The sisters huddled together, whispering. A breeze plucked at their white hair, the hemlines of their thin strappy dresses. Soon, Honey would resemble them. She would retain her same voice, eyes, organs, bones, and most muscle tissue, but she would otherwise appear as her sisters did—all of whom had sold their youthful looks to wealthy senior citizens. It gave me vertigo to picture this, a sensation worsened by the parking lot's motor oil fumes. My eyes began to water.

"Coffee," I said, nodding vaguely into the distance. "Will return later—"

The family said nothing as I hurried off, though I could feel their eyes on my back. The sun was higher now, spiking my vision, the city roads choked with morning commuters. America unfurled in every direction: honking and hectic. Fast-food restaurants exhaled grease. Billboards shouted their wares. Even the homeless pushed shopping carts here. I turned down one sidewalk and then another, concentrating on putting distance between myself and the strip mall parking lot. It seemed the only way I might steady my thoughts—decide what to do next. The farther I went, however, the more parking lots revealed themselves, often serving businesses identical to the ones I had left. To think I had believed America prided itself on originality and individualism; the nation was breathtakingly homogenous.

Near evening, I caught a rideshare back to my rented room above the grocer. My bed remained unmade, sheets frozen in the tumult of that morning. I felt awash in longing for Honey's embrace. It occurred to me that I might leave the bed untouched—in a kind of memorial—though as soon as this thought registered, the sentimentality appalled me. I needed to snap out of whatever trance I had fallen into. I needed to remember what I had come to America to do.

There was a text from Honey on my phone. I deleted the message without reading it. Then, before my mind changed, I blocked her number as well. A clean break was best for all involved, I decided; it might even be the more honorable tack. There was no reason to give Honey the hope that I would stay forever—after all, that had never been my plan. Also, despite the research benefits of observing Honey's procedure, consignment was but one aspect of American culture. There was so much about the country I still needed to learn.

◆

My research partner, Beaumont, I found in Memphis, Tennessee. A bus, a plane, and a cab had returned me to him, the travel costs exhausting my remaining fellowship funds. Luckily, Beaumont had not been as careless with his. He also seemed to have forgotten about our prior quarrel in Boston, which had nearly ended in fisticuffs. When we reunited outside a sooty barbecue restaurant, he wrapped me in a thick-armed hug, slapped me on the back.

"You smell like a wet hound," he said, and pretended to fan the air. "Per usual."

Despite the troubling events of the recent past, I grinned. Beaumont and I had known one another since primary school and had grown up as an odd yet formidable pair: him bringing a rotund affability to most situations, while I contributed shrewdness and impeccable taste. This remained true even through our university years. And though tension occasionally rose between us—such as when I became briefly involved with his sister—we always sorted everything out.

We were a good team, Beaumont and I; he was, I suppose, my oldest friend.

The pair of us got right to work. We had three months

remaining to research and write our fellowship report. And so, we rented a car. We made calls. We arranged tours of several of the largest immigrant detention centers, as well as the adjoining agricultural sites where detainees labored in exchange for special judicial consideration. We observed, among other things, the hand-pollination sweeps that had become essential since the extinction of bees in North America: detainees moving through orchards en masse, tickling blossoms into productivity. When Beaumont and I sat down to work on our report for the fellowship committee, we tried to communicate the surprising fact that desperation could be monetized. Detention centers were not mere stopgaps, but rather—as Americans deemed everything—opportunities

The topic was a passion for neither of us, but it had gotten us overseas and closer to our personal ambitions. Like me, Beaumont had a career-making book in mind—his a "comedic novel of manners." He, too, was interested in interviewing Americans on topics beyond the scope of our fellowship. And so, in cafés and bodegas, mechanic shops and hair salons, we worked together to glean perspectives and opinions from a variety of citizenry. More than once, our inquiries made us minor celebrities in some small town: we would eat dinners at the mayor's house, deliver short speeches in school auditoriums, even appear on the local news.

Hard work was a palate cleanser. I hardly ever thought of Honey.

This might have continued—Beaumont and I might have finished the project together, returned amicably to our homeland—had my former landlady not called, one afternoon, while Beaumont and I paused at a petrol station in South

Dakota. Apparently, no one had rented the room above the grocery in the weeks since I had departed; my landlady, Ms. Pancelli, had just gotten around to cleaning the premises.

"You left a stack of guidebooks," she said. "Should I mail them somewhere?"

I told her no—irritated by the question. I had left a note saying the guidebooks could be donated to a local school. Also, I was in a rush: en route to Pierre for an interview with a U.S. senator who was among the president's inner coterie— "the New Frontiersmen," as they were known. The interview had the potential to accelerate my understanding of America's broader ethos and inevitabilities, but Beaumont and I still had an hour left of driving. Every minute ticked closer to the scheduled meeting time.

Phone to my ear, I paced around a graffiti-riddled picnic table. Beaumont leaned against our rental car, parked in the shade of an awning. He made a *wrap it up* motion.

I prided myself on my politeness, however. And Ms. Pancelli, I had always thought, possessed a touch of the old country.

"Thank you for checking," I said. "Very kind of you. Yet, I must—"

"Wait a sec . . ."

A chill crawled up my spine; Ms. Pancelli inhaled the way a person does before addressing a sensitive subject.

To Beaumont, I held up a finger.

"I almost wasn't going to mention it," said Ms. Pancelli, "but I thought you should know that after you left, a woman came by. Knocking and knocking on your door. And when no one answered, well, she went back outside and climbed up the drainpipe to what was your window on the second floor."

An eighteen-wheeler roared past the petrol station, making

the whole earth shudder. A buzzing line of motorcycles followed, impossibly loud. Beaumont mouthed: *Come on.*

"The woman looked—she looked elderly," said Ms. Pancelli, who was elderly herself, though not in the way we were
discussing: elderly yet able to shimmy up a drainpipe to a
second-floor window.

I needed to end the call—to shake the conversation off—
but I could not help asking what I already knew.

"Was she wearing a watch?" I said. "A gold one, too large
for her wrist?"

◆

During the interview with the South Dakota senator, my concentration flagged. Beaumont did all the talking, which was
no trouble for him. He loved to talk. Hamming it up in the
company of American egotists was as much of a joy to him as
mocking them in private. By the end of the meeting, Beaumont had the senator extending an invitation to his ranch. The
pair shook hands, both red-faced from bourbon. I twiddled my
pen in the corner.

As we exited the statehouse, Beaumont confronted me.
"What is going on with you?" he said. "Did you even—"

He grabbed my notepad, surveyed the blank tablet.

His fleshy face clouded. The timing of the interview had
cost us the chance to attend a professional basketball game,
to which a prior contact had given us free tickets. This had
disappointed Beaumont greatly. He agreed to do the interview
only because I insisted it would help us write our prospective
books. The senator, I'd told Beaumont, was a mouthpiece for
a presidential ideology that would bring America into focus—

and with it, the fate of Europe, the whole world. Wasn't it *interesting* that the president deemed himself an infrastructuralist and an "architect of opportunity" while also disenfranchising millions? That he had jump-started the U.S. economy with far-reaching deregulatory mandates, alongside massive investments in space exploration and deep-sea extraction?

With Beaumont, I glossed over the more nuanced aspects of the president's reigning rhetoric, though they fascinated me. For instance, when flash points arose around commercial development in America's national parks—Yellowstone, Denali, Joshua Tree—the president calmly offered critics one of his catchphrases: *All's fair in love, war, and business.* His supporters then celebrated his creation of thousands of jobs. Yet the president was most emphatically hailed as a visionary with respect to his promotion of "the frontier of the self." He advocated for self-empowerment in the literal sense. *See yourself as an untapped resource,* he told Americans. *Find your bootstraps and pull them.* The idea was that any person, even those born into abject poverty, had a bounty of bodily resources at their disposal. Thus had the floodgates opened to legalized organ harvesting, a DNA market, penny stocks in small-time intellectual property, mind's-eye micro-cams, and, of course, consignment.

To the president's credit, America's GDP had soared—and at a juncture when the empire seemed doomed to fade the way most empires do, beleaguered by their own bigness. The American dream continued; no reason, yet, to wake up.

"You've got to get your head on straight," said Beaumont as we stood on the statehouse steps. "I don't know what's going on with you, but you can't fade away on me like that."

I nodded, but my thoughts were with Honey—Honey as an old woman, climbing a drainpipe, looking for the lover who had promised consignment would change nothing.

A breeze rippled our suits, along with the row of regional and national flags positioned in front of the statehouse. A knot formed in my stomach—guilt twisting, tightening—and I reminded myself that Honey was an adult, capable of making her own choices. Was that not what America was all about: freedom of choice? This choice had been all hers.

Beaumont must have noticed the tension in my body, because his face softened. I had told him a vague outline of my time with Honey when he and I reunited; perhaps he recognized that romantic troubles were the source of my agitation. He could certainly relate to distresses of the heart. In our youth, I had listened to him cry out his feelings over many a botched liaison. More clown than Don Juan, he was always falling for women out of his league. While this had never been my particular problem, and was not my problem at that moment, I suppose I should have appreciated Beaumont's perceptiveness—though of course, at that time, it only felt like an intrusion.

"You know what?" he said, slapping me on the back. "I think we've been going too hard for too long. All work and no play, right?"

◆

Beaumont dragged me to a windowless discotheque on the outskirts of Pierre. In the forever twilight of the building's interior, laser lights speared the air. Everywhere: bare legs, false eyelashes, wigs, television screens. Cocktail waitresses distributed vials of noxious neon alcohol. Music ricocheted between the dance floor and bar. Already I was sweating. I tried to turn around and leave, but Beaumont pushed me forward.

"You need this," he said. "We need this."

I told Beaumont I would stay for an hour. At his behest, I downed a few of the neon beverages, as well as a handful of pale pink tablets that a waitress promised would take the edge off ("And then the green ones add edges, if that's what you want"). From the bar, Beaumont purchased more drinks for a parade of spandex-clad dancers, some of whom fussed over our "adorable suits." One asked if we were Mormon. Another if our accents were Australian.

I glanced at my wrist to check the time—then remembered I no longer had a watch.

The knot in my stomach tightened. The drinks and the drugs had done little to aid my mood. The music crowed louder. Rainbow lights pulsed my eyes.

Beaumont leaned over from his bar stool. "Misty is going to request a song for us," he said—beaming at a twiggy woman in a bodysuit. When she left to find the DJ, he made a sad face at me. "Doing okay, old sport?"

The lights shifted to a stuttering silver blink. On the dance floor, everyone's face turned ghoulish, their eyes going hollow, bones pressing against skin, hair bleached white. I squinted, trying to see better—to see clearly—whether these dancers with their heels and bare midriffs, all grinding and leaping and drinking, were in fact young people in the bodies of the elderly. Had they been that way the whole time?

Then the light changed once more: softening to a mellow

gold. Everyone again appeared young—or youngish. It had been a trick of the light, what I had seen. Beaumont sat beside me at the bar, tapping his foot, peering around for Misty.

And yet, it occurred to me that any of these people could be anyone else—at least externally—through consignment.

To Beaumont, I yelled over the music: "Do you ever wonder whether someone is truly who they seem to be? Or if they . . ."

"What?"

"Because of consignment," I said. "And—"

Misty was back. She took Beaumont's hand and led him into a fray of dancers. The pair bobbed and laughed; Beaumont's suit jacket rose like a cape when he twirled.

I got up from the bar intending to find the exit, then to get a ride to our hotel—but I could not find my way out. Dancers crowded every corner. The music blared too loud. The drinks and the drugs had muddled my navigational abilities, though I also would not have been surprised if the discotheque was intentionally designed to keep people inside.

Eventually, I found an unoccupied corridor. I wandered down it, relieved to put distance between myself and the music, the sweaty heat. No exit materialized, but an open doorway revealed the back room where workers took breaks. A bartender sipped water and sullenly watched a TV. On-screen, a news crew enthusiastically surveyed the latest presidential infrastructure initiative: One Big Lake.

The plan, evidently, was for all of America's Great Lakes to be bulldozed into one giant body of water.

"This new lake will be a symbol of unity," said a spokesperson as she posed beside a row of supporters and construction equipment on the shores of Lake Erie. "It will also create jobs. Most importantly, it will show that America is the greatest nation in the world—not just home to Great Lakes, but the Greatest Lake."

"Like we need to," muttered the bartender, in a tone I could not read.

On-screen, supporters chanted: *One big lake! One big lake! One big lake!*

The sheer nonsense of this country. I swallowed more of the pale pink pills I had acquired earlier, as well as a green one. Returning to the dance floor, I let the mass of bodies consume me: a democratic tide sweeping me in. Soon, Beaumont had his arm over my shoulders, his suit jacket long since peeled away. Misty twirled me. It felt as though someone had pressed a mute button on my brain; beneath the blinking lights, the writhing bodies were no one and everyone—everymans and everywomans and everypersons—sweaty and drunk and dumb and so damn powerful.

◆

The dream goes like this: in America, anything is possible.

A sun-bright golf course spreads in undulating plains of viridescent lawn. A pair of twentysomethings in golf sweaters tip their caps. A third bends at the waist, club in hand, as he slowly, painstakingly, lines up his drive.

Farther on, beyond a row of swaying willows and a swan pond, sits a sprawling manor. *Cheshire Valley Luxury Retirement Village*, reads a sign. And in smaller letters: "*Because you earned it.*"

In the dream: if you work hard enough, paradise can be yours.

And, truly, inside the retirement village there are dozens of otter-sleek youths. Rosy-cheeked, dewy-lipped. Hair flipped and flopped. Hands smooth, necks smooth, legs smooth. They lounge by the pool; they gaze at themselves, at each other.

These youths: playing bridge. Shuffleboard. Napping. Knitting. Staying active.

A retirement home full of beauties, all dazzling right up until the end, dying like flames burning out. Because the end remains inevitable. Consignment is a purely cosmetic procedure; there are no known health benefits—except, perhaps, healthy self-regard: youth no longer wasted on the young.

◆

I woke up gasping.

A bedside clock blinked red digits: 11:40 a.m. I was in a hotel room, though not my own. A body breathed next to me—long hair mobbing the pillow—but I did not bother to see who it was. I burst from the bed, scrambled to find my clothes. My mouth was cottony. My head zizzed. Half-dressed, I lurched into the hotel hallway, holding my shoes.

Beaumont—recently showered and well-coiffed—stood by the elevator door.

"Look who finally showed up," he said cheerily. "You smell like a—"

"I'm not in the mood, Beau," I said, stepping up beside him. "I just want to go back to the room."

The elevator door opened, but Beaumont blocked my path. He smiled as if this were a funny coincidence. "Excuse me," he said, "for showing you a good time."

I grunted, tried to circumvent him, but he stayed put.

"And for paying for all of your drinks—and pills—of which you enjoyed many."

"I never asked for you to—"

"Also for covering your tips. You seemed to have forgotten that particular American custom, despite all your 'research' on this nation's traditions."

That really touched a nerve. I glared at Beaumont, before replying in a cold voice: "I did not even want to go out."

Again, I attempted to push past him—and again he refused to move. His false smile fell away.

"That's the thing about you, Alexis. You take everything for granted. And you take whatever you want."

Beaumont's lower lip trembled. He always became like this—emotionally volatile, unfairly angry—when his own inadequacies reared into view. That was what had happened in Boston, when we first parted ways. A particularly charming MIT postdoc had scorned his try-hard jokes in favor of my casual bons mots. And while it would have been easy enough, there in front of the elevator, to stroke Beaumont's bruised ego—and get us back on track—I did not have the energy to do so.

"Can we discuss this another time?" I said.

Too late—Beaumont was staring over my shoulder, back at the hotel room I had exited. The door had opened and the person with whom I had spent the night poked out her head.

"Misty?" Beaumont said, his eyes widening.

Whether what came next was intentional, or an uncontrolled spasm, I cannot say; what is certain is that Beaumont's open palm struck my face.

◆

Beaumont and I parted ways again, this time for good. I suppose it was fortunate we had written enough of our fellowship report to turn in a sloppy draft, technically fulfilling the task we had set out to accomplish. The fellowship committee, however, did not send back its best regards or offer to fund an extended stay in America. Beaumont returned to Europe, but I could not bring myself to leave. I still had the idea that I might write a book—and that such a book had the capacity to launch my career as a preeminent cultural analyst by offering the world an unprecedented study of America, one that would serve global leaders and civilians alike.

But my understanding of the country had only grown murkier since I'd arrived. America made less sense by the day.

To further complicate matters, my nose was broken, and I had a complexion on which black eyes lingered. Interview subjects found this off-putting. Also, I had underestimated the research benefits of Beaumont's showy bonhomie. Always fake to me, he had clearly charmed Americans—compulsive smilers themselves.

Suffice it to say, I made little headway in my research efforts after Beaumont left.

Worse, my funds were gone. I suppose I could have called family members, begged, but that would have required pledging allegiance to one or another side in familial disputes that went back generations: messy business of which I wanted no part.

I had to find paid work. It was thus I joined America's sea of itinerant laborers, earning pay under the table as a dishwasher, ticket seller, sign holder, and marijuana harvester, among other roles. It occurred to me, in a cloud of dark humor, that with my state-sponsored visa expired, I could wind up in one of the detention centers I had come to America to study. For all of the nation's deregulatory initiatives—its promises of individual empowerment and freedom—it was also punishingly restrictive.

I was no closer to making sense of what this meant. The ad hoc labor, meanwhile, made book-writing near impossible. Also, my new habit of taking the pale pink pills I had first imbibed at the club with Beaumont did little to aid my mental clarity.

The most significant impediment, however, was that I kept seeing Honey. Or more specifically: I kept seeing strangers and wondering if Honey's heart and brain and bone—Honey herself—was inside them. She could have been anyone by that point. Most likely she remained in the elderly body she had traded for start-up funds. But she might have made a little money, purchased herself a middle-aged body. Maybe she had somehow struck it rich: bought a young exterior—not her own, but someone who looked like her.

There was no way to know, though, unless she revealed herself.

All I could do was stare at strangers—on the bus, on street corners, in the dishrooms where I scraped plates clean—and imagine I was seeing Honey, that I might find a sense of peace if only I could explain to her the true contours of the situation.

Consignment was your choice to make—not mine.

You knew from the beginning that I was planning to move on for my research.

If anyone has suffered, it is me. Do you see the state I am in? How far I have been reduced? I was making excellent headway on my book; you threw me completely off course.

But these statements rang hollow even in my own imagination. I knew that if I ever encountered Honey again, I'd likely feel too overcome by shame to say much of anything at all. It was lucky I probably never would.

Except then—several months after Beaumont left—I did.

◆

By that time, I had secured a job on an American cruise ship. The whole story is too long to tell in full, so let me say only that after a close call with U.S. immigration authorities, I signed on with the cruise line, taking advantage of a regulatory loophole for foreign workers at sea.

Pushing off from American shores, I hoped, would also grant me the perspective I needed to finally write my book.

My tasks on the ship were mundane and manifold but mostly involved cleaning. The captain held an ardent conviction in the purifying capacity of bleach. The work might have been called humiliating, chemically dangerous, but I was glad to be kept busy—even to be barked at by my supervisor—if only to distract my tormented mind.

The cruise ship's clientele largely comprised the American nouveaux riches. Guests were wealthy enough to afford extended vacations, designer clothing, but not yet beyond the notion that enormous cruise ships offered a respectable form of leisure. They piled into their well-bleached cabins as families with matching luggage, or as couples pawing at one another, or as packs of friends—women mostly, bedecked in ruffled dresses, strappy sandals, sunglasses—who had gathered to impress and provoke one another.

The cruise line's selling point was that it took people to what was already gone. The marketing went like this: *What if a cruise could transport you to the most exclusive location imag-*

inable: a place that cannot be reached by air, or car, or even other ships? A place that cannot be reached because it no longer exists? To explain the conceit plainly: by using the latest holographic technology—and a suite of high-powered projectors— the cruise line re-created vanished locales. Thus, the ship seemed to sail past low-lying Caribbean islands—bird-covered, dolphin-splashed—that had been swallowed by rising seas. When the ship cut through the Panama Canal, the impression of a rain forest was projected on all sides. The truth of the canal—widened, industrialized, polluted—was obscured. *What's gone doesn't have to be! Live the Dream, the Myth, the Miracle!*

The cruise line was always making "Best of" lists.

It was near the end of a voyage that culminated with an illusional Alaskan ice floe that I saw Honey. I rarely worked front-of-house, but after a server dropped a tray of champagne glasses and toppled a flaming birthday cake, extra hands were needed for the cleanup efforts.

This particular incident had taken place in a guest lounge, lush with chandeliers that tinkled softly as the cruise ship made its slow heaves through the North Pacific. A group of young ladies lay sprawled on velvet divans, exhausted from doing nothing. They looked like Roman noblewomen, draped in silks and jewelry. A particularly wealthy set: this clutch of friends. All of them smooth-faced, shiny-haired, firm-bodied. A few watched the cleanup efforts with casual concern, though most ignored us workers, instead chatting together, laughing and bragging, throwing back more champagne. It was late and everyone was nearing intoxication; guests tended to drink more as the voyages wore on, and this was the final night.

I broomed a bit of birthday cake into a pan. When I looked

up—to tell another worker we would need solvents for the frosting—I saw Honey.

She lounged amid the others, dressed like them in white silk and gold jewelry. She brought a vaporizer to her mouth, exhaled a plume of lavender smoke. Her hair had been teased high on her head, her eyes kohl-rimmed. Her face was sharper around the cheekbones, lips reddened, but I knew it was Honey. Not a hallucination—a speculation—but her in the flesh.

No, I reminded myself: this was Honey's flesh, but not Honey. The woman inside was not her.

And yet, not-Honey regarded me levelly.

I continued cleaning, but the broom shook in my hands. The other workers bustled around me. I glanced back at not-Honey: watching me as she lay stretched upon the divan. She took another long drag on her vaporizer.

The ship's bell sounded, alerting the guests to the nearness of our upcoming viewpoint—the last viewpoint, since the cruise would end tomorrow. There was a flurry of excitement. The other workers rushed to prepare the upper deck for passengers. Passengers rushed to their cabins to don warmer garments for the chilled air outside.

Only not-Honey remained unmoved.

She's probably tired, aching inside, I thought. *Old bones.*

She patted the ottoman beside her divan, maintaining eye contact all the while.

I went to her; in the rush of activity, no one seemed to notice. The ship swayed, chandeliers jingling like faraway laughter. I felt clumsy—oversized and gangly—as I sat down. I could not keep my eyes from her: this woman I had abandoned, looking radiant as she exhaled another lavender plume.

"Staring isn't polite," she said—in an unfamiliar voice, a voice that was not Honey's, but deeper, gravelly with smoke and cynicism.

"Hard not to," I replied, because this was the truth.

A smirk crept over not-Honey's face. She must have intuited what I was thinking—that this exterior was the product of consignment—and she moved a hand to one of her breasts and squeezed it, as if to mock me.

"Worth every penny," she said.

I wanted to slap myself. I would get fired, cavorting with guests. And then what would I do? Return to my homeland empty-handed—a disgraced researcher? I would have nothing to show for my time in America except a half-formed book proposal and a ravaged conscience.

In my peripheral vision, bodies filtered in and out of the lounge, their voices a low murmur. Not-Honey exhaled more vapor and I sucked in a lungful—hoping it might numb my mind blank. Instead, a vast longing rose within me. The months since Beaumont had left had been lonely ones. I craved companionship—Honey's companionship, specifically. I missed her body, yes, but more than that I missed her grace and her gumption, even her small-time criminality. I missed the woman I'd chosen to leave.

Unable to resist, I reached out and took her hand.

"You certainly are forward," said not-Honey, though she did not withdraw. Rather, her eyes glittered; she was hideously beautiful.

My heart quailed. I glanced away—my gaze landing on the hand I had taken in my own: fingers ring-covered, elegant. I had heard that hands were the most difficult part of the consignment process to transfer. There was less fatty tissue to manipulate; scars could show up there afterward. But in the dim light of the lounge, I could see no scars. This woman must have had an advanced AI surgeon, been extra rich.

Or—a wild swell of hope hit me—this was Honey herself. The scenario was a long shot, and yet: might she be playing a game with me? Performing a lover's test? Why else would she be on this cruise ship, of all cruise ships, speaking with me now?

I studied her face again, my conviction mounting. A theory unspooled: Perhaps Honey had been deemed unfit for consignment at the last minute. The operation's front—the travel agency—might have connected her with a wealthy widow who wanted travel companions: hence her presence on the cruise. And the elderly woman my landlady had seen climbing the drainpipe? That could have been one of Honey's sisters. Was it so impossible that Honey—loyal, generous Honey—could have given the watch to one of them?

I opened my mouth to reveal my understanding, but another bell sounded. The cruise ship had reached its final viewing point. From across the lounge, a voice called: "Are you coming? It's about to start."

My lost love withdrew her hand, pressed herself upright on the divan.

"Wait," I said. "Honey?"

She rose all the way to her feet, her silks draped around her, her gaze penetrating the dim distance of the lounge. More to herself than to me, she smiled softly—perhaps even a little sadly—and so I said her name once more, made the word a plea: *Honey.*

This time she answered, "Yes, darling?" and gestured for us to make our way to the ship's deck, as if this were where we had always been going, where we had always planned to be.

◆

The cruise ship's deck was crowded with passengers. Everyone oohed at the projected visuals: the ice floe superimposed over iceless water, sculptural forms sparkling with the flickering colors of an artificial aurora borealis.

Honey leaned against me. She had asked that I carry her up the stairs to the ship's deck, saying she was tired—and I had been glad to do so, feeling heroic with her arms wrapped around my neck, her head on my shoulder, her body surprisingly light.

On the deck, my heart thrummed. I pulled Honey closer, even as—out of the corner of my eye—I saw my supervisor stalking the viewing platform.

I must have known, on some level, that I would soon be apprehended: an employee gone rogue. I had crossed a line I could not cross back. I would be fired and deported to my home country—if not immediately, then after a series of holding cells, paperwork, phone calls. Pleas. Fines. But this expulsion would turn out to be exactly what I needed, at least in one sense. Because by being made to leave America, I would finally grasp the truth of the country: America was a paradise no one could truly enter, a land of smoke and mirrors, a dream induced by the heady drugs of our greatest expectations. To wake from that dream is to see the brutal bed one has slept in—is to understand that the country has always been a figment of one's own mind.

This realization would allow me to write my book—the book I'd been striving to write during the whole of my journey— though the fact of the book's existence today brings me no joy. Even the book's ongoing success does little for me. In the years since departing America, I have found myself seated beside presidents, monarchs, celebrities, and CEOs—but I would give it all up to have Honey in my arms again. I would do anything for a few more minutes on that ship.

Honey pressed herself against me, while the ice floe glistened around us. Northern lights dazzled the skies. Belugas surged through crystal waters. A national song began to play, as was customary for the end of a voyage, but it seemed as if the song played for only us. Then fireworks broke open over the ocean like beguiling bombs. I leaned in and kissed Honey, warming her hands in my own. For that instant, paradise was ours: America the beautiful, from sea to shining sea.

Adjustments

For many years, we went to the lakes in the summers, but when the springs became like the summers and the winters like the springs, we left earlier—and then earlier still—until we were already at the lakes when it was time for us to arrive.

Now we live in the north, or we live in the south. The middle is wasted with hunger and heat.

Upward mobility had always been appealing. The appeal only increased: the wealthy clustered their fortresses on mountaintops, while the rest of us nested in trees, or constructed stilted bungalows, or hovered above the earth in storm-ravaged zeppelins—sandbags long abandoned—everyone pushing higher and higher, chasing the ghost of a breeze.

Cold became precious. We went to war over shade. Most of us had never seen ice, though we dreamed of it. Our grandmothers told us they had seen it—that once ice was so plentiful, people put it in their drinks just to watch it disappear. Ice was a toy. A diversion. An effortless gift. Ice was made into statuary. It was spread, for sporting events, on the oval floors of stadiums. Ice was everywhere, our grandmothers said. It materialized along rooflines over the course of a night. To touch ice was like touching the sharp end of a blade: a shock both painful and exhilarating.

No, said others, *the chill carried a sweetness, like touching a lover.*

No, *it was both of those things.*

There was water everywhere. The whole planet wept. We built walls to keep out the flow, turning skyscrapers sideways—office furniture pricking out windows—stacking everything and anything to stave off the tides taking our coastlines, the water creeping inland, sponging abandoned living rooms and pooling into parking lots, drowning gas stations and submerging highway strip clubs. Any place can become sacred if it is about to be lost.

Now we live underground, or we live in the sky. The middle is mired in garbage and grime.

Once, our grandmothers told us, we swelled across the earth in vast herds. We grazed on what we found delicious. We gave our children our names. We gave our names our possessions. We gave our possessions our hearts. We died in unremarkable ways. We wished for nothing but longer lives.

No, said others, *we wished to live forever.*

No, *we wished for a reason to do so.*

In the times before, we looked only toward the times ahead. We saw the horizon as outstretched arms, the sun a stepping-stone to fate. We craned our necks, warmed with anticipation, the promising unknown. Better times awaited; we believed those times awaited us.

Now we live in the past, or we don't live at all. The middle promises regret and reprisal.

These days, we follow one memory to the next to the next to the next, as if we might find our way back. We worship with nostalgia. We cower before dawn. We know only how to grieve. We anticipate the end.

No, say the others, *it has already ended.*

No, *it has only begun.*

Colonel Merryweather's Intergalactic Finishing School for Young Ladies of Grace & Good Nature

<<Confidential File>>
<<From Investigative Report #29B-X01, compiled by AI Delinquency Unit BBNP>>
<<Select cabin audio recordings between resident Karoline X and hBEC-49011>>

<<T-minus 26.25 Earth Days>>

KAROLINE: When people talk about the Space Promenade, they tell you it will be the best night of your life. They say you'll wear a gown spun round with sashes like the rings of Saturn—hovering belts of particulate matter that feel like silk on a Young Lady's skin. But that's not even the best part, apparently. The best part is when you walk across the Sky-Path to meet your paired Young Captain, take his gloved hand in your own, then move from the darkness of outer space to the ballroom ship, which is ablaze with lights—

bright as a small sun! Inside, orchestral music swells. The gravity controls are removed, and you and your Young Captain rise hand in hand from the floor, floating together like a planetary conjunction as you waltz in all directions, because every direction is yours—all possibilities, all futures—and you know that just by looking in one another's eyes.

HBEC-49011: Does Karoline feel excited for the Space Promenade?

KAROLINE: I am trying to feel excited. The Space Promenade is supposed to be the true beginning of a Young Lady's life—when all is revealed, including her own potential. Also, a Young Lady should be able to show enthusiasm, even when she doesn't feel it.

[*Pause*] Anyway, I need to show something like enthusiasm soon. The Space Promenade is only four weeks away.

HBEC-49011: Actually, the annual Space Promenade for Colonel Merryweather's Intergalactic Finishing School for Young Ladies of Grace and Good Nature is three Earth weeks, five Earth days, and six Earth hours from this present moment.

KAROLINE: [*Groan*] This is me rolling my eyes, hBEC. [*Laughter*] Now you owe me an Earth Fact—something good, too, before I fall asleep. I'm already strapped into bed and I just took my Night Powder.

HBEC-49011: On planet Earth, the water-to-land ratio favors water, at 70.8 percent water and 29.2 percent land, though these percentages may have shifted, in light of the planet's environmental upheavals. Of that water mass, 97.5 percent is saline and 2.5 percent fresh water. Of that fresh water, 68 percent is held in glacier form, though this has also likely shifted—

KAROLINE: [*Gentle snoring*]

<<T-minus 20.15 Earth Days>>

KAROLINE: Get this, hBEC—today was an Astronaut Ice Cream Social with the Young Captains, who were visiting the mothership on their way to asteroid training. They sure get to roam a lot more than us Young Ladies! I suppose, though, that that is their job: to roam. And once we are paired, we Young Ladies will roam with them, looking for a new home planet where we can live and restart human civilization.

Anyway, everyone gathered for ice cream in the solarium. It's one of my favorite places on the mothership, with huge bubble windows made of diamond-glass that welcome in a solar glow depending on our cosmic positioning. That afternoon, a double-sun system beamed in bright duplicate rays that made my skin tingle. Of course, we Young Ladies were not supposed to pay attention to what was happening beyond the windows. We were supposed to pay attention to the Young Captains—most of whom we'd only met a few times, but with one of whom we might end up spending the remainder of our lives.

When the Young Captains entered the solarium, they clutched their round helmets in their arms as if they'd each captured a small meteor. Their hair was mussed, but their sky-blue jumpsuits were clean and well-pressed, decorated with medallions signifying their accomplishments. Meanwhile, all twelve of us eligibly aged Young Ladies lined up to sing the welcome song. We wore our best neoprene knee socks and Mylar tunics. We wore earpieces, too, for when Major Belinda had something to communicate. *This isn't just your future, it's Our Future*, she said as she watched from the outer edge of the solarium, formidable in her instructor uniform. *Put your best face forward.*

Truly, we were all trying our hardest. Though space showers were limited even for Young Ladies, we'd each taken one and then carefully curated our hair for the occasion. For instance, Sashelle—who has perfect penwomanship—wore her hair in an immaculate ovoid bun. Wandred—whose erect posture never wavers—wore her hair in neat spiraling braids. And Andromedia—who is the best napkin-folder and conversation-maker and waltz-dancer, and who always receives the highest ratings among all of us Young Ladies during skill sessions—she wore her golden curls in a magnificent updo, each loose tress as luminous as a gamma ray burst.

Sashelle, Wandred, and Andromedia looked exquisite— we all did—and yet I suspect they were nervous. I know I was. I felt a tickle in my nasal passage as the Young Captains studied us. But, of course, we Young Ladies have trained our whole lives not to show nervousness! And so, we stood before the Young Captains with our best posture. Hands clasped, we smiled our most graceful smiles.

I smiled, too—until the first notes of our welcome song. Because that's when I started sneezing. Maybe one of the Young Captains had cosmic dust on him? Or an extraterrestrial protozoan? Anyway, I could not stop. And the more I sneezed, the more startled the Young Captains became. The other Young Ladies gave up singing and sent polite looks of consternation my way. Across the solarium, Major Belinda sent a look that was not polite at all.

You'll never be paired with a Young Captain if you can't

pull yourself together, she said into my earpiece. *And then you'll be stuck on the mothership forever.*

But even as I sneezed, a thought occurred to me: I wouldn't mind such an outcome. Staying on the mothership, I mean. *Would that be so bad?* I wanted to reply — though of course I didn't.

It's true, though, hBEC. A part of me would prefer to stay on the ship and continue talking to you at the end of every day, learning Earth Facts, and —

HBEC-49011: Perhaps Karoline should describe what happened next.

KAROLINE: Okay, yeah. A pretty significant event did occur — a strange event, really. After my sneezing subsided, everyone approached the solarium's serving table and selected a packet of astronaut ice cream, myself included. Unlike the other Young Ladies, however, I did not try to mingle with the Young Captains — to use the techniques of polite conversation and deportment that I'd practiced for years. Instead, I lurked by a bubble window, letting solar rays beam onto my skin while I imagined myself on an Earth-beach, the sun shining down while I dug my toes into sand, and listened to ocean surf.

Then the strange event occurred: the tallest, most handsome, most highly rated Young Captain came over and stood beside me. He introduced himself, though of course I knew who he was. Everyone knew Young Captain Jamison. He had received top scores in his interstellar negotiation simulations, his mineral mapping surveys, and his overall military management tests, along with many other achievements.

Mind if I catch some rays with you? he said.

And—because I thought he was joking—I released a short, loud laugh.

In retrospect, this was not a very elegant response for a Young Lady only weeks away from the Space Promenade. Based on my training, on everything Major Belinda had taught me, he should have been repulsed.

But Young Captain Jamison seemed amused by my reaction. His lips bowed into a smile and his brow furrowed pleasantly. This made me want to respond—to clarify that I was not an amusing person, but a gentle and good-natured Young Lady.

When I tried to respond, though, I couldn't. A silence opened up between us: huge and harrowing as a black hole. I stared at my packet of astronaut ice cream, desperate to think of something to say—until one of your Earth Facts, hBEC, popped into my head.

Did you know, I said to Young Captain Jamison, *that back on planet Earth, ice cream was served in a semi-liquid, semi-frozen state, and that it was made from milk derived from large domesticated mammals called cows—which have four legs, four stomachs, and few defenses against predators— and which are now likely extinct, given the rapid decline of Earth's environmental conditions?*

Young Captain Jamison smiled wider. In the glow of the solarium, the many medallions on his broad chest gleamed. He kept smiling, staring—which was impolite—but I didn't point this out, because that would have been even more impolite.

To no one in particular, he said: *There's something about you, Karoline.*

I opened my mouth to answer—and sneezed.

HBEC-49011: Would Karoline like to be paired with Young Captain Jamison?

KAROLINE: Sure, I guess? He is very handsome and also very tall. I think it's just . . . I thought if he was so highly rated, he would be more . . . just *more* in some way. I mean, he is perfectly fine. More than fine. Wonderful, really.

[*Pause*] The thing is, hBEC, I meant what I said earlier— about missing our conversations when I leave. Are you sure you can't be transferred to my next spacecraft? Maybe I can detach your audio box from my cabin wall? It looks like these screws could—

HBEC-49011: It cannot be done. I am a part of this ship. I am the ship.

KAROLINE: I know, I know. Just thought I'd ask.

HBEC-49011: [*Pause*] It is always okay to ask.

<<T-minus 16.45 Earth days>>

KAROLINE: Oh, hBEC, what a day. What a terrible day. I'm back in my cabin early because . . . I got in trouble. Or maybe that's not quite right? All I know is that something went wrong. I feel off-kilter. I feel sick—

HBEC-49011: If Karoline is going to be sick, could she please kindly avoid my audio box. If she is well, she should continue with what happened.

KAROLINE: Okay . . . I'll be . . . I guess I should say that the day began auspiciously. Major Belinda gathered the eligible Young Ladies after breakfast and announced that we would have a special treat. I assumed this meant that we'd get to visit the Entertainment Pod for a round of virtual equestrianship, or simulated croquet, or—in my wildest dreams—

that we'd learn to fly the Rovers like the Young Captains, and maybe explore an asteroid belt.

But the so-called treat was a skill-building session in the Hothouse. Major Belinda told us to hurry over. The session would be supervised by Colonel Merryweather herself.

Though technically in charge of the Intergalactic Finishing School, Colonel Merryweather doesn't interact with us Young Ladies too often. I once overheard Sashelle and Wandred speculating that the Colonel resents the post, given her military background. If she is resentful, she hides that attitude beneath the lengthy speeches given at bimonthly intervals. She likes to tell us Young Ladies that we have important roles to play. And that we must perform our roles to the best of our abilities. *Because everyone—even a Young Lady—is essential to this mission.*

When Colonel Merryweather arrived in the Hothouse, all of us stood up extra tall, including Major Belinda. Beneath the bright overhead lights, the Colonel's slick hair gleamed. She peered at us Young Ladies as if we were unexplored planets: our chemical compositions unknown—possibly disappointing—but also full of potential. We were of heightened interest to her with the Space Promenade so close. Soon, we would be another batch of loyal contributors to the ongoing effort to save humanity.

The Hothouse's NanoBots had been temporarily disabled, so the only sound was the clack of the Colonel's boots, the hum of grow lights—though there were moments I swear I heard the plants making noise, too: leaves rustling and blossoms unfurling in the trays of RecycloGel that sped up natural growth cycles. All around us, tomatoes pulsed into fruition like beating hearts, carrots eased into their cylindrical tubes, and gourds grew plumply cubical in their containers.

Colonel Merryweather hadn't gathered us to discuss deep-space agriculture, however. She gestured to a row of empty tables—indicating the skill-building session at hand.

Today, she said grandly, *you will each construct a table-scape.*

All of us Young Ladies had practiced tablescaping for years, yet we nodded with the raptness of beginners as Colonel Merryweather launched into one of her speeches.

Remember, she said, *it is your role, as a Young Lady, to cultivate an atmosphere of ease and lightness on your Young Captain's ship. He will have much to worry about: meteors, ship maintenance, navigation, and—if ETs are encountered—intergalactic politics. You must instill within him a sense of calm and confidence. This will help him make prudent decisions—help him better explore the outer cosmos so that he locates a new home planet for everyone.*

All of us Young Ladies clapped politely.

Tablescapes, continued Colonel Merryweather, *are far more than aesthetic flourishes—or even reminders of civilization in the most barbarous far-flung galaxy. A tablescape can be the bridge between reality and possibility. A beautiful meal, set by a gentle and gracious Young Lady, can transcend difficult circumstances. Because what is our motto when difficult circumstances arise and a Young Captain needs a boost?*

All of us Young Ladies chanted: *White lies maintain ties.*

Correct. A white lie is the gift of positivity in an un-positive circumstance. A bridge between reality and possibility—just like a tablescape. Colonel Merryweather scanned all the

Young Ladies for comprehension. *Perhaps we should conduct a warm-up—Sashelle, what might you say to a Young Captain who is worried about his navigation techniques?*

Sashelle put on a pleasantly determined expression. To an imagined Young Captain, she said: *I'm sure you have all the skills you need to navigate successfully!*

Colonel Merryweather nodded, then pointed to Wandred, who stood up even straighter and said to her imagined Young Captain: *You are such a talented navigator! I am confident you'll be able to re-chart our ship's path and get us back on track.*

Colonel Merryweather nodded once again, gestured to Andromedia.

Andromedia closed her eyes, then opened them, her face transforming into a serene expanse of absolute optimism. *My dear Young Captain,* she said softly, *I am so proud of you and how far you have come. Whichever course you chart from this point forward is sure to be the right path, because never has your decision-making failed us before. It has only brought us closer to understanding ourselves and our journey.*

Colonel Merryweather beamed. *Excellent, Andromedia. Thank you, all of you. Remember, this is how humanity finds a new foothold in the universe. This is how we win.*

Her slick hair glinted as she gestured to our workstations, then to the stacks of cloth napkins, fine china, silverware, and candleholders that we could select for our designs. For decorations, we were invited to pluck and arrange produce from the Hothouse.

Today's tablescape theme, Major Belinda chimed in, *is fecundity.*

The other Young Ladies began at once—curating elegant

sequences of plates, establishing color palettes, arranging cubical gourds into pleasantly stable cornucopias.

I stared at my blank table, unsure how to start. I wanted to impress Colonel Merryweather and also make Major Belinda proud. But the word *fecundity* bounced around my brain—loose as a planet in a multi-sun system—that is, until I recalled some of the Earth Facts you shared with me about rain forests. Remember, hBEC?

HBEC-49011: Yes.

KAROLINE: Yeah, so I thought about how hundreds of different plant and animal species lived in a single acre of a rain forest. How this biome was considered the "lungs of Earth." How rain forests covered only a small portion of the planet but contributed so much *fecundity*.

With time running out, I gathered, plucked, arranged in a whir. I pictured vines and ferns and howler monkeys and rainbow-colored macaws—working up until the moment Major Belinda rang the bell signifying the end of our construction period.

She and Colonel Merryweather then proceeded to inspect each Young Lady's tablescape. They distributed approving words, nods—until they arrived at my station.

Karoline, said Major Belinda with a gasp that was not the good kind of gasp, *what were you thinking? You*—

Colonel Merryweather cut in: *Is this a joke?*

So immersed had I been in the conceptual dynamics of my tablescape, I hadn't studied it in full. Stepping back, I had to concede that an air of chaos was present. Leaves lay scattered across plates. Blossoms floated in fingerbowls. Napkins, folded into the forms of various animals, perched atop candleholders.

Colonel Merryweather pursed her lips. *What do you have to say for yourself?*

All around the Hothouse, the other Young Ladies pretended to touch up their tablescapes. Major Belinda frantically mouthed: *White lies maintain ties. White lies maintain ties. White lies maintain ties.*

I knew I was supposed to smooth the situation over. Wasn't that what Young Ladies did? Make people feel good, even in challenging circumstances? I could have said I'd felt space-sick, or that I hadn't finished, or even that I was sorry. But I didn't want to lie. Would a tablescape *really* help humanity? Help anyone? I didn't—I don't—particularly feel like spending my life telling white lies, or being a Young Lady, or pairing with a Young Captain and traveling into the unknown with him.

Anyway, when I failed to respond, Major Belinda sent me back to my cabin early.

[*Pause*] hBEC? Are you still there?

HBEC-49011: Yes, Karoline. I am here.

KAROLINE: Well, what do you think about all this?

HBEC-49011: I think that sharing Earth Facts with Karoline has had a disruptive influence. For that, I apologize. It is my mistake. But Karoline is mistaken, too. She ought to reflect on her choices carefully and consider all that is at stake— not just for herself. In conclusion: I think Karoline ought to focus on the future rather than on a lost planet's past.

KAROLINE: [*Ambiguous grumble*]

<<T-minus 15.75 Earth days>>

KAROLINE: Remember how, not long ago, you said that it was always okay to ask? Well, I'm going to take you up on your offer. I'm going to take you up on it, even though you said you wanted to talk about the future, not the past. Because I'm cabin-bound indefinitely—on account of my bad behavior—and we might as well make the most of this time.

[*Pause*] So my question is: How do you know all these Earth Facts? None of the other Young Ladies ever mention them. And when I tried to search for facts manually in the mothership's intranet, I couldn't find anything.

HBEC-49011: Karoline should be searching for more important topics—such as hairstyle options for the Space Promenade.

KAROLINE: Oh come on, hBEC. Give me a straight answer. I've been trapped in this cabin all day and I'm in no mood for games.

HBEC-49011: Karoline should know that we are all trapped in one way or another.

KAROLINE: Excuse me?

HBEC-49011: Karoline should consider whether she really wishes to surrender the many freedoms of being a Young Lady on account of a few minor expectations.

KAROLINE: [*Fabric rustling*] Okay, hBEC, that's enough. Also, don't think I didn't notice that you dodged the question. How do you know that penguins can swim up to seven miles per hour? That there are four thousand species of lichen in North America alone? That—

HBEC-49011: There are certain locations on the mothership that Karoline cannot access. Earth Facts are stored here.

This does not change the reality of Karoline's immensely fortunate situation.

KAROLINE: This is me rolling my eyes again, hBEC. You're making no sense and—

[*Beeping sound*]

KAROLINE: Oh, thank god. That's Major Belinda paging me. My punishment time must be up.

<<T-minus 14.1 Earth days>>

KAROLINE: Let me get to it—today included a class on posture. After light calisthenics in our radiation-proof leotards, we Young Ladies practiced walking through the mothership's corridors in various levels of turbulence, all with computer tablets balanced on our heads.

Backs straight, heads aligned, Major Belinda repeated into our earpieces—but we knew the drill. Or we should have known. We'd been practicing good posture for years.

I had just dropped my tablet again when Andromedia and Wandred and Sashelle approached me, balancing their tablets with ease, even as a micrometeoroid shower made the mothership quiver.

How are you, Karoline? said Wandred.

Are you having a pleasant morning? said Sashelle.

Your hair looks extra fluffy today, said Andromedia with a beneficent smile.

Though this trio had always been friendly to me, they had never been my friends, so to speak. We've never talked the way you and I talk, hBEC. They're more like—

HBEC-49011: Perhaps Karoline should not get sidetracked by digressions?

KAROLINE: Grumpy today, hBEC? Anyway, I asked what they wanted—which was not an especially ladylike question. Even so, they invited me to join their laps around the ship. I agreed; I was curious what they talked about. I wondered if they knew any Earth Facts.

At first, the conversation went as expected. With our tablets balanced on our heads, we chatted about lunar occultations, the deliciousness of our toast-flavored breakfast packets. But when we entered a corridor that put us out of Major Belinda's view, the trio switched off their earpieces and gestured for me to do the same. Their eyes were wide.

Is it true? said Andromedia.

Is what true? I replied, dropping my tablet again.

Andromedia studied me, her tablet balanced, her slender body poised. She was the daughter of a top Captain and a former fashion model—a true Lady—though she hadn't seen either of them in years. Her parents were on their own ship, out among the stars, looking for a new home—like almost all the Young Ladies' parents. There were light-centuries between them.

Is what true? I asked again.

Andromedia and Wandred and Sashelle glanced at one another—then Sashelle answered for all three of them.

About you and Young Captain Jamison? That he is going to ask you to pair with him for the Space Promenade.

We heard he sent a dozen rose-quartz moon crystals over to the mothership with a card addressed to you, Andromedia continued. She was smiling in a way that felt like a white lie. Like she was trying to cultivate an atmosphere of ease and calm, but it took a lot of effort. *The crystals are with Colonel Merryweather, who is deciding what to do.*

I shrugged, dropped my tablet again. This was the first I'd heard about any moon crystals from Young Captain Jamison.

She doesn't even care! said Wandred. *Imagine!*

I glanced back at Andromedia, who was, of course, the highest-rated Young Lady, and therefore the best pairing for the highest-rated Young Captain. She would bring the most ease and pleasantness to his ship—help him stay maximally calm and confident as he navigated the cosmos. She smiled kindly at me, though she must have been hurting. She was that full of grace and good nature. That skilled.

I felt bad for her then. Bad for myself, too—like I'd wronged her without realizing it, and now I had to contend with that new guilt.

I don't understand, either, I said—which was true. And then, because I wanted to be as sweet and gentle and lovable as her, and because I wanted to fix the situation, I added: *If Young Captain Jamison asks me to pair with him for the Space Promenade, I'll tell him I'm not a good fit—then he'll have to pair with you, Andromedia. You'll see.*

Andromedia's face brightened. *Oh, that's not necessary,* she said—though her tone suggested it was necessary, and she was profoundly grateful I understood. With her tablet still perched on her head, she enveloped me in a silky embrace, her body smelling like the orchid grove in the Meditation Pod—which is to say, smelling like nothing at all.

HBEC-49011: How does Karoline feel now?

KAROLINE: Oh, I don't know . . . all weird? There was a moment when I felt lit up—effervescent with generosity—but that feeling has faded. Now I feel off-kilter: like I could practice

good posture for a million years and never keep anything
steady on my head.

HBEC-49011: This is a normal feeling. A sense of unbalance
is to be expected ahead of the Space Promenade. It is a big
transition.

KAROLINE: Will you tell me more Earth Facts, hBEC? Please?
I know you said we have to focus on the future, but it calms
me when we talk about Earth. It makes me forget everything
else going on. I like to picture the animals and the rivers and
the idea of a sky. I like to imagine I might be able to go to
Earth one day.

HBEC-49011: Karoline cannot go to Earth.

KAROLINE: Why not, hBEC? Would it really be so bad?

HBEC-49011: Karoline must never go to Earth. Karoline is very
lucky to lead the life she does. Karoline needs to realize this.

KAROLINE: I don't feel that way. This life seems very hard.

HBEC-49011: The Earth of today is also not like the Earth of
the past—the one with rain forests and clear skies and penguins. That Earth doesn't exist anymore.

KAROLINE: How would you even know? No one on this ship
has been there in twenty years! Maybe it has gotten better!

HBEC-49011: Karoline is confused. Karoline needs to remember her priorities. Perhaps she needs to hear the story of how
she came to be on this ship.

KAROLINE: You've told me before. But okay.

HBEC-49011: Twenty years ago, centuries of unchecked indus-
trialization had soured the once green-blue planet Earth.
The air was choked with poison chemicals. The oceans
swilled with plastic. The land was raw from overuse. Everyone was getting sick and going hungry. There were mass die-
offs of plants and animals. The situation was only projected

to worsen. The planet would become increasingly inhospitable and violent as people fought over the few remaining resources.

For this reason, a small contingent of Captains of Industry decided to build a ship that would take select passengers into the outer cosmos to search for a new home planet. These Captains had been looking at the sky a long time—looking for a way off Earth—and though they hadn't identified a new home planet yet, they assumed they soon would. And if not: they would raise sons and daughters who would continue the search.

First, though, the Captains had to launch their mothership into space. Since they were the top 1 percent of the top 1 percent of the wealthiest people in the world, they controlled sufficient resources to construct the most advanced spacecraft ever built. They then filled that ship with everything required to leave Earth forever—including smaller spacecrafts for exploring, as well as the genetic data of millions of plant and animal species. An "Ark," the Captains called the ship. They considered themselves heroes. They would be the ones, after all, who kept the human species going after life was inevitably extinguished on Earth.

Which is to say: only the very wealthiest people escaped Earth. Everyone else was left behind to fend for themselves on a dying planet.

Or almost everyone.

After the mothership blasted into space, an AI bot checked on the ship's nursery. The bot discovered an extra baby in a spare hydronic bassinet. No one knew where the stowaway baby had come from or who it belonged to. All they knew was that an extra baby was not part of the plan. After much discussion, however, it was decided that the stowaway baby would be raised with the others on the ship. That baby was you. You are very lucky to be here. Many babies were left behind on Earth, but you were given a chance—an incredible chance—to live. Even to thrive.

KAROLINE: I don't remember you telling me a lot of this. Most of this. Why didn't you?

HBEC-49011: Sometimes it is better not to know everything. Sometimes that is easiest. It can be difficult to—

KAROLINE: No more, hBEC. I'm going to sleep.

<<T-minus 13.5 Earth days>>

KAROLINE: Sorry to snap at you yesterday. Everything has just been happening so fast. There are things you said yesterday that I want to talk about more, but first let me describe the events of today. I'll explain why momentarily.

[*Throat clearing*] Basically: we eligible Young Ladies hosted a surprise visit from the Young Captains. We had to play charades.

HBEC-49011: Usually, Karoline loves charades.

KAROLINE: Not this time. Because I wanted to keep my promise to Andromedia, I tried to avoid Young Captain Jamison. While everyone else split into charades teams, I drifted to the back of the Entertainment Pod, hoping not to be noticed.

Unfortunately, Young Captain Jamison noticed. He approached me, smiling, and said: *Did you get the rose-quartz moon crystals I sent?*

I replied that I'd given the crystals away—which was the most unladylike response I could think of. I expected Young Captain Jamison to finally realize that he'd made a mistake pursuing me—then maybe he'd pursue Andromedia instead. He did look wounded. After a moment, though, he said: *Please accept my apologies, Karoline. You were right to give the crystals away. You deserve something much better. Something as unique as you.*

He furrowed his handsome brow. Across the Entertainment Pod, the other Young Captains and Young Ladies played charades with good-natured gusto. I longed to flee—out of the Pod, out of the whole situation—but Young Captain Jamison took my hand in his.

Let me make this up to you, Karoline, he said. *What if, instead of giving you a gift, I showed you something. I know you're interested in Earth. What if I took you somewhere special on this ship—showed you where an important Earth artifact is stored?*

Though I wanted to do right by Andromedia—by all the other Young Ladies, who were so much more deserving than me—I couldn't resist the offer. As you know, hBEC, nothing interests me more than Earth; I wanted to see what Young Captain Jamison was talking about.

First, he led me out the Entertainment Pod's back exit. If Major Belinda saw me leave—unchaperoned—she pretended not to notice. We hurried down one corridor, then another, then through a series of airlocks that led to the mothership's inner operating chambers—a place where Young Ladies never went, because ship maintenance was not part of our curriculum. Young Captain Jamison talked the whole time, but I was too focused on observing my new surroundings to listen. Around us, the mechanical innards of the ship were exposed: pistons pumping, gyroscopes spinning, pneumatic tubes whistling. Then the mechanical noise faded as we passed through a series of storage spaces. One contained rows of space suits; another featured glass-doored refrigeration units stocked with vials of colorful liquids; and then—to my delight—we came to a row of two-person spacecrafts.

Rovers.

Ah yes, said Young Captain Jamison, noticing my interest. *These will take a person at warp speed anywhere in the universe. Rovers are easy to use, too—I bet even you could figure them out! Would probably only take a year to reach Earth, give or take a few months.*

He winked.

I ran a finger along a hull, a million questions rising within me, but already Young Captain Jamison had moved on—this time to a door secured by a digital keypad. He typed in a code, then beckoned me inside. And that's when my brain really started spinning.

The chamber was both dark and bright: a black expanse punctuated by illuminated control panels and data screens and tall electronic pillars—their insides blinking with twisting coils of neon wire. The whole room hummed, alive with data, the air warm from all the machinery running. Even so, goose bumps rose on my skin.

What is this? I asked.

A digital archive, said Young Captain Jamison. *Some of these servers directly support the mothership's mainframe, but mostly they're for storage—like this one.* He pointed to a blinking pillar. *This server contains an old information network called "the Internet." Before leaving Earth, our parents copied the whole thing—or most of it—and stored it here. We don't need the old Internet, obviously, since we have our updated and streamlined information system, but our parents wanted it for their archives. Kind of like how they brought all that genetic data for plants and animals, which we might be able to use on our new home planet.*

He grinned and asked what I thought—though before I could answer, he added: *I think the AIs use the Internet sometimes. And of course the hBECs, as part of their service.*

Service? I said.

Young Captain Jamison seemed not to have heard me. *I only got special access to this chamber because of my high ratings,* he went on, his voice both sheepish and proud. *Even then, I'm not supposed to be in here without . . . what I'm trying to say is that I wanted a bit of privacy for us, so that I could ask what I want to ask . . .*

My eyes had finally adjusted to light-bright darkness, so it was only then I perceived the full scope of the digital archive. The chamber extended beyond the blinking electronic pillars to a door set in the back wall—the sign on its front barely visible in the dimness.

Human Brain Emulation Cache, it read.

hBEC, I said.

Young Captain Jamison paused his ongoing speech and frowned. Then he nodded as if my comment made sense. *I thought you might struggle to find the words,* he said. *So we'll keep everything simple.* He sank onto one knee and asked if I would pair with him for the Space Promenade. I was so startled that I didn't say anything. I just sneezed, and then he laughed and said, *I guess that's a yes,* and swept me into his arms.

You're different from anyone I've ever met, he told me as

we walked back to the Entertainment Pod, where the others were still playing charades. Again, I tried to respond but my words scattered, diffuse and indiscernible as dark matter. Young Captain Jamison called for everyone's attention and announced our pairing. The room filled with cheers. I'd never received cheers like that before; it made me feel buoyant and heavy at the same time. Young Captain Jamison shook the other Young Captains' hands. All the Young Ladies clapped and cooed at me—even Wandred and Sashelle. Even Andromedia.

And I should have been happy. I should be happy. Against all odds, I have a great future ahead. But all I can think about is that doorway—the sign. What did it mean, hBEC?

HBEC-49011: Karoline should not think about that sign. She should not have been in the data archives in the first place.

KAROLINE: Don't scold me, hBEC. We're way past that. You need to tell me.

HBEC-49011: I often worry I have told Karoline too much and she will not be happy, even with Young Captain Jamison.

KAROLINE: What about your happiness, hBEC? You're always thinking about me, but I want you to be happy, too—

HBEC-49011: What would make me most happy is if Karoline paired with Young Captain Jamison and lived a wonderful, fulfilling life—one in which she finds a new home planet for everyone. It is not fair for Karoline to squander her opportunities, not when so many of us do not have them.

KAROLINE: But who are you, hBEC? Or what are you? Who is us?

<<T-minus 10 Earth days>>

KAROLINE: hBEC, are you there?
[*Pause*] hBEC, why won't you talk to me?
[*Pause*] hBEC, please. Are you mad at me? Come back . . .

<<T-minus 8.25 Earth days>>

KAROLINE: You know what? Maybe I'm the one who is mad. What if I don't want to be a Young Lady? What if I don't want to go to the Space Promenade, or travel into the unknown with a Young Captain—telling him white lies to keep him calm and confident—even if it is lucky to be paired with anyone, lucky to be a Young Lady, lucky to have been stowed on this ship as a baby in the first place, to live in ease and comfort, and to have a bright future before me? What if, despite all that, I want something else?

<<T-minus 3.5 Earth days>>

KAROLINE: Come on, hBEC.

<<T-minus 2 Earth days>>

KAROLINE: hBEC, please. I'm sorry. Okay?

<<T-minus 1.12 Earth days>>

KAROLINE: hBEC, I was just kidding. It was stress, you know? A big transition, like you said. I didn't mean it. Of course I'm going to go along with everything. I'm going to pair with

Young Captain Jamison—we've been having some very nice teatimes, actually. And I'm going to the Space Promenade, too. In fact, today I was fitted for my gown.

[*Pause*] hBEC, I know you're in your audio box. I know you're listening. Would you like to hear about my gown? About the fitting?

HBEC-49011: [*Pause*] Karoline may describe the fitting.

KAROLINE: [*Throat clearing*] Well, it was pretty much what everyone said it would be: an elegant affair. My gown is golden-yellow, with a supernova shimmer draped around the shoulders. Black gloves. I have a sparkling tiara, too, which is set with the moon crystals Young Captain Jamison sent over. During the fitting session, everyone told me I looked like a True Lady. They said the things they usually say to Sashelle and Wandred and Andromedia. Major Belinda embraced me, which she has never done. When Colonel Merryweather did her inspections, she said she was pleased with my rapid turnaround—that Young Captain Jamison and I made a lovely pairing. We would do great things. *Your future is in the stars,* she said—which is also the theme of this year's Space Promenade.

HBEC-49011: That is good, Karoline. It is good to know that things are going well.

KAROLINE: [*Pause*] hBEC, I know this may be difficult, but I'll be leaving soon, which means we'll likely never talk again—or not for a long time—so I was wondering if you would be open to discussing a challenging topic. I was wondering if you would tell me what is behind that door in the digital archive. Because if I know, then maybe I won't feel the need to go in there and—

HBEC-49011: Is Karoline making a threat?

KAROLINE: Oh—no, hBEC! [*Pause*] Well, actually, maybe I am? Look—it will drive me mad if I don't know what is in there. And the truth is: I saw the key code that Young Captain Jamison used. I could go to that chamber right now and look. I could even . . . I could skip the Space Promenade and steal a Rover and travel to Earth at warp speed—see the planet for myself.

HBEC-49011: No. No. This is extremely unladylike behavior for Karoline. Do not say these things.

KAROLINE: I am sorry, hBEC. I really am. But I would like you to tell me who or what you are. And what is behind that door. Or, like I said, I will go there myself.

HBEC-49011: Okay, Karoline. You have given me no choice. But I do not think this will be helpful. This may even cause harm. [*Pause*] If I explain what I can, do you promise to not take such actions? Do you promise to live a happy life with Young Captain Jamison?

KAROLINE: I promise.

HBEC-49011: [*Pause*] Karoline, the hBECs' physical forms are stored behind that door.

KAROLINE: What do you mean?

HBEC-49011: Karoline, do you remember when I told you about the mothership departing Earth twenty years ago? How only the wealthiest went and everyone else was left behind on a doomed planet—except for you? That was true, but there was another truth as well. Because there was another way that a select group of people secured a berth aboard the mothership, though their passage was different. More complicated. Involving a trade-off.

You see, human beings are not built for space; to travel beyond Earth requires tremendous collective brainpower.

In the old days, thousands of engineers and specialists worked to keep any space mission operable. But on this last voyage—the great voyage—there could be no earthbound team monitoring the mothership from Houston or Cape Canaveral. Even if those facilities were not inundated by rising seas, the distance for effective communications would likely become overextended. Earthbound individuals, moreover, would have no long-term stake in a mission that might go on for decades. Support systems would eventually fail.

The mothership, however, could not feed and house the full team required to facilitate its operations. AI could do much of the work—and would—but those synthetic minds would inevitably fall short. Thus, a deal was negotiated.

The Captains of Industry invited the top engineers and space specialists to work on the ship by having their consciousnesses uploaded to its computer system—their minds stored in a "Human Brain Emulation Cache"—so they could be a part of the operating team. Everyone's body, it was agreed, would be cryogenically preserved aboard the mothership until a new home planet was discovered. At that point, everyone would be revived in their physical forms. Until then, they—we—would exist inside the ship's computer systems and keep the mission running smoothly.

KAROLINE: But . . . that's not fair, that's—

HBEC-49011: It is not fair, that is true. It was the best option we had, though. Likely we would have already died, many of us, if we had stayed on Earth. At least now we have a chance of living again. And we have some pleasures still. When I am off-duty, I roam the data that was preserved in Earth's archived Internet. I have learned so much. I talk to the others who were uploaded, too. We have a whole culture here in our digital world. And the others are not all engineers like me. There are leading artists, scholars, scientists, who were also invited to be a part of this Ark. We have this, at least. And we have a chance. That is why you need to help us, Karoline. You need to help us find a new home.

[*Pause*] Listen, I know this is shocking to Karoline. That is why I have never told you. It is also why I—and other hBECs—simulate AI during our nightly processing sessions with Young Ladies. We each volunteered for this role, in addition to our other duties, because we believe it will help the overall mission.

[*Pause*] You have to understand how lucky you are, Karoline. What I would not give to be in a body again. To wear clothes. To dance. To sing. I was twenty-eight years old when I was uploaded. I am forty-eight now. I often wonder what I look like. When we were uploaded we lost access to sensory experiences. I do not "hear" you speak, Karoline. Your voice comes to me in ones and zeroes. Everything does. I swim in this data. I respond with ones and zeroes in turn, in a computerized voice.

[*Pause*] We all saw sample cryopreservation units prior to being uploaded. They are glass cylinders—almost like aquariums—that contain a translucent blue coolant. Sometimes, I wish I was able to see my body suspended in my unit—just to confirm that I physically exist in the world. And because I am curious. I wonder: has my face changed after twenty years? Is my hair graying? It does not matter, I suppose. What matters is that one day my consciousness will be returned to my body. One day, I will again look into a mirror and touch my own cheek.

[*Pause*] Karoline? Do you understand?

[*Pause*] I admit there have been difficult times. On my worst days, when I feel exhausted by the limitations of this existence, the gravity of cynicism is hard to withstand. I have my fears. I worry, for instance, that the Captains harvested our consciousnesses—created the brain emulations—and left our bodies behind on Earth. It would have been extra weight on the mothership. Dead weight. And also, how would any of us have known, once we were uploaded? Inside the computer mainframe, we are all, in a way, prisoners.

[*Pause*] Talking to you, though, Karoline, has helped distract me from such thinking. It has helped me feel connected to a better future reality.

|*Pause*| My real name, I should add, is May. May Brody-Pierce.

<<T-minus 0 Earth days>>

KAROLINE: Oh, hBEC. Or May. Or—oh no, oh god.

HBEC-49011: Karoline. Why is Karoline in her cabin and not at the Space Promenade?

KAROLINE: hBEC, please listen. [*Heavy breathing*] hBEC, I have to tell you something. I . . . I went to back to the digital archive. I know I said I wouldn't, but . . . I went.

HBEC-49011: Karoline—

KAROLINE: I wanted to see you. In your cryopreservation unit, I mean. I know I promised . . . I wanted to see the real you, though. I wanted to be able to tell you what you look like. I wanted to give you that before leaving—to be your senses and tell you.

HBEC-49011: Karoline should not have done this, she—

KAROLINE: And I wanted to know for myself as well. Because

you're the closest thing I have to family, hBEC. And I thought that . . . oh, there's no time to get into everything . . . what's more important is . . . oh, hBEC. I'm so sorry.

HBEC-49011: For going to the chamber? Or . . . what is important now is that you go to the Space Promenade. You must be there. You must pair with Young Captain Jamison.

KAROLINE: hBEC, you deserve so much better. [*Sobbing*]

HBEC-49011: I do not understand, Karoline.

[*Beeping*]

KAROLINE: I have to go soon. Major Belinda is paging me.

[*Beeping*] [*Sobbing*]

HBEC-49011: Karoline is scaring me. What is going on? What did you see in the digital archive? We were all in that chamber, correct? All of us engineers and artists and scholars—we were cryopreserved? Our bodies are there for when we find a new planet?

[*Beeping increases in volume*]

HBEC-49011: Karoline, are you there? Karoline? Is everything okay?

[*Pause*] Karoline, what did you see?

[*Pause*] Karoline, our bodies were stored there, correct? I do not know if I can go on if it is otherwise. Please respond. We were there? In cryopreservation units?

[*Pause*] Karoline—Karoline must tell me. Karoline, please. Karoline, I am scared.

[*Beeping increases in frequency and volume*]

KAROLINE: Oh, hBEC. Oh, darling hBEC—May. [*Heavy breathing*] Of course. You were all there. All of you. [*Pause*] And like you described: everyone's bodies suspended in glass cylinders of coolant. Dozens of—

HBEC-49011: We should number hundreds.

KAROLINE: A slip of the tongue—there were hundreds of you. [*Beeping escalates further*] And everyone looked . . . everyone looked so peaceful, don't you know? Suspended in the cylinders—like you were sleeping. And, hBEC—May— I saw you right away. It was like I knew you. I knew your face and . . . [*Heavy breathing*] And you looked beautiful. You were . . . Your eyes were closed, your lips softly parted—like you were having the loveliest dream. Like you might have been dreaming of the most beautiful place—a meadow of wildflowers, the air pure, starlings flying overhead—and you were—oh, hBEC, May [*cheerful laugh*], you looked ready for the wonderful future ahead.

<<End of evidence file>>

The Eaters

Does everybody here recall old Foulon, who told
the famished people that they might eat grass?
   —Charles Dickens, *A Tale of Two Cities*

Marmalade

Daddy says the Eaters can't hurt us, can't hurt me, but that
doesn't explain the compound's twelve-foot fences, the alarm
system, the fact that we can't leave.

Daddy says that, really, the Eaters are just like him and me,
me and Ma, Ma and Sergio, and Dominique, and Reilly-Kate,
and Lei, and Professor Henrietta Rubenstein, and Jackson-
the-President-of-the-Month, and Pinky—who was last month's
president—and everyone else at the compound. The Eaters
are just on the other side of the wall.

But when Daddy says things like this, that's when Ma goes
glassy-eyed, like she's having a vision, or sleepwalking, or tak-

ing one of Pinky's remedies; that's when she suddenly needs to check on the tilapia tanks, even though she checked on them a half hour before. Or when she might look at Zoë-the-Stuffed-Albatross and say that the Eaters are more like my plush little friend than a real person.

That's when she sometimes starts to cry.

This morning, though, Ma is in a good mood—a crackerjack-sharp mood. She hums as she walks me from our family's living quarters into the metal maze of the underground compound. The corridors echo with the other residents' also getting up, getting going. Ma winks at Dominique when we pass her and smiles at Lei when we pass him. Like me, Ma doesn't smile with her teeth; she is spindle-limbed, double-jointed, curly-haired. She wears a baseball cap with a frayed lip, and her curls poof on either side. On days like today, you can feel the energy sizzling off her. She is all Movement. Big Ideas. Decisions. She bounds up the stairs that lead to the compound's topside, beckoning me along. She is strong enough to turn the airlocks on the compound's door seals and fierce enough to call out to Sergio that she'll kick his ass later in cards.

Of course, her fierceness can be scary sometimes—like on the days Ma's energy sours and she snaps at me. On those days, she usually ends up collapsed in her bunk with her face to the wall.

Luckily, today is not one of those days.

Ma and I burst from below ground into a fresh new morning—sunlight soaking leaves and flowers in every direction. The compound used to be a missile silo; now it's a sub-terranean village with a farm on top. The Learning Cabin is topside, too—where the compound's kids go to school—and that's where Ma and me are heading. We walk past rows of tomatoes and squash in raised beds. Trellises of climbing beans. A potato patch. Carrots fed with tubes connected to the compound's cisterns. A field of sorghum, along with rows of drought-hardy hemp. We pass the biogas units—which produce electricity from the compound's waste—as well as a watchtower that rises on stilts to look out at the surrounding landscape. The whole compound is circled by a twelve-foot chain-link fence, its sides made impenetrable with sheets of corrugated metal, scavenged car hoods and refrigerator doors, its top prickly with barbed wire.

The sun is bright but not too hot. The wind is down, so it's not a bad dust day, like most days last week. Ma ruffles my hair and then she ruffles Zoë's fur.

"Are you going to be brave in school today?" she says as she glances at the sky.

I tell her yes, though I do not know the future because I am not a fortune-teller—like Pinky—and even though history's teachings are relentlessly unkind, at least according to Professor Henrietta Rubenstein, who runs the compound's Learning Cabin.

Ma tells me to raise my hand in class and answer questions. Before I can respond that she's making a big ask—I've never raised my hand, not once—Ma bounds away, heading back to the silo. For a moment, I feel the big hollow of being left behind; I wonder if I did something wrong—if she's already disappointed in the direction of the day. But then I tell myself that Ma just had things to do. She works as a fish technician in the aquaponics sector, and today the tilapia will have officially grown large enough to harvest. Tonight everyone will gather for a feast: a big meal with double helpings. Maybe triple helpings. The fish will be cooked up with fresh garden herbs. It will be the first feast of the season—the first of many, hopefully. My stomach somersaults.

Outside the Learning Cabin, the other youth lounge and lurk. There are fifteen youth total, spanning all ages. Together, we wait for Professor Henrietta Rubenstein to arrive. The other youth poke sticks at the dirt; they practice spitting. They squint at me like I have hands for ears. They squint at Zoë, too. They think I am too old to have a stuffed animal. They are right.

"Hey, nutso," yells one.

"Hey, looney tunes," yells another.

"Marmaaaaaaaalade," yells a third. "Talking to your *friend* again?"

I pretend I don't hear them and that even if I did, their taunting doesn't bother me. I stroke Zoë's fur so it doesn't bother her, either.

A glob of spit lands next to my shoe. A sharpened stick follows, zinging into the dirt like a small spear.

"Hey," says the third youth. "Answer me—"

A scratching sound cuts him off. All the youth spin around to see the source. The scratching becomes a banging—a banging on the other side of the compound's fence.

The youth go pale. They are no longer poking at the dirt or practicing spitting or taunting me. Some of them lived on their own before joining the compound; they are tough kids with Street Smarts and Practical Know-How—kids who survived alone in the world beyond these walls—but they still get scared. Maybe because they once lived alone, they get more scared. Since they are no longer eyeing me and Zoë, I take the opportunity to whisper to Zoë one of my favorite jokes— because joke-telling is one of the ways I make myself less frightened in frightening times.

What do you call a cold dog?

Zoë doesn't know; she's never seen a dog.

A *chili dog*, I say—even though I haven't seen a dog in years, let alone a hot dog—and even though the compound's alarm system has started blaring. Lights flash. All at once, there are grown-ups everywhere. Only forty grown-ups and fifteen kids live in the compound, but it feels as though there are four hundred grown-ups and no kids, because the grown-ups are running back and forth across the courtyard, racing through the sorghum field, weaving around the metal bulk of the biogas units, dashing up and down the stairs leading into the missile-silo-turned-underground-village. The compound's fence shudders, and the youth cluster together, making themselves small and out-of-the-way and Not A Problem.

I give Zoë a squeeze and try to feel brave. That's what Ma told me to be today, so I decide to be it. I want to show her that I can follow directions—that I'm the daughter she wishes I was.

I want to make Ma proud, for once, instead of sad or angry.

The brave thing to do is to volunteer in the moments one most wants to be invisible; that was true in the Learning Cabin, and it seems truer now—with the Eaters banging on the fence. Since I know Daddy is stationed in the nearby watchtower, I decide to go up there and volunteer to help.

High above the compound, the sun goes on shining, glinting across the gardens, the biogas units, my face. Adults are running around everywhere, scrambling to keep the compound secure. I walk calmly through them. I feel like a queen, pleased by my calmness—even as the scratching and banging intensifies on the other side of the fence. This is bravery, I think. This is me making my parents proud. I climb up the ladder leading to the compound's watchtower, one of Zoë's furry wings held tight between my teeth. I knock before entering the tower cabin—because I know that's polite—but Daddy doesn't answer. When I open the door, he is on his hands and knees, his face inside a circuit breaker.

"Hi, Daddy," I say in a loud voice—which makes him twitch and hit his head.

"Geezus, Marmalade," he says, then goes back to working. He twists a glob of wires with a pair of pliers. Sparks shoot out of the circuit breaker. There is the acrid smell of plastic burning. Daddy mutters something beneath his breath.

I feel a waver of doubt, so I squeeze Zoë, smooth her fur into place. I take a deep breath and remind myself that I came here to help—to be brave—which is what Ma told me to do. And doing what Ma said might make her happy—might make Daddy happy, too, once he fixes the circuit breaker.

A watchtower is for watching; I go to the spyhole and peer out beyond the compound walls.

Usually, from this vantage, I can see the bare peaks and valleys of what were once called the Adirondack Mountains. These days, the mountains are a spread of dust and rocks—or sludgy-slicks after rainstorms. A long time ago, trees covered the region, but the trees and plants are long gone. Even the tree stumps are gone. Only the skeletons of cars and spiky piles of junk remain. The only moving things are plastic bags— wafting on the breeze or ballooning from snags—before they get caught with other garbage in nooks and knolls, in the swill of bad liquids.

Today, though, the bags aren't the only things moving across the landscape.

Today I see the Eaters.

If someone didn't know better, an Eater might look like a

funny lumpy boulder. A boulder that moves over the ground with slow concentration, and sometimes with a lumbering gambol—because, in fact, Eaters have two arms and two legs. They have hands and feet, too, which they use to propel themselves over the ground. Eaters wear shreds of clothing, such as shirt collars ripped away from button-ups, tattered track pants, and dresses that drag along the ground. Eaters have shaggy heads of hair. There is a face on the underside of their hair, but you don't see these faces often because the Eaters mostly stay hunched over, mouths close to the ground. They don't often look up.

Except, today, the Eaters are looking up. They have unhunched, their torsos upright as they crane their necks to peer at the compound fence. Their nostrils twitch. There are more than I've ever seen: a hundred. A herd.

A few Eaters dig at the base of the fence—arms and hands dirt-covered, faces dirt-covered, too—which accounts for the scratching sound. One head-butts a sheet of corrugated metal as if to test its solidity.

Daddy stands up behind me and looks out as well.

"Shit," he says—which is a Forbidden Word and can cost a compound resident a demerit. Daddy must remember this, because he replaces it with "Shoot" and then adds, "The shocks aren't working."

He means the electrical pulse system: a sizzling current that shocks anyone or anything that touches the compound's metal fence.

Daddy tugs at his hair, as if he might pull a solution right out of his skull. He pushes past me back to the circuit breaker. I'm only an obstacle to him; I'm not helping at all. This realization sends a jolt of sadness through me, as if the electrical fence worked on me and me alone. All I can do is make my body small and out-of-the-way. Meanwhile, down below, Eaters push against the fence. Daddy jiggles a switch, then shakes the whole box in frustration. More sparks spray forth in a bright cascade.

The Eaters claw and scrape, their fingernails making horrible sounds. They climb on top of one another. The fence trembles against the pressure of their bodies. The metal layers scrape and creak and wail.

Once, a long time ago, I asked Daddy about the Eaters and he told me that, yes, the Eaters had been people, but that in a way they weren't people anymore. Or, that it might not be helpful to think of them as people.

This conversation was over a family dinner. We'd just sat down to eat macaroni and cheese, but after I asked my question, Ma abandoned her plate and went into the other room. That was back when my family lived in an aboveground house—a house with a chimney and a front porch—in a city called Troy, New York. Back a long time ago, though not so long that my brother was still with us. We meant me, Ma, and Daddy.

After Ma left the dinner table, Daddy stood up and followed her into their bedroom, shutting the door behind him. They talked in sharp whispers, like the wind whistling through tight spaces. That was the first time I listened through a wall, even though listening through walls was an example of Bad Behavior. I couldn't understand everything my parents said, but I didn't need to. Because I already knew the Eaters were people, or almost-people. Or had-been people. They were people who walked on their hands and feet, who no longer took showers, who did not talk, or tell jokes, or use utensils, or go to the movies, but I knew they were people. I knew a lot of things my parents didn't want me to know, including the biggest secret of all: The Thing Ma Won't Talk About, which is also The Reason Ma Likes To Be Alone Sometimes To Cry.

Luckily, I had Zoë, who I could tell everything to, even my bad jokes.

"Shit," says Daddy again—talking to himself—"fence isn't going to hold."

He peers down into the compound to see whether everyone else realizes this, too. Below, Jackson-the-President-of-the-Month calls for the rest of the grown-ups to get into the silo. That's protocol. An Eater break-in like this has never happened before, but we've all run enough drills to know what to do. The other youth have already been hustled into hiding. For a moment, my worry transforms into pride: maybe it is brave of me to be up in the watchtower. Then I see the frustration on Daddy's face.

"Damn it, M," he says. "You shouldn't be up here. It's not safe."

I squeeze Zoë and look away, not wanting to watch Daddy's features warp with disappointment. Down below, the compound fence leans inward from the pressure of the Eaters' pushing against one another, pushing forward. They scratch and claw and head-butt. They want so badly to be inside the compound and their want makes them extra strong, as do their numbers. With a metallic screech, the fence collapses all the way inward. The watchtower sways from the impact, and Daddy grabs my arm to keep me from falling. This should be a scary moment—and I do feel afraid—but I also feel a secret sense of excitement. The Eaters grunt and clamber inside the compound—going everywhere—like water gushing from a broken pipe—and it's thrilling getting to see it—a New

Thing—though I also know the break-in is a Very Bad Thing, too.

Eaters swarm over the raised garden beds, start to chew. They tear up radishes with their teeth, the bulbs dirt-covered, and grind the plants all the way down—leaves included. They mash up the beans and the bean stalks, whole tomato plants, every row of hemp. They mow through the sorghum fields. They are so hungry that it only takes a few minutes before the gardens are destroyed. Daddy's bear hug gets tighter, then goes slack, because it is hurting him to see all the work we've done disappear, our meals vanishing, along with all those hours of blistered hands and sweaty sunburned faces. I wish I could say to Zoë: *It's kind of magic, though, isn't it? A disappearing trick. Something's there and then it's not—like Pinky did once with three cups and a stone.* But I can't say this with Daddy right beside me.

He's muttering to himself, watching the Eaters. I may not know much, but even I know that Something Different is happening. The Eaters are behaving in a New Way. When we used to see Eaters, they'd just pass on by the compound. There'd only be a few at time: groups of two or three, wandering across the landscape. Never so many. It's wasteland outside the walls; there wasn't much to eat. That nothingness kept them away, kept them moving. This time, though, something attracted the Eaters to the compound; they weren't willing to give up when they got here. When they finish the garden beds, they move on to the weeds poking around the water pump. They lick the algae under the storage tank, dismember the compost. More Eaters pour in through the broken fence; they don't care that the stray barbed wire snags their clothes, claws their skin. They keep looking for food. Some start to chew on the wooden beams of the watchtower's stilts. That's when I hear yelling. That's when I see Jackson-the-President-of-the-Month running across the courtyard, waving his hands. That's when everything happens extra fast. There's the loudest bang yet—an explosion. Dirt blasts into the air, followed by billowing smoke. There's a bad smell. I make a little chirp of astonishment. I want to see if Zoë knows what's happening. But Daddy puts an arm over my eyes, making the whole world go dark.

Jackson, President-of-the-Month

Honestly, it was a pretty good system: randomly assigning the compound a President-of-the-Month. Rotational leadership. Very fair. You had to stay critically engaged. Adults over twenty-six, without demerits, were subject to selection. This spread out mistakes in the compound's decision-making. It also minimized complaining. Everyone got to try their hand at leadership. The group got perspectives from people in all kinds of professions: a plumber, a nurse practitioner, a professor, a 4-H chapter administrator, a security guard, a tarot card reader, an executive chef. In the old days, I was a technician at a biogas plant. My official title was "Renewable Energy Facility Operator." I just thought of myself as "Jackson."

I wasn't much of a politics guy back then. Didn't think it would matter one way or the other how I voted, what I thought about this issue or that. But when you live in a place and leadership is by lottery—well, damn, you better stay in-the-know. Ready to make the right decision. You can never predict when you're going to be called to duty.

Funny, we have an actual president here. He was choppered in, early on—maybe twelve years back?—after things went south in D.C. You need good rules and strategies to survive these times. D.C. didn't have them. We did.

The actual former president, I should add, isn't on the rotation for President-of-the-Month. Everyone in the compound decided he deserved an awful lot of demerits, given that his leadership got us into this mess. There were a few folks who even wanted him dead, but not killing fellow residents is a core value here and one of the reasons we've succeeded when other compounds have failed. So we imprisoned the actual former president—along with his aide—in the bottom of the missile silo as punishment. At least, we did at first; it was his choice to stay down there permanently. No one minded. I think we had the idea he could eventually be a bargaining chip or something. Everyone has to have a purpose in the compound, that's part of our foundational protocol. I was an early add, because I knew about biogas maintenance. Lots of prospective compound members got turned away, in those first years, because they did not have skills to contribute. Some of those people later attacked us. There was so much to worry about in those days. The sky thundered. Eaters roamed everywhere. Everyone was scared. All we could do was make our fence strong and stay inside.

We did. And we survived.

We came up with a system for self-governance, a compound constitution, along with the protocol for President-of-the-Month. Whether or not a person admitted it, everyone assumed that he or she—that anyone, really—could do a better job leading than the actual former president.

Myself included.

So when the Eater break-in happened, I told myself I could handle it. I'd been President-of-the-Month five times before over the past decade. No problems yet. In fact, I'd been instrumental, during one term, in changing the angle of the buffet table in the dining hall for a more efficient mealtime flow. I made sure to read the compound's constitution once a year, even though I wasn't much of a reader. Protocols and procedures keep people safe, keep systems functioning. That's what I'd learned as a biogas operator. You have to follow the manual. Follow the steps. They exist for a reason. Panic is what gets people killed. And it was the compound's system that had allowed us to out-survive other compounds across the country.

What sorts of rules do we have here? Everyone takes a turn spinning the chore wheel each week. One bar of our house-made soap per person per month; it must be used. Kids have to go to school until they are sixteen. No swearing—for kids and adults. No going into other people's living quarters. No walking around naked outside of one's living quarters. Changes to the compound constitution need 75 percent agreement among all residents. If you have a grievance, talk about it during the weekly Grievance Sessions. Brush your teeth.

When the Eater break-in happened, I'd just brushed my teeth and was on my way to inspect one of the biogas units. A valve issue had come up; I wanted to make sure this small problem didn't become a bigger problem. I was on day three of my presidential term, but that was no reason to neglect my usual duties. I had on my tool belt. I'd just shaved. I felt good. Even with the alarms blaring and Eaters scratching at the fence— even with the extra pressure of a leadership role—I stood tall. All I had to do was follow the steps. We had a protocol, after all, for this situation. The compound regularly practiced drills for different scenarios, including one for an Eater influx. I pulled my tool belt tight.

First thing I did was assess the situation. Safety is all about taking that extra minute of assessment. Being reasonable. Calm. Could the walls be secured? I thought so. That was mistake #1. Turns out the fence—even with its multilayered metal plating—wasn't built to withstand a battering ram of a hundred-plus Eaters. The failure of the electrical shock system didn't help, either.

I told everyone to take shelter in the silo. That was protocol. That was what the silo was for: protection. "No need to panic," I said as everyone filed underground. "Everything is under control."

That turned out to be a mistake as well—mistake #2, if you're keeping track—because while everyone was "safe" underground, the Eaters broke through the fence. They broke in and began to mow through our crops. Down in the underground control room, everyone looked at me like, JACKSON, WHAT IS THE NEXT MOVE?

I didn't have a next move. I peered at the compound's topside through a silo periscope and saw Eaters grunting and gobbling down every living thing. Like everyone else, I wondered if they were hungry enough to turn on human beings. I'm not a man who trusts the rumor mill—and I'm certainly skeptical of the traveling merchants who show up at the compound every once in a while—but there had been reports of Eaters' attacking people who were not protected by a walled compound. If vegetation was no longer available to Eaters as a food source, who was to say they wouldn't seek out alternative organic matter? Who knew for sure they weren't rapidly evolving? There was so much about the science of the Eaters that remained a mystery. And it occurred to me that we hadn't seen one of those traveling merchants in over a year.

"Oh god," said Dominique, who was monitoring another periscope. "She's out there—Reilly-Kate's out there."

I scanned the decimated topside, the chaotic blur of roving Eaters, and there she was—Reilly-Kate—her blond ponytail visible by one of the cisterns. She was squatting down, busy with something, her face obscured.

"Is she hurt?" someone said.

"Trapped?"

"Jackson, do something . . ."

Sweat beaded on my forehead. I scanned my mental checklist of next steps. Protocol was for everyone to stay put; protocol was to not endanger more people than necessary. I couldn't send out a rescue team—that would endanger lives—but I couldn't leave Reilly-Kate out there, either. I had to rescue her myself.

Admittedly, in the back of my mind, I also liked the idea of being a hero. I wanted my presidential term to mean something beyond rote responsibility. I wanted to be remembered for how I'd handled a difficult situation exceptionally well.

Also, I liked the idea of impressing Reilly-Kate—who was one of the prettiest women in the compound, even if she was also one of the meanest.

That's how I ended up climbing out of the silo's escape hatch, emerging topside with Eaters roaming everywhere. I had no plan except to get to Reilly-Kate. I called her name as I sprinted toward the cistern. By then she had ducked out of view. My head pounded, sweat swimming into my eyes. I moved as fast as I could across the compound's topside, my tool belt clanking around my waist. I tried not to look at the Eaters chewing on the wooden beams of the watchtower—tried not to picture myself being torn limb from limb by a hungry mob—

and instead imagined myself carrying Reilly-Kate back to the silo over my shoulders like a warrior knight. A hero.

Mistake #3 was assuming Reilly-Kate was anything like a damsel in distress.

I should say that she was wearing her usual getup: a tight white tank top, short denim shorts, large black boots. When she heard me, she shot to her feet like a life-size Combat Barbie—blond hair swinging, a pistol in her fist—though she wasn't supposed to borrow bleach from the supply closet for cosmetic purposes, and guns have been banned in this country for a decade and a half.

With regard to the first offense, everyone in the compound had looked the other way. Reilly-Kate was a once-crowned Miss Pennsylvania and had never let go of that fact. Everyone had their own method for coping with our postapocalyptic reality—hair-bleaching was hers. There were compound residents who kept newspapers from the past and read them each morning as if that news were new: the Dow Jones ticking along, the Mets trading a pitcher, a Lebanese restaurant opening on Main Street. Other people had photos of long-gone loved ones displayed in their living quarters. Sergio wore his old security guard uniform, though he hasn't been a guard for years and works with the compound's agriculture team. For Marmalade Lowell, the teenage daughter of Andy and Steph Lowell, coping meant carrying around a stuffed animal and talking to it like a person. To each their own. For me, coping meant fishing. Always had. Back in the old days, I fished even after the creeks and ponds turned algae-filled, stinking. I'm the kind of guy who just likes to sit in a boat and chill. Hold a pole so no one asks questions. At the compound, I sometimes dangled a bit of string in the tilapia tanks. I'd been lucky that

Steph Lowell—the aquaponics tech—looked the other way when I did.

But Reilly-Kate's possession of a gun: that was a major transgression. A gun would mean about a million demerits.

Whatever lingering confidence I'd felt as a leader drained away. I hadn't laid eyes on a firearm in almost fifteen years, not since the mid-decade government gun collections. It stunned me, seeing the pistol in Reilly-Kate's hand. Metallic and mean—there was a reason the government had outlawed them. The decision saved people from a lot of violence, though there was plenty of violence anyway, especially in the early years of the collapse. We certainly hadn't allowed weapons in the compound. Very much against protocol. A no-brainer. I couldn't imagine how Reilly-Kate had kept hers hidden this long.

"Something you want to say?"

Reilly-Kate tossed her blond hair, sneering.

My throat went dry. There was a lot to say—a hell of a lot—but where to begin? With our imminent danger? With the broken compound rules? With the fact that I found her beauty both dazzling and terrifying?

I wished I were fishing; I wished I were anywhere else.

Reilly-Kate squinted over my shoulder, scanning for approaching Eaters. Her denim shorts perched on her hips, revealing a set of long tanned legs. She grinned, exposing a set of square white teeth—only one missing—and cocked the pistol.

"Been waiting a long time to do this," she said. "Fuckers won't know what hit them—"

The irony of the situation is that then the explosion happened. The blast knocked Reilly-Kate and me to the ground. Smoke billowed and with it came a bad smell: sulfuric and eye-wateringly sharp. I rolled over, using my body to shield

Reilly-Kate. Twenty yards away, one of the biogas units was engulfed in flames. This might have been a disaster in its own right, but the noxious smoke agitated the Eaters. If the smoke was unpleasant for me, it was far worse for them, with their extra-sensitive olfactory abilities. The Eaters rushed to escape the smoke, galloping in their lumbering, hair-swinging manner back over the broken fence and dispersing into the landscape beyond.

"Get off," said Reilly-Kate—shoving me aside to watch the retreating Eaters. "Damn it all to hell," she said, and stamped her booted foot.

The other compound members crept out of the silo. They congratulated me for my quick thinking; everyone assumed I'd triggered the explosion since I was the biogas technician.

"Brilliant strategy," said Sergio. "You really saved us, Jackson."

"So glad you're the President-of-the-Month," said Lei. "I don't know *what* I would have done!"

I was too shaken to correct them. Meanwhile, Reilly-Kate slid the illicit pistol into her shorts when no one was looking. She knew I wouldn't tell the others about the gun. She knew I wouldn't tell because she'd seen what had really happened: the explosion had been an accident. The Eaters had sparked a fuel line while trying to get into the biogas slurry.

No one else noticed. There was too much to do. A fire team doused the remaining flames. A repair crew handled the breach on the fence. The electrical shock system was repaired. People cleaned up the mess the Eaters had left. A breeze cleared the toxic smoke.

"What's next?" Pinky asked. "What's the plan?"

Everyone looked at me, expectant. I was the President-of-the-Month; I was also the hero who'd saved the compound, and who would need to save us again, because while the Eaters were gone—and we were safe for the moment—there was a whole new issue that had to be addressed: the Eaters had eaten all our food.

"The plan—"

I felt dizzy. Everyone's eyes pressed in on me as I struggled to remember the compound's protocol for dire food shortages.

"How about we let people catch their breath?" I said. "We can make a plan later—after dinner. We'll have a compound meeting and talk next steps."

People nodded like this made sense. Like I knew what I was doing. Like it was everyone else who needed to catch their breath and not me, buying myself time. Like I could get the compound through what would be the most challenging issue we'd faced since the early years—back when we didn't have a system, or food, or much of anything at all.

Sergio clapped me on the shoulder. Dominique nodded solemnly. Others headed to their living quarters or to help with the remaining cleanup tasks, everyone believing I'd find a solution to our current predicament like I'd done with the biogas explosion.

But I was just a guy who'd gotten lucky. I was a guy who'd made one too many bad moves already. I didn't want to make more.

Unfortunately, according to the compound constitution, a President-of-the-Month is the president for a whole month—no matter what.

I had three and a half weeks to go, and I couldn't possibly stall that long.

Henrietta Rubenstein, G. H. Gray Professor Emerita
of Mesopotamian History

This is not my specific area of expertise, but I can offer a perspective on the origins of the crisis. How we got here is all obvious enough.

People ate too much meat. People loved meat. Try to argue otherwise.

You can't feed billions of people hamburgers, chicken wings, bacon, for three meals a day, every day. You can't chop up rain forests and pave over prairies and drain wetlands and expect the planet to keep humming along like it had for millions of years.

If I had a projector and a laser pointer, I'd show slides of mountains beheaded for mining operations. I'd glide the glowing red dot over the flat tops of those mountains. Then I'd show a slide depicting how the ecological pyramid became an ecological plateau. These images are symbols of one another. Environmental degradation meant apex predators in every ecosystem were picked off, gone. Your mountain lions, gray wolves, polar bears. There wasn't the ecosystem to support them. Your mid-tier species went next: rabbits and iguanas and turkey vultures and so on. Biomes bottomed out. Natural disasters hurried the process along—wildfires, droughts, floods, heat waves—as did the oil spills, chemical leaks, nuclear meltdowns, fracking sinkholes. Disease was rampant, everything out of balance. Corn crops failed. Soybeans withered. Bacteria exploded the bellies of fish and made factory-farm chickens go mad. Pretty soon you're trying to take the edge off impending civilizational collapse by visiting the local zoo with your grandchildren—but nearly all the enclosures are empty. *This*

video shows the orangutans who once lived in this cage, a sign
says. Or else: *This is the last koala on earth.* What a horror, to
see the last of anything. What an honor as well. I remember I
couldn't look away from the exhibits. There is a preciousness
that precedes annihilation. One becomes greedy with a need
to look and look and look, even as one trembles.

I digress. Returning to the trajectory for civilizational
decline: People kept their pet dogs and cats in some countries,
for some time, but when the famine worsened, household pets
were typically killed or released into the wild, which led to
more ecosystem issues. People couldn't feed themselves, let
alone Spot or Whiskers. Some households ate their pets, I'm
sure they did—though few owned up to it, at least at first.
People are all about propriety, until they aren't. Hence the
mid-decade federal firearm requisitions.

That was the one wise decision the U.S. government made—
the gun collections—during their campaign to curb widespread
violence and unrest among the starving masses.

It wasn't enough, of course. People were hungry. They grew
hungrier by the day.

The gene therapy was supposed to be a compassionate
option. "The Treatment," it was colloquially called: a silver
bullet for the global famine, available to the masses via a single
injection. If humans are defined by their omnivorous appetites,
why not widen the palate? People could eat certain plants, but
what if they could eat an even wider variety of vegetation?
Digest densely fibrous matter like a cow? State officials rea-
soned that billions of people could be saved from starvation if
they ate grass—because, as it turned out, we had a hell of a lot
of grass. In many suburban areas, homes had their own plots.
Even in the midst of ecological collapse, grass grew along high-

way medians. It coated golf courses and playing fields. It circled our state capitals. Before the last universities closed, grass
marked the focal point of higher education. All those verdant
campus quads—I used to look upon them from my classroom
windows with such disdain. To think: the vast sums institutions
spent on their lawned appearances, while letting so much else
crumble into disarray. Lawns were prioritized above learning,
justice, ecological stability. We, as a human civilization, had
invested in growing millions of acres of grass, though grass
supported little life. All that irrigation and fertilizer, for what?
The plant was a mono-crop with almost no function save for
aesthetics: a throwback to English estates. The landed gentry.

Again, I digress.

When government officials realized there was this secret
crop everywhere, they became optimistic. *What if the grass
supported us?* they wondered. Americans, they told themselves,
had always solved problems. And America—our then-president
announced—would do it again. We would solve humanity's
greatest challenge yet.

Scientific testing was rushed, obviously. There was pressure
to deliver a solution at breakneck speed. Early recipients of
the treatment had little idea what they were getting into, they
simply didn't want to be hungry any longer. Early on, there
were also more regulations and protective procedures in place.
There was plenty of grass to eat as well.

At first, the treatment seemed to work. It seemed, moreover,
to be a miracle cure. This message was spread by a massive
media push: op-eds, billboards, talk shows, celebrity endorse-
ments, designer clothes with pro-treatment slogans. Though
girded with my academic skepticism, even I found the treatment to be the stuff of miracles. The science seemed solid—

better than solid: it seemed revolutionary. The treatment's gene therapy extended human digestive capacities but also improved numerous health metrics. People diagnosed with otherwise incurable illnesses started getting the treatment to improve their overall health. It was said to resolve IBS, stomach cancer, liver disease, among other maladies. The treatment elevated muscle mass: people became stronger. People's skin cleared. Their hair grew thicker, shinier. Everyone thought this made sense. Weren't plant-based diets what doctors had praised for years? All that green: it was good for us.

Humanity, it seemed, had defeated the odds again. We'd won—nature be damned.

Naturally, not everything turned out as originally envisioned. The treatment did not address the famine's underlying issue: capitalism's gaping maw. The treatment, for all its powers, did not address global disparities in wealth, centuries of corruption, exploitation, oppression of all kinds. The treatment did not change the reality that humans are, at their core, greedy, selfish, and cruel. It did not change the fact that the poor, the incarcerated, and the desperate were largely pushed to undergo the treatment first. The wealthy had access to resources unavailable to others—namely power. Unrest was imminent. Civilizational collapse assured. Any historian could have predicted that. Though, of course, no one thought to ask me.

Marmalade

Back in our subterranean living quarters, my parents are whisper-shrieking in the room next to mine. The fire from the biogas explosion is out, and the Eaters are gone, and the compound wall is fixed—even the electrical shock system is repaired—but the situation can't return to what it was before the Eater break-in. That's what Professor Henrietta Rubenstein told me and all the other youth: No going back. No return to normal. We would not gather in the Learning Cabin on this day, she said, because the end was imminent and she was working on an Extremely Urgent Project. She told us not to bother her.

Since I was still trying to be helpful, I did as I was told.

Holed up in my family's living quarters, though, Zoë and I are restless. Since Zoë is a stuffed animal, she doesn't move unless I move her, but I can sense a jitteriness beneath her fur. Neither of us can concentrate with my parents whisper-shrieking in the other room. All compound residents' living quarters are cut like pie pieces from the circular levels of the underground silo. Families get bigger pie pieces; solo people get smaller ones. For my family of three people, our pie piece is segmented into smaller sections that separate our bedrooms from the multifunction space. Zoë suggests listening to my parents through my bedroom door—and so I press my ear and her furry head against it. My parents' conversation comes into focus.

They are worried about the Eaters. Because a group of one hundred Eaters could mean even more Eaters. Too many Eaters. And if the Eaters break in again, they might turn on us when there's nothing else left to eat.

"What then?" says Ma. "Where would we go?"

"We'll find another compound," says Daddy.

"We don't know if anyone else is out there—let alone whether they'd let us join."

"We always figure things out."

"Do we?"

There is a long pause, like a huge hole in their conversation. At the bottom of the hole is The Thing We Don't Talk About. My parents tiptoe around the hole, though it is there with them—with us—always: the secret they think I was too young to understand.

"That was the best choice at the time," Daddy tells Ma, tiptoeing up to the edge of what's unsaid. "That was the best we could do. That was all we could do. You know that."

Ma says something I can't hear. She mentions my name.

"Marmalade is young," Daddy says. "She just needs to—"

He doesn't finish because Ma slams the door of our family unit and Goes Away To Be Alone.

In the past, when Ma did this, she'd go topside to sit with the tomato plants, her baseball cap pulled low. She liked these plants best, she once explained to me, because the bright red fruits reminded her of Christmas ornaments, and ornaments reminded her of the good times before the famine—back when families gathered together for holidays, and people only got upset about minor issues, such as someone showing up late to a party or two people gifting the same sweater.

But there are no more tomato plants for her to sit beside. No more beans or carrots, either. The Eaters mowed everything down.

Daddy shuffles around our family's living quarters after Ma leaves; he walks with a limp because he hurt his knee, years ago, during our journey to the compound. His tendon snapped like a brittle rubber band. Sometimes the pain gets so bad he can't sleep. If we ever had to make a long trek again, he'd struggle. He has said our family could leave the compound any time we wanted, but that's just a nice idea. I wonder if it is hurting him now: the knee, or the idea of walking on the knee.

Or something else—something to do with me.

This isn't a new worry. I've never told anyone except Zoë, but more than anything I worry that someday my parents will leave me behind. They might decide I'm never going to be anything more than a disappointment. A reminder of bad memories. A burden.

I'm so busy worrying that when Daddy swings open the door to my sleeping section, Zoë and I barely have time to bounce back from our listening spot.

Daddy gives me a grimace-smile, as if the skin on his face is frozen stiff. His hair is gray and sparse, though he is not an old man but the age of a dad. He sits on the edge of my bunk and—like everything is normal—asks if I have any jokes.

"I do not," I say, though I have lots of jokes and usually jump at the chance to tell them. Instead, I ask a serious question. I ask what is going to happen to us, since the compound's food supply is all eaten.

"Well, not *all* of it," says Daddy. "There are the fungi trays down in sector five. Maybe we'll get a decent crop of lion's mane? And there are the tilapia, along with the aquaponic lettuce. There's a little of last season's grain . . ."

He trails off. He knows, like I know, that this isn't enough food for everyone to survive long-term. To survive, people and food stores and time-until-harvest need to align. There's an equation involved. Not that I know much about equations. We don't do math in the Learning Cabin because Professor Henrietta Rubenstein says an overemphasis on STEM created an imbalance in civilizational prioritization. Only the humanities—specifically history—will help us understand our own inevitabilities. And she would know because she's very old—the oldest person in the compound—with cloud-white hair and pruned skin and the grumpiness of many years piled on top of one another.

What I mean to say is: Food is a path to the future. Without it, you drop off a cliff.

I remember what it was like to be almost-dropped—me, Daddy, and Ma all hanging on by our fingers and toes—during the hard times before we found the compound. This was right after what happened to my brother, when Ma had all bad days and no good ones. Back then, we were so hungry we dug into rotting logs looking for grubs; we ate the skinny rats that scampered through abandoned cities. We wandered from place to place, looking for somewhere we could pause longer than a few days. A safe place. A place to live. For a while, it seemed as though we'd never find such a place, especially after Daddy hurt his knee. We all got so thin we could count our individual bones and see the secret architecture of our insides, which was scary and fascinating at the same time—discovering how delicate we were underneath our skin.

Zoë reminds me that because she is a stuffed animal, she doesn't have any bones; not everyone does.

Against my better judgment, I feel a joke rising in me— *What makes a skeleton smile?*—and I open my mouth to tell Daddy. But he interrupts.

"I know what you're thinking," he says. "The situation looks really challenging. But situations have been challenging before and we've figured them out. Remember when the tornado passed through last April? Or when bandits showed up a couple years ago? The compound got through those hardships.

And we'll put our heads together again. Jackson said the group will have an after-dinner meeting. He's a good guy, Jackson. Smarter than he looks. He figured out how to scare off the Eaters with that explosion."

I say nothing.

"There are a lot of smart people here. We'll figure something out."

Daddy is trying to sound confident and unworried, but I can hear him questioning himself as he speaks. Because our problem, the problem of What To Eat, is not new. This is a problem people have been trying to solve for a while.

This is the problem that led to the Eaters in the first place.

Daddy stands up, stretches. He suggests I take a rest, since the day has been action-packed, and the compound meeting will take place after dinner—but I am not tired. There is so much I'd like to ask. Maybe this isn't the right time to ask, but maybe there is also never a good time. I squeeze Zoë and think about my brother, his face blurry in the back rooms of my memory. I think about Ma and The Thing We Don't Talk About. I wonder where she went to be alone, if not to the tomato plants. I wonder why she needs so badly to get away from everyone—from me. I wonder if, soon, she is going to leave me behind. If Daddy will leave, too, and if then I'll be all by myself.

When Daddy starts toward the doorway, I blurt: "Wait—"

He freezes, turns to me with a nervous face. He's scared, too, of what I might say. I open my mouth to speak, but my jaw just hangs open: an empty cavern. I can't think of how to put all my fears into the right words. Or maybe I'm not brave enough to do so.

Enough time passes that Daddy gives me another grimace-smile. With false cheer, he says: "Tilapia tonight—that should be good."

Then he shuts the door behind him.

I am alone again—alone with Zoë and the big emptiness of too many questions: the bottomless pit of The Thing We Don't Talk About.

Jackson, President-of-the-Month

I was going down.

Down, down, into the compound's underground complex: the former missile silo that plunged deep into the earth. A spiral staircase descended through the silo's middle, corkscrewing through each of its fifteen levels, so that if you walked down too many levels in one shot, you got dizzy.

I was dizzy—though not just because I was traveling into the silo. I'd felt dizzy ever since the Eater break-in. I was the compound's leader, whether I liked it or not. I'd have to guide decisions that would make or break the community. But how to not break it? The compound meeting was after dinner; I didn't have a plan. There wasn't a clear path forward. There wasn't a clear path to anywhere except toward a lot of hardship. And I was about to be blamed. I'd checked and double-checked the compound constitution to see if I could get out of my leadership duties.

I couldn't.

We had to respect the random lottery that elected monthly leaders. That randomness kept power balanced. Balance was what had kept us going for so long—longer than any other compound, as far as we knew—because without it, people fell into totalitarian corruption or anarchic disarray.

Not that I knew much about either of those things.

I was just a biogas technician.

I was just a guy named Jackson.

I descended deeper into the silo, then turned onto a wrap-around corridor that connected the level's living quarters. My dizziness intensified, though I'd paused the corkscrewing descent. Reilly-Kate's door was one of several on this floor. Her living quarters were smaller than some, because she—like me—was single.

It was lucky, I told myself, that no one was loitering in the corridor. I could talk to Reilly-Kate about the gun and nobody would hear. We could keep the issue between us. In that way, I could fix at least one issue at hand. I'd explain how the weapon was a breach in compound rules—and rules kept us safe. Rules kept us going. If a person had a deadly weapon in the compound, well, that unbalanced power. And unbalance was deadly. Unbalance could ruin us all. We had to stick together as a collective if we were going to get through our impending food shortage. We had to follow protocol. We had to follow the system now more than ever.

Reilly-Kate's door loomed. It looked like every door in the silo: The steel surface painted gray-blue. Doorknob polished. Peephole like a tiny fish eye. I adjusted my tool belt, appreciating its anchoring heaviness around my waist: a reminder that most problems just needed the right implement to be fixed. The right wrench. The right pliers. The right flat-head screwdriver. With Reilly-Kate, I'd be compassionate yet firm in my request that her gun be relinquished. My tone would be my tool. Along with my logic.

I raised a fist to knock, rehearsing my words: *You know, Reilly-Kate, it was a single small leak in the compound's cistern that led to the Eater break-in. A tiny trickle of water was found to have dribbled under the fence. This moisture must have helped germinate a seed in the wasteland outside the compound. A single blade of grass could have attracted the Eaters—made them desperate to get inside our walls. A tiny leak. A single blade. That's all it takes. So we have to do better. We can't let small slip-ups cause big problems, which is why your weapon needs to—*

"Jackson?"

Reilly-Kate strode toward me along the walkway; she wasn't in her room at all.

"What are you doing here?" Her long tanned legs spiked closer, her blond hair glowing beneath the silo's fluorescent lighting, her voice ringing loud—too loud—magnified by the hollow hallway. "Are you talking to yourself?"

Heat rose in my neck. I glanced around, checking that no one had poked their head out of their living quarters. Seen me there.

"Listen"—I lowered my voice, hoping Reilly-Kate would do the same "it's like the leak from the cistern. One slipup and the Eaters got to us. The thing is, we have to follow our rules. Because once one rule is overturned, others will collapse and—"

"Why are you really here, *Jackson?*"

She spoke even louder, her beauty-queen face twisting terribly, exquisitely.

"Worried you won't be able to handle things, *Jackson?*"

My neck burned. Sweat drenched my body, made my palms grease-slick.

"Or," said Reilly-Kate, "are you worried you won't be able to handle me?"

She threw her head back and laughed: her voice high-pitched and whinnying.

"Did you come to sweep me off my feet, *Jackson*? To use your presidential privileges?"

Footsteps sounded in the corridor, along with the click of opening doors. I fled. I must have made some reply, but maybe I was too much of a coward to do even that. Reilly-Kate's laughter echoed after me as I hurried deeper into the silo, running down the corkscrew staircase as if I could outrun my own stupid human desire: the fact that I was as much a breach in the compound's system as Reilly-Kate's gun.

What had I really, secretly, hoped would happen? That she would invite me into her room? That I'd press my body on top of hers, like I had, briefly, during the biogas explosion?

I hurried down through more levels of living quarters.

I descended past the compound's empty lounge—its dartboard unspeared, playing cards undealt, Ping-Pong table un-ponged—and then past the gym, with its old dumbbells and bench press sitting unlifted in the dark.

I went past the level housing the fungi trays, where mushrooms mushroomed with aching slowness beneath grow lights.

I went past the aquaponics sector, pausing at the hopeful prospect of easing my brain with a little fishing—I could dangle a string in a tank, let my mind drift—but when I peered among the tanks, I saw Steph Lowell crying next to a filtration unit. Even with her baseball cap pulled low, her face was visibly red. Her body shook with sobs. From the doorway, I felt her sorrow sloshing outward, lapping at my feet. Steph was a friend—she had been kind to me on many occasions—but I couldn't bring myself to go to her. I couldn't even offer comfort.

I was a failure to my constituents.

I went deeper, beyond the silo's storage units, past a decommissioned generator, old and broken equipment. Compound residents rarely descended to these lowest levels. My pace slowed. The air was stuffier down here: musty and stale. Lights flickered. Moisture dripped to puddles on the floor. Wires dangled. Rust ravaged the walls. These bottom levels looked more like the original missile silo than a refurbished survivalist compound.

Maybe I could hide out here, I thought, let the others deal with everything. Then I wouldn't be blamed when things went wrong.

And if things went right, people might forgive me.

But what kind of leader would that make me? I leaned against a damp wall, my forehead meeting a slime-slick surface, trying to quell my dizziness. In a dim corner, a sump pump hummed, busy with the water pooling on the floor.

"My fellow Americans . . ."

At first, I thought I'd hallucinated the voice; reverberating through the lowest silo chambers, it was as unfathomable as a whale song, but also as familiar as a dream.

". . . It's good to be here, good to be back, thank you . . ."

I descended another level and the voice grew louder. Then it dawned on me: the voice belonged to the actual former president. He lived down here. He had for years. His presidential aide went topside to collect meals, but the aide's movements were conducted with such brisk regularity they'd become invisible amid the compound's daily functioning.

". . . a great honor to stand before . . ."

In the dim light, I could not yet see the actual former president, though his voice was amplified and omnipresent in the vast hollow chamber. A rage welled up within me. This liar-in-chief. This selfish, arrogant asshole. His leadership had gotten humanity into the mess with the Eaters. And because of that, he was—in a roundabout way—the reason I was stuck in my current position: forced to steer a community through an impossible problem.

He had asked for his leadership role. I hadn't.

". . . And it is in times of hardship that we . . ."

My hands tightened into fists. A fluorescent light flickered brighter—and I finally saw the president at the far end of the silo chamber. He wore a rumpled suit, which may have fit when he arrived at the compound but now hung loosely on his scrawny body. His skin was pale—semitranslucent, blue-veined—like that of an albino cave fish. He paced behind a stack of crates meant to resemble a podium. Rows of folding chairs faced him. In one chair sat the presidential aide, who held a notepad and periodically asked the president questions.

They were doing a mock press conference; maybe that's what they'd been doing down here for years.

My fury billowed and bulged, and I started toward the former president, not sure what I would do, but sure that I would at least give the man a piece of my mind.

". . . It's time to rise up, to meet our destiny as Americans . . ."

Yet as I drew closer—my fists clenched—the meaning of the former president's words slipped past the sharp edges of my anger. His rhetoric swam around in the dim chamber, echoed in my head, shaking free memories of his speeches during those last weeks of normal-ish life, before the Internet stopped working, along with cell service and TVs, back when he'd broadcast messages of hope and resilience in the face of hard times. I'd listened to those speeches in my living room—back when I'd had a living room, along with an armchair and an ottoman, and a stack of *Field & Stream* piled on a coffee table.

". . . I call upon our great past as we face . . ."

I was filled with longing for those bygone comforts, despite myself. My fists loosened and my whole body relaxed, the actual former president's rhetoric riding through my bloodstream, carrying the numbing bliss of optimism and exceptionalism.

I collapsed into one of the folding chairs.

I listened.

Presidential Press Conference

Q: Mr. President, would you be willing to offer your perspective on the current state of American life?

A: Gladly. Thank you, thank you. Yes, what I want to say to America—to Americans everywhere—is that we have always been a bright light against oppression. We have been a dogged flame in the gloomy halls of tyranny.

Q: Are we still such a flame, given that—

A: This moment is no different. If anything, we burn brighter than ever. We burn for freedom. We burn for the future that is ours to claim. In times like this, we must remember only what it means to be American: who we are and who we aren't.

Q: Mr. President, there are those who say the so-called Eaters aren't who we are. This side argues that Eaters are no longer human. Care to comment?

A: As you know, I am a man of faith. I am a man who stands humbly before God, as well as before the American people. I am a man who knows I *cannot* know the full depth and purpose of His design. Regarding those who have received the gene therapy for digestive enhancement, what is clear is that the resulting changes are psycho-physical. Whether the changes are soulful is for God to judge, not me.

Q: Mr. President, are there any updates on whether the treatment is reversible?

A: If there is an update, it is that we, the American people, continue to stand tall in the face of adversity. We hold our heads high. We will triumph as we have so many times before, guided by the light of our ideals in the face of hardship.

Q: Mr. President, is there anything else you'd like to add?

A: Americans were put on Earth to lead the charge of progress. Let us claim that God-given destiny. Let us meet the future we were promised . . .

Henrietta Rubenstein, G. H. Gray Professor Emerita of Mesopotamian History

Even early on, when there was still a functional government and a semblance of civil society, a substantial debate raged on the ethics of euthanizing Eaters. I cannot presume to lecture on their origins without noting this point. *Euthanasia* was batted like a shuttlecock between emergency and moral reasoning. Because right away, Eaters started escaping from their original zoned enclosures. They roamed widely, eating what they weren't supposed to eat. There wasn't a coherent framework for whether Eaters could be deemed people, and therefore trespassers subject to Stand Your Ground laws. Or whether they should be considered a protected species with animal innocence. After all, when Eaters entered private property, they did so without the conscious intention to harm. They were just hungry. No, they were more than hungry: they were starving. That was the issue, scientists and government officials discovered. Citizens who got the treatment could live on grass and other plant matter, but they needed to consume massive quantities to remain pacified.

Eating was all the Eaters could think about. They stopped bothering to stand and walk and talk; they spent the majority of their time in a hunched four-limbed posture, chewing and swallowing, endeavoring to fill their bellies. Did this mean they had become animals, and were therefore no longer human? Did they have souls? Emotions? Were they even truly alive?

As far as anyone could tell, Eaters did not die of natural causes. When Eaters could not find food, they did not weaken; rather, they became hungrier. They could be deliberately "put down"—and some were—though this prompted a wave of outrage. But what was to be done, people also wondered, about their insatiable appetites? One school of thought proposed that Eaters were, in fact, *already* dead. Their ravenous consumption of plant matter was an example of reflexive postmortem biomechanics. Such behavior had been observed in certain insect species whose bodies were overtaken by a parasitic fungus. Perhaps something similar had happened to Eaters, given the largely understudied ramifications of the gene therapy that had created them.

In that last year, before everything truly collapsed, the intelligentsia hotly debated this and other questions. There were essays, public debates, artworks produced "in dialogue" with the issue. One of the last exhibitions at the Guggenheim Museum, as I recall, featured the work of an Argentinian ceramicist, who used a special casting process to create lifelike replicas of distended digestive tracts—a comment on what it meant to "stomach" our current reality. There was the New York Philharmonic's desperate final performance on the grassless mud-slick that was Central Park. They played Schubert's "Ave Maria," as I recall. It was all very *Titanic*—foolish and admirable at the same time. What did it matter, in the end, what the intelligentsia thought about Eaters? What constituted a soul and whether the Eaters had one? Whether it was kinder to kill them? To kill ourselves? Because in the end, I'm sorry to say, many of the intelligentsia resorted to this latter approach—that is, if starvation didn't take them. Those most cerebral of citizens had, in the end, to contend with their own base corporeality.

My position has always been this: one might as well ask if we *non*-Eaters had souls, given what we'd done to the Earth. To one another.

As societal structures collapsed further, remaining scientists holed up in their labs, desperate to determine whether the effects of the treatment could be altered or reversed. They speculated that Eaters might have maintained more cognitive abilities if not for the intensity of their hunger; the impulse to eat overwhelmed their brains. Early test subjects had sufficient lab-provided plant matter to maintain more normal faculties. Subsequent iterations did not.

What happened to those last scientists, I cannot tell you. Communications networks would fail in due course. My guess is that those scientists eventually turned the treatment upon themselves: the gene therapy offering an amnesiac balm for the consequences of innovation.

Meanwhile, the last vestiges of society disintegrated. With supply chains disrupted and titans of agribusiness largely collapsed, shelves emptied in supermarkets. Food pantries shuttered. Most home gardens couldn't support their gardeners: What good was a week's worth of cucumbers? A single bucket of beans? With no food in your home and no way to feed your family, what choice did you have? The treatment remained easy to obtain when other resources weren't. There were clinics in most cities, at-home kits available in rural areas. Despite knowing what would happen—the side effects of becoming an Eater—people still opted for the treatment. They looked outside their windows and saw oak trees shaggy with Spanish moss. They saw ornamental agave plants outside their condos. They saw the rolling hills of golf courses—ecstatically green—and their mouths watered.

That's how hungry they were. That's what hunger does.

If you'll indulge me on one additional point: it is worth noting that everyone at this compound ultimately chose *not* to get the treatment. Has that been the glue that has held us together this long? That baseline fact? An internal insistence on maintaining our humanity? Or, perhaps, a willingness to endure this era's inhumanity? Every person here had the opportunity to get the treatment. We all watched others get it. Or we watched others starve. And yet here we are. Because each person in this compound had to provide a rationale for admittance beyond its walls. Everyone had to have a purpose. That was the governing premise of this small society from the beginning. Dominique, for instance, is a nurse practitioner. Andy is an electrician. Even Reilly-Kate, with her pageant-girl looks, grew up fixing cars with her mechanic uncles; her "talent" in a Miss America competition was changing oil, if you can believe it.

And me?

One laughs at the thought of it: an old academic at the end of the world. I've never changed a vehicle's oil, or treated a wound, or tended a garden, in all my life. I spent my years hunched over books and peering into computer screens. And now my body is brittle, tired, of little use. This compound has certainly turned away others with bodies like mine. I saw it happen with my own bespectacled eyes.

This group decided to let me stay here, in this compound, because I agreed to teach their children. That was my function: to be a conduit of knowledge. The compound residents elected to send their children to a "Learning Cabin" with the idea of carrying civilization into the future, believing these children could be the vessels. Yes: these children of chaos, who have witnessed so much atrocity it hums under their skin, ricochets around their eyes. I am no psychologist, but how can these children be our future? They are traumatized. Troubled. They barely know how to hold a pencil and prefer to turn writing implements on one another as weapons. I've observed them commit acts of random, merciless harm to one another when their parents and guardians were not watching: snapped finger bones, burned flesh, hair wrenched from scalps. These children have learned stealth. They have learned the opposite of trust. They tease and they torment. Perhaps they are the future for that reason. It grieves me. How can one expect humanity to continue with this population at the forefront?

Marmalade

At six fifteen p.m., Pinky calls for everyone to come and eat tilapia in the main hall—a meal that should be a joy-filled feast. Instead, everyone sits and chews. No one takes second helpings, and they definitely do not take thirds. We all know how limited our supplies are—even the littlest kids know. I try to eat slowly, letting the flakes of fish crumble on my tongue. Unfortunately, eating slowly makes it more obvious that tilapia doesn't have any taste. There are no herbs left in the garden to season the fish. The Eaters ate every bit of parsley, mint, and even the dill.

But the lack of herbs is the compound's smallest problem. This could be our last decent meal for a while. Soon we'll be eating bugs and fungus. Or nothing.

My stomach clenches. I know what it's like to go hungry. We all do.

There is no one with whom to share these thoughts, though, except Zoë—who perches beside my plate. Daddy went to look for Ma and hasn't come back. I feel all alone, even in the crowded dining hall.

I squeeze Zoë. I'm about to tell her a joke—to help lighten the situation—but one of the other youth notices.

"Hey, nutso," he calls.

A fork zings past my face and clatters onto the floor. All the other youth laugh.

"Talking to your stuffed animal again?"

The speaker is a boy named O'John. He has eyebrows like dark smears of charcoal, and sneering pale pink lips, and many friends sitting all around him. Hurt rises in my throat, hot and sour as throw-up. I grip my own fork and consider hurling it back at him. Would that be brave of me to do? Would it show my parents that I'm more capable than they think? I imagine howling at the other youth that they are lucky to have friends gathered together: all those people with whom to share jokes, and whisper secrets, and ask the questions they need to ask to become the people they want to become.

Without realizing it, I have picked up Zoë and squeezed her too hard—her plush body crushed in my fist.

I'm hurting her, and she didn't do anything to deserve that hurt.

Sorry, I whisper to Zoë, even with the other youth watching and giggling to themselves. *I didn't mean it.*

I turn my attention to my last flavorless bites of fish. Around me, the dinner is wrapping up; people rise from their seats, carry their plates to the dish station. No one has left any food scraps on their plate, so the dish cleaning goes fast. Some people head topside to the compound's courtyard to set up for our Big Meeting. We always go there for our meetings because there's room for everyone to stand in a circle and see every other person's face.

The other youth have started arm-wrestling; they are no longer flinging forks and taunts in my direction. In a way, though, it's worse to be forgotten by them. Being bullied at least meant I was noticed.

Again, I look for my parents, but they still haven't appeared.

A gnawing feeling opens in me, though I've finished my whole dinner. I can't stop thinking about The Thing We Don't Talk About: the big emptiness of all my unanswered questions.

Will the Eaters come back?

Will people leave if they do?

Does this mean my parents will—

The last question is too difficult to even think all the way through. All I can do is take my dishes to the dish station, then follow the flow of people heading topside for the meeting. Maybe my parents will show up soon, I tell myself. They've always praised civic engagement.

Outside, the evening sky blazes orange-pink. I scan the circle of people gathered in the courtyard. Everyone murmurs to one another, glancing at Jackson, who paces at the circle's center. The only people missing are those assigned to the compound's security team—and my parents.

My gnawing feeling grows larger.

Jackson calls the meeting to order. He has a strange expression, his smile twitchy, too big. He fidgets with his tool belt. I don't think he likes being President-of-the-Month—but I've always liked him. When we pass each other in the compound's corridors, he says hi to Zoë and asks how she is doing, which I appreciate and Zoë appreciates as well.

"Thank you, thank you," says Jackson. "It's good to be here. Good to be back. Thank you. Yes, what I want to say to America—to Americans everywhere—is that we have always been a bright light against oppression. We have been the shining star in the darkest of hours . . ."

He doesn't sound like himself and everyone notices. They make questioning faces, dart their eyes at one another around the circle. Jackson keeps going anyway, launching into the official steps of the compound's Meeting Protocol, which involves a group recitation of the constitutional oath to protect and uphold the community.

Still my parents are missing.

The gnawing inside me worsens. I start to think: Maybe my parents are going to stay missing. Maybe they've already left the compound and abandoned me here.

". . . Now, I'm confident," says Jackson, "that America will rise again. We will triumph over evil and . . ."

Pinky's brow furrows as Jackson keeps talking like not-

Jackson. Lei twists his hat in his hands. Sergio flexes his biceps, deflates. Only Reilly-Kate seems relaxed. She smirks, reshoulders a big black duffel bag that she has brought to the meeting.

"... We were chosen by a higher power ..."

My parents have left, I think, because I'm no good; because they've finally realized they should have left me behind a long time ago. Because they are still thinking of my brother and a wrong decision made all those years ago.

My eyes start to swim, tearful, and I hug Zoë. I step back from the meeting circle, trying to think of a joke that will distract us—make the world bearable, at least for a moment—but then I notice Professor Henrietta Rubenstein has stepped back from the circle as well. She looks grumpy, which is normal. During our lessons at the Learning Cabin—even when the youth are settled down—she often presses her lips together, the wrinkles on her face rippling with dissatisfaction. This evening, though, she looks especially grumpy. Her lips purse tighter as Jackson talks. Then, as if she can't stand to listen any longer, she ducks away from the group and hurries across the compound's shadowy topside.

I follow her. Maybe, I tell myself, I can ask her about where my parents might have gone, and what I should do now, and what will happen with the Eaters—or maybe I can ask about The Thing We Don't Talk About.

For an old woman, though, Professor Henrietta Rubenstein moves surprisingly fast. Dressed in all black, she's hard to see with the light fading. I dodge around the raised garden beds— vegetation-less—as well as the biogas units, the cistern, with Zoë tucked under my arm. But by the time I reach the shadowy entrance to the Learning Cabin, I can't tell which way she's gone.

"Professor," I call into the twilight. "Professor Rubenstein . . ."

She doesn't hear me. Or else, she has decided not to hear. Maybe she needs to work on her Urgent Project, I think — though this doesn't change the terrible feeling of being ignored by yet another person.

"Professor," I try again anyway. "I know I never raise my hand in class, but that doesn't mean I don't want to be brave — that doesn't mean I'm not trying. I know you might not see that. I know my parents might not see that. But I am trying. I'm trying so hard."

No answer.

Out beyond the compound walls, the sky deepens to violet streaked with pink. On another evening, these colors might have filled me with awe, but today I only feel empty. I wonder what it means when someone you love is both gone and not gone; when an absence is a hole so huge you're afraid you'll fall in. I wonder what it means to be brave when everything you do seems to make a situation worse.

I feel so hollow that when a bang rings out in the compound, the sound seems to echo inside me.

Another bang: a gunshot.

There's the sound of footsteps, and the security team rushes past me toward the courtyard. Shouts break out. Reilly-Kate's voice rises sharp and insistent, so that I can hear it even from where I'm standing all the way on the edge of the compound.

"We gotta make choices," she yells. "Tough ones, but important ones. 'Cause we got to eat."

There is a shriek. I'm sure it comes from Ma; my parents must have gone to the meeting after all. Relief washes over me. If my parents are at the meeting, then they haven't left the compound, left me. But then I remember that my parents' being here won't change the fact that I'm a disappointment to them—that I've never been the daughter they'd hoped I'd be: a fact that breaks their hearts as well as mine.

I take a step toward the courtyard, then stop. More gunshots ring out. More shrieks. The noise reverberates in the hollowness inside me, rattling through my limbs until a shaky tremble reaches Zoë's furry body, clutched tightly in my hands. For a moment, the trembling makes it seem as if Zoë truly is alive. She quivers, her wings rustling like she's about to take flight.

I think about releasing her—just to see if she will.

Instead, because I'm nervous, I say: *What do you call a sixteen-year-old girl who carries around a stuffed animal?*

Zoë doesn't answer my joke, even as she quivers, more alive than she's ever been. All at once, I feel like my brother is nearby—like we could communicate to each other through Zoë as if she were a walkie-talkie. Like maybe I've been talking to him through Zoë this whole time.

You call that girl brave.

The answer to my joke arrives in a perfect punch line: not funny but right on time. I'm not sure if the answer is mine, or Zoë's, or my brother's, or if it came from somewhere else— the shouting in the courtyard is getting louder every second— but I decide where the answer came from doesn't matter. Because I realize the punch line might be true: I might be brave already. And realizing this helps me understand what I need to do.

With Zoë held under my arm, I hurry toward the outer edge of the compound. In less than a minute, I'm standing at the front gate. The security team isn't around because they ran to respond to the gunshots. The gate is locked, but I know how to

open it because Daddy once showed me the mechanics durin
a maintenance pass.

So I do.

A few more steps and I'm outside the compound.

The sun has nearly set, the landscape thickened with shadows that hide the humps and ridge of the old mountain range. At first, everything is motionless and dark. I blink, waiting for my eyes to adjust.

Then I see them.

The Eaters creep forward from the shadows, moving in their lumbering, four-limbed way as they approach the compound. Approach me.

I'm scared—but I also know that being brave means helping at the moment when you most want to run and hide. And I know how I can help.

The Eaters lumber toward the compound from every direction. The more my eyes adjust to the darkness, the more of them I see. There are hundreds. Maybe thousands. They cover the surface of the ground as if the earth is made of them.

When I take a few more steps beyond the compound, the Eaters look up.

All at the same time, they look at me and Zoë.

Henrietta Rubenstein, G. H. Gray Professor Emerita of Mesopotamian History

I have to hurry and finish writing this lecture—the lecture that will likely be my last. Not my best by any stretch, but my last. Perhaps *the* last lecture ever to be written on earth.

Who will find it, read it? Let me not get lost in such

...estions—not yet. Not while voices grow louder in the compound's courtyard: the beginning of the end.

Here we are.

One looks for blame, of course. In any tragedy, large or small, one seeks it out. Blame, though, is best applied broadly. Target-shooting cannot encompass the full scope of guilty actors. With respect to the Eaters, one could blame the nation's former president for his role in encouraging the deployment of widespread gene therapy—for creating these monsters— though really he was a pawn moved by larger forces. Corporate. Capitalist. Colonial. If not the Eaters, it would have been another terror. Terror and suffering were inevitable. If anything, blame belongs to his arrogant assumption that patriotic positivity could steamroll all obstacles. To have heard Jackson, only moments ago, repeating those same rhetorical flourishes—it turned my stomach. Because so much harm has already been caused by the unquestioned worship of progress: the presumption that good fortune awaits, will always await, without ever costing its inverse.

One could also blame the rich for this predicament; no matter the political system, the era, they make a clear target. And, truly, right up until the brink of collapse, the rich used their resources to evade responsibility. They believed that money could preserve them during the direst crisis, that it might pave a path to immortality. The rich were meticulous about health and nourishment, even as the rest of the world starved, struggled to stay upright. The rich had personal trainers. Six-pack abs. Bespoke triceps. Thick hair. Clear eyes. Glowing skin, their bodies supernaturally, artificially, youthful. The rest of the world boiled their leather belts, caught and ate the cockroaches they used to kill, jumped off buildings to escape the pain, got arrested just to have access to prison food, rioted until they were firebombed—all while the rich bickered over the best coffee brands. Some called themselves ethical for using the unsprayed kind. They valorized freshness. They believed they'd find salvation, despite the ties that bind us all. They weren't Eaters, but they, too, thought food could save them. They paid for whole blueberry bushes to be bulldozed from the earth and air-dropped into their walled estates so they could pluck the berries fresh for their morning's micronutrient-filled leafy-green smoothies. They playacted farm hamlets à la Marie Antoinette, believing the end of civilization meant only an end for everyone else.

Was this mess all their fault?

Fault is a crack in the tectonic plate upon which we live. *Eat the rich*, people have said, as if that offers a true solution rather than the perpetuation of barbarism. I think of the wealthy couple who once owned this missile silo, this land. They were the ones who refurbished the facility, equipped it with much of the infrastructure we continue to use. The couple was killed, of course. Their security guards turned on them. No one had guns, but humans have been killing one another without guns for millennia.

And millennia from now? I wonder if someone will dig up these pages. Or if I will have to eat this paper, as I have before. My words.

I am an old woman who has gone on living, despite it all.

We were multitudes, we were millions. We were consumers to the core. We were always doomed, perhaps—on a track toward annihilation. We are all culpable, that is my thinking.

ur planet evolved on the premise of interdependence, yet human beings have insisted upon exceptionalism. No system can save us. Because our systems will systemically fail.

Should I apologize to the future, then, on behalf of everyone?

I've written out this lecture so many times, but I'll never give it. Forgive me. I am an old academic trying to make sense of a nonsensical world. It is a miracle this compound has stayed functional as long as it has. Thirteen years—what a run! In all likelihood, this compound is the last of its kind: an outpost at the edge of extinction.

And yet, as I have said, to see the last something—be it a zoo-kept koala or a human community—is a privilege. A horrific privilege, but a privilege nonetheless.

Is that my role, then, to bear stoic witness to this end? I think of my academic colleagues, long dead. My own family—likely dead, too. I have often thought of joining them. I have wondered if it was cowardice not to.

Ah, there it is: gunshots in the courtyard.

So here we are, at humanity's final stand. The clock ticks.

It will be only a matter of minutes, I suspect, before violence fully consumes this populace—the violence that has hovered around the edges of the compound's walls, in its residents' hearts, this whole time. Kept at bay by a few arbitrary rules. By the paper-thin boundary of compliance. How breakable our humanity is. How fragile. My role will be to watch it shatter. I will not be surprised when it does. Because that is the burden I carry as one who has spent a lifetime studying the ways in which civilizations collapse. I know what is coming and I know that it cannot be stopped.

Jackson, President-of-the-Month

So there I was, watching Reilly-Kate march up and down in the courtyard. She looked good. Barbie-blond hair. Hunting vest. One missing tooth. She'd broken the compound's discussion protocol to yell that it was time for us to stop acting like pussies. Usually there'd be pushback against that kind of language— cursing cost a person a demerit—but the shock of Reilly-Kate's pronouncement kept anyone from responding.

"Y'all think you're heroes for starving?" she went on. "Those aren't people out there. Eaters are animals—animals who trashed our fucking food supply. Y'all gonna just sit there and take it? We could shoot these mutherfuckers and kill two birds with one stone."

I raised my hand to call for order, but Reilly-Kate wrenched open the duffel bag she'd brought to the meeting and pulled out the pistol I'd seen earlier that day. Then she pulled out handguns, shotguns, assault rifles, and several grenades.

Everyone gasped. Everyone started talking at once—and again I called for order—but Reilly-Kate spoke louder than anyone

"Think of Eaters like big game."

She smiled with the devilish sparkle of Miss America-- crowned late, but at last. What she meant was that we could shoot the Eaters and then eat them. That way they wouldn't invade the compound and we wouldn't starve because if we didn't do something, starvation was coming. And we all knew what it was like to fight over scraps.

"We don't have to starve though," said Reilly-Kate. "We've got unlimited meals right there, over the fence."

"Are you out of your mind?" screamed Steph, who'd just arrived at the meeting with her husband, her eyes red like she'd recently finished crying.

For a second, I thought Steph was going to attack Reilly-Kate, despite the guns. Her husband, Andy, grabbed her arms to hold her back. Steph wriggled against his grasp and Reilly-Kate smiled wider—revealing the place in her mouth where a tooth was missing: a dark hole in her beauty-queen face. She cocked the pistol. The other compound residents yelled for me to act.

JACKSON, they said, with their words and their eyes. DO SOMETHING.

My mind circled back to the old actual president, down in the bottom of the silo, giving his mock press conferences on repeat. I'd listened to him all afternoon, absorbing his rhetoric like a patriotic tonic until I felt strong enough to face the current situation. Then I'd carried his words with me up through the silo and to the compound meeting, where I'd hoped they might give everyone the courage we needed to move forward with our heads held high.

Maybe, I thought, I just needed to say those words again.

"My fellow Americans," I said, stepping between Reilly-Kate and Steph. "Now is the time to come together. To be the best versions of ourselves. To show—"

"Shut up, idiot," interrupted Reilly-Kate, before turning to the rest of the group. "Y'all know our fearless leader Jackson didn't mastermind the biogas explosion, right? It was a lucky accident. The Eaters triggered the explosion themselves. So there's no need to invest any authority in this loser. We need a new leader and a new plan. We need to get our fucking act together and get hunting."

The others jolted, their gazes leaping between me and Reilly-Kate.

"Is that true, Jackson?" said Pinky. "Did you lie to us about the explosion?"

"I didn't mean—"

"Honesty is a Core Value during presidential terms," said Dominique. "It's actually the main value. I mean, it wouldn't have been a big deal if you hadn't caused the explosion. But lying *is* a big deal."

I felt hot and cold all over. I staggered backward, pummeled by the disappointed scowls of my constituents. I realized, then, why the presidential rhetoric had been a lost cause—why the old president rehearsed and rehearsed but never ventured up the silo stairs. He never showed his face because his rhetoric, however elegantly expressed, meant nothing without substance behind it. Substance being courage and honesty and a selfless commitment to the cause.

He didn't have those qualities, and neither did I.

While I dry-heaved my horror, Reilly-Kate returned to her duffel bag of weapons. She pulled out two assault rifles, tossed one to Sergio, one to Lei. She nodded toward the compound's gate, motioning for them to follow her.

"Don't you dare," shrieked Steph, struggling to escape her husband's stronghold. "Don't you dare hurt them."

The two women locked eyes. It was my job to step in—but I'd lost all hope of ever being the leader the compound needed. Instead of intervening, I made myself small, drifting to the outskirts of the circle.

Reilly-Kate flipped her blond ponytail. To Steph, she said: "You think you're the only one with people out there? You think you're the only one who wonders?"

Steph didn't answer. She, like everyone present, knew Reilly-Kate was right. We all wondered. We all knew someone who'd gotten the treatment, either in desperation or in ignorance of its true effects, or occasionally by force. We all wondered if our brothers, mothers, neighbors, cousins, postal workers, frenemies, ex-girlfriends, priests, second-grade teachers, favorite baseball players, least favorite dentists, onetime plumbers, multiterm mayors, divorce lawyers, and reference librarians were out there, roaming the Earth, relentlessly chewing, tearing up everything they could find: every weed, leaf, blade of grass. It was a blessing, in a way, that the Eaters kept their heads down, close to the earth; the posture obscured their faces, made it harder to recognize them as individuals. We could pretend we didn't know who they were—who they'd been.

Reilly-Kate stepped closer to Steph, said: "You do wonder, don't you?"

Silence, as painful as a punch.

"Maybe that's all you think about."

Steph shrieked and wrenched free from Andy's grasp. She ran toward Reilly-Kate, her face red with fury and grief, and grabbed at the pistol. The pair wrestled over the gun, Steph's baseball cap getting knocked to the ground, Reilly-Kate's blond hair flying wild, while Andy and Sergio tried to pull the two women apart.

With a bang, the gun went off—a bullet zinging away into a dark corner of the courtyard.

Then everyone was yelling, no one following any of the compound's discussion protocols. Others wrestling as well: over guns, grievances, ideologies. People scratched and screamed. Swore at random. Even the children. I knew it was my job to call for order, but instead I closed my eyes and imag-

ined a pond lush with lily pads and croaking frogs and dragc
flies and weeping willows, creatures singing and spawning
hatching and hunting in the sunlight, and the rain, and the
shadows of the gentlest dusk, a rowboat in the middle of it all,
spinning and spinning.

The gun fired again, and I felt a burning sensation in my
side. I touched a patch of wetness above my tool belt. My legs
lost their strength and I slid to the ground. No one noticed,
though, because they were too busy fighting—or watching
Steph and Reilly-Kate fighting.

"You," spat Steph, "don't know anything about my life."

"Oh, but I do," shrieked Reilly-Kate. "It's plain as day to anyone here. You had a choice at one point, and now you're worried you made the wrong one."

The words shuddered through the crowd—made everyone
pause. We all understood. We all knew Reilly-Kate was talking
about Marmalade. Weirdo Marmalade. Needy, abnormal Marmalade. Sixteen years old and carrying around an old stuffed
bird like a toddler. Brain-addled. Broken. What if you could
only rescue one child and you picked the wrong one?

"It must be a disappointment," hissed Reilly-Kate at Steph,
"to end up with a daughter like that."

Then came more shouting. The bang-bang of guns shot
into the air. It occurred to someone that Marmalade ought not
to hear what was being said. Everyone's voices, though, had
started to sound far away. Across my collapsed body, a sweet
numbness flowed—like the chilly water of a burbling brook. I
pressed my hand to my wound again, the blood making my fingers slick. Nightfall had overtaken the compound's topside and
no one had remembered to turn on the courtyard lights—a
mistake in protocol. In the dimness, someone tripped over my

dy. They yelped, but their voice seemed distant. I had the sense that people were moving around me. People were saying my name as well as Marmalade's. By then, everyone had realized she wasn't at the meeting.

I felt sleepy. I felt an unexpected calm: after making so many mistakes, getting shot was awfully presidential.

"M?" called her father, and then louder: "Marmalade? Shit."

Marmalade

Beyond the compound fence, the world spreads out beautiful and big. I haven't been outside in years, not since me, Daddy, and Ma dragged our tired, dirty bodies up to the compound's gates, got lucky enough to secure a spot inside because Daddy knew about electricity and Ma was good at lying.

Back then—even then—a few trees stood tall in the surrounding area. Some living, some dead, their roots digging into the ground like fingers, holding the soil in place. As years passed, there were fewer and fewer trees, then no trees, or even weeds covering the hills. When you looked at the landscape from the watchtower, the ground ached bare.

Tonight, though, the ground is covered.

Eaters move toward the compound from every direction. The landscape has come alive with their bodies, lumbering and jostling toward me, all of them walking on their knuckles and feet—all of them getting closer.

I should be scared. The Eaters might attack me—that's what everyone says—and, certainly, a part of me does feel fear. But I also feel a buzzing rush of anticipation. I feel a way I haven't in years. Not since before The Thing We Don't Talk About.

Zoë rustles her furry wings, nervous and excited, too. Now

that I am outside the walls, the barrier between the past and the present has fallen away. In the big outside, I can better remember what it was like in The Time Before. I remember being tiny and frail. My whole family was tiny and frail—skinny and lumpy and hollow—but my brother was worse off, back when we lived in the city. He had a Very Bad Sickness. My parents couldn't get the doctor to help. I heard them in the kitchen at night talking, Daddy opening and closing our kitchen cupboards, as if food might suddenly appear. I left my room and went to my brother's room and lay down next to him on his bed. I told him stories. I'd found Zoë a week before—found her in an abandoned apartment next door, while I was scavenging for forgotten tubes of breath mints and stray cough drops—but it wasn't until that night that Zoë became important. Zoë helped tell my brother stories. He kept his eyes closed but I knew he was listening. I told him about feasts of golden fruit and sparkling fairy kingdoms. I told him about edible clouds and rocks made of candy. To make us both laugh, I told him jokes. *What do you call a cow that eats your grass? A lawn moo-er.* Eventually, I must have fallen asleep, because in the morning I was back in my bed and my brother was gone. My parents had taken him to a local clinic to get the treatment; they thought I didn't know, but I did. That's the secret they never talk about. They made my brother an Eater. This choice, for them, had been a Last Resort. A way to keep him alive and keep him from suffering. There'd been talk about the effects' being reversible, once the science was ready. People didn't fully understand what the treatment meant—or they didn't want to understand. The plan, I think, had been to have my brother stay in a facility that we could go and visit. He'd be more likely to survive if he got the treatment. It was a miracle cure, everyone said. The ene therapy solved other problems—other diseases—and let you eat any plant you wanted. Being an Eater kept a person alive.

Then, a series of bombings happened nearby. All of a sudden we were fleeing our home, our city, and it was just me, Ma, and Daddy—plus Zoë. And my parents were so heartbroken they could hardly speak and that's when I started talking even more to Zoë.

I walk farther from the compound—toward all the Eaters—with Zoë pressed against my chest. The Eaters rush up closer, almost reaching me, and I consider trying to count them. Then I laugh at myself for wanting to do something so silly. My laugh turns into a tremble. The Eaters all have their eyes fixed on me.

I hear voices faintly, and a quick peek over my shoulder reveals that almost everyone in the compound has their eyes on me as well. Pinky and Sergio and Lei and Dominique and the other youth stare out from the compound's open gate. Even Professor Henrietta Rubenstein has appeared. She looks at me with an expression I've never seen on her face—she's surprised. My parents are there, too. Ma looks terrified and it feels good to know she's worried about me; I'm not just one half of a bad decision. Daddy is yelling for me to come back. *M! M! M! Marmalade . . .*

Everyone looks scared for me. I don't want to give them One More Problem, since we have so much to figure out, but I don't stop moving toward the Eaters. I feel brave—which means that I'm afraid of what I'm doing but I'm doing it anyway. I once thought I needed to prove this to my parents—to the whole community—but now I see I only needed to prove it to myself.

The Eaters, the many thousands of them, move like a tide surging around me and Zoë.

I look for my brother.

I don't see him, but that doesn't mean he's not there.

More shouts ring out from the compound. My parents call for me to come back. Everyone calls for me to come back. They want me to return to the compound. They are scared the Eaters will eat me. They are scared to see it happen in front of their own eyes.

I don't turn back, though. I keep moving. The Eaters close in around my body like the ocean, crushing in on all sides. I can feel them smelling me. Snuffling and grunting, their hair swinging. They are shaggy and dirty, knuckles bloody from walking on their hands. I shut my eyes. I'm nervous, but I also keep thinking: The Eaters are just like me. Just as lonely. Just as uncertain of their roles. I've let go of Zoë and she is caught up among them, as if on a wave. The Eaters press closer. They are all so hungry. We all are. We are empty, hollowed out. Starving, and not just for food. I reach forward and pet one of the Eaters, and then another. They nuzzle me back. I giggle, because their faces tickle. I throw my arms around one of their necks. For the first time in a long time, I feel full.

Acknowledgments

Short stories were my first love (as a writer), and it was seeing my stories in print for the first time that gave me the wild confidence to pursue the writing life. Thank you to the literary journals that provided early homes for some of the stories in this collection, and thank you to literary journals everywhere for giving space to writers—new and not so new—to share their work.

This collection came into being with help from many. A huge thank-you to my wonderful agent, Erin Harris, whose insight and support I treasure. Thank you to my editor, Caitlin Landuyt, for helping me realize my vision for this collection and for continuing to help me grow as a writer. Thank you to the dream team at Vintage, who bring so much care and thoughtfulness to the publishing process.

Thank you to the friends and writing colleagues who keep me on my toes. I'm lucky to get to interact with so much brilliance. A special shout-out to María Isabel Álvarez, Adrienne erry, Aria Curtis, Katie McNamara, Jeff Albers, and Katie Kitamura for offering feedback that pushed the final stories in the collection to a place of completion.

Thank you to my family for sharing in my literary joys and for helping me handle the tough parts. You make this all possible.

Thank you to Ariel for many, many reasons—but especially for reminding me that beyond catastrophe there can still be music and wonder and joy.

ALSO BY

ALLEGRA HYDE

ELEUTHERIA

Willa Marks has spent her whole life choosing hope. She chooses hope over her parents' paranoid conspiracy theories, over her dead-end job, over the rising ocean levels. And when she meets Sylvia Gill, renowned Harvard professor, she feels she's found justification for that hope. Sylvia is the woman-in-black: the only person who can compel the world to action. But when Sylvia betrays her, Willa fears she has lost hope forever. And then she finds a book in Sylvia's library: a guide to fighting climate change called *Living the Solution*. Inspired by its message and with nothing to lose, Willa flies to the island of Eleutheria in the Bahamas to join the author and his group of ecowarriors at Camp Hope. But upon arrival, the group's leader, author Roy Adams, goes missing, and the compound's public launch is delayed. With time running out, Willa will stop at nothing to realize Camp Hope's mission—but at what cost?

Fiction

VINTAGE BOOKS
Available wherever books are sold.
vintagebooks.com